Ghost Track: Melissa

By David Graffham

Book One of the Ghost Track Series.

Copyright © 2015 David Graffham

All rights reserved.

This book or any portion thereof
may not be reproduced or used in any manner
whatsoever without the express written permission of
the publisher except for the use of brief quotations in
a book review.

ISBN-13: 978-1505567830

ISBN-10: 1505567831

Facebook.com/ghosttrack14

Twitter.com/actionwriter75

I never could have known when I began writing this book for NaNoWriMo in November 2014 that the dedication page I was considering back then could have changed so dramatically to the one I present to you now.

To those who didn't judge me. To those who helped me to where I am now. To those who never gave up on me. You know who you are and I cannot express in words my gratitude and love for you.

To Mum. We all miss you so incredibly.

I know I would probably have got a slapped wrist for using some sweary words in this book, but I went easy on them really with that in mind!

The pain of you being taken from us so suddenly I don't think will fade for a very long time, if ever. The void left behind could never be filled. Our love for you could never weaken.

One.

Monday mornings heading to the tube seemed busier than Leyland Francis remembered them.

A damp and breezy start to the day didn't bother him so much despite the fact that it was mid-August. The crowd of bobbing heads up ahead made Leyland nervous.

He hadn't tackled the tube crowds since the accident and moving along on crutches was still a struggle for him.

Under normal circumstances it would have been a ten minute stroll from his flat on Ebury Bridge Road to Victoria station, but given his predicament it was taking longer. He had to be cautious.

One wrong move and he would be falling head over heels in front of the rush hour punters, and he really didn't want that kind of embarrassment today.

Nor did he want to dirty his suit on his first official day back to work and look like some sort of tramp.

As he held that thought Leyland couldn't help but check his appearance when he passed the window of the Ideal Cafe.

His five foot eleven wiry frame reflected back at him, jet black hair styled and parted neatly.

He had lost significant weight during his rehabilitation, and as someone who always took his gym time seriously, that was concerning.

His suit was immaculate and his shoes shining like he was on first name terms with Messrs spit and polish.

The reflection did little to reassure him. He looked good. He had inherited his style from his late mum.

He had most certainly inherited her nose as well. The Italian bloodline evident in him with his jet black hair and slightly olive complexion.
She would have looked great in a flour sack. It was the fact that he looked so drawn and he could feel the pressure already.
Enough attention would be on him that day as it was without any snipes about his fitness. Or lack of.
That and the thought of tackling the escalator had Leyland's heart thumping and his guts tightening.
He had never really felt nerves like this before. Not in a long long time. Like starting a new job. At least he had the advantage of knowing a lot of people where he was going. That'll definitely help, he thought to himself, but it was still daunting.
Victoria tube station used to be like a second home to Leyland, but since the accident he hadn't been there for six months at least.
He was now treating its walls and shiny floors with the caution of them being potential muggers. Ready to set him off balance. Steal his dignity and confidence for the day.
He moved along so very slowly, allowing firm contact with his crutches on the floor before putting his faith in them and leaning his weight forward.
He got angry with himself if his heart jumped at any slight potential slip or movement of the crutches as he made his swing. It was just making him more nervous and he could feel sweat under his arms was likely forming nice cringe worthy patches ready to be revealed and scrutinised upon removing his suit jacket.

After a sterling effort Leyland found himself at the escalator. A deep breath. A shuffle. A little sideways turn. Slight forward manoeuvre and Leyland was on. Relief.

Quickly hooking the crutches over his left wrist he clung on for dear life with his right. It seemed a hell of a lot steeper than last time he was here and then would not be the time to mash his leg up any further than it already had been.

Deeper down he travelled and the fumy breeze began to brush across his face as the air pressure of trains coming in and out of the tunnels was pushed around.

Far from fresh but, like an old friend, much missed over time.

Indeed there were many occasions during his time in hospital that he longed to escape underground for a little while. Looking out of the window on his ward he would daydream about face watching on his journey to and from work and wondered about people's stories.

As he neared the bottom of the escalator, Leyland prepared well for the step off when the sound of a real live saxophone breezed deliciously through the tunnels and massaged Leyland's ears.

It was a beautifully soulful and warming sound and made him smile. As he got closer he recognised the busker. He didn't know his name. But he knew the face from a hundred journeys.

It wasn't unusual for Leyland to pop the odd quid or two into his sax case and take in five minutes or so of a particular classic that took his fancy at that time. Soaking in the atmosphere. Some of his friends thought it a little weird but it reminded Leyland of what he loved about the underground and all of its spots, patches and character.

There would be no stopping on that day, but as Leyland drew closer to the sound he couldn't help but make eye contact with the busker. Almost like seeing an old friend after a period of absence.

Stupidly, when the busker returned eye contact to Leyland and smiled warmly, he went to raise his hand as he very briefly forgot about his balance predicament. His left foot slipped out and right leg crumpled weakly. He cracked the back of his head on the cold stony floor and Leyland Francis lost consciousness to the dulcet saxophone rendition of Louis Armstrong's 'We have all the time in the world'

Two.

"Hey Buddy."
"Hey, you O.K.?"
Leyland came too.
The busker was standing over him. Leyland tried to get up.
"Hey, take it easy, hell of a tumble you took there."
He offered Leyland his hand. Leyland winced. His head hurt and his bad leg was throbbing. He had to get off his back.
"You accident prone or something buddy?" Stan chuckled pointing to Leyland's strapped up leg.
Leyland took the buskers hand and shuffled onto his backside, slowly and gingerly spun around to lean his back against the wall.
He rubbed the back of his head and looked at his hand. No blood. Huge relief from Leyland.
"Gonna be one hell of a lump there," said the busker.
"You need an ambulance?"
"No! No, thank you," replied Leyland anxiously but politely.
He looked down at his suit trousers. No visible damage, which relieved him immensely.
"Maybe get checked out when you reach wherever you're heading?"
Leyland had never spoken to Stan before now. He found his Louisiana accent surprising, soothing and very cool.
Standing beside him the busker towered Leyland. He was six one, maybe six two in height and built like a

brick shithouse. He could have been intimidating but his smile was warm.
Leyland just made out the badge on his t shirt.
'New Orleans Pelicans' partly obscured by his three quarter length leather jacket. His hair protected by a pork pie hat.
He wondered how and why he had ended up playing the saxophone on the London underground.
"This fell out your pocket."
Stan handed Leyland his warrant card back.
"A police officer huh?"
"So how'd you get to be in this state?" Stan was looking at Leyland's leg brace again.
Leyland was feeling slightly less shaky now, but he didn't want to get into the explanation.
"Long story. Work injury," he answered shortly trying to get to his feet dizzily.
Stan held his crushingly big hand out to Leyland as he struggled to coordinate his crutches and legs.
Leyland paused briefly and, reluctantly, took the help that was being offered.
"Thank you so much," said Leyland. There wasn't generally much by way of obvious humanity in the morning rush hour down there. Leyland was inwardly very grateful for this third crutch at that time, as hard as it was for him to even briefly admit that he needed it.
Stan gently pulled him up. Leyland noticed that despite his massive hands he had a strong, yet warm grip.
Stan helped straighten him up a bit and Leyland was soon stable on his crutches again.

"God dam slippery floors," said Stan

"Be the death of someone down here...but not you today fella. Let me grab my sax and I'll walk with you to the platform."

Leyland nodded a weary agreement.

"So, where you headed to officer?" Stan asked as Leyland moved along gingerly.

"Vauxhall " he answered.

"Oh yeah, Vauxhall huh? So you headed for Tinworth Street? You a big shot down there?"

Leyland was taken aback by his spot on synopsis of Leyland's destination.

"Well as you can see, nothing big shot about me," answered Leyland neither confirming or denying where his journey would take him.

"First day back in a while," he added, not really comfortable at talking about what he did for a career to a stranger.

Not that he was embarrassed by his job, but more the fact that he was a very private person and really didn't know this guy from Adam. As kind as he had been.

"Because of your leg?" asked Stan.

"Yeah mostly because of that," he nodded.

The leg was the most obvious of his injuries. The psychological impact of the accident was just as painful. And not as easy or quick to fix either.

He had made very good progress. His career depended on it. If he didn't progress even further then he could kiss his hard work goodbye. He would be riding a desk forever or collecting his pension early. Neither of those options thrilled Leyland Francis compared to getting back out on the squad.

They slowly continued to the platform. Leyland nearest the wall and Stan in a funny sort of way protecting him from the bump and grind of the passing impatient travellers.

Leyland's head was ringing. He looked at his watch wondering how much time his little tumble had cost him.

He had missed his preferred train and was starting to feel the frustration of a messed up morning rise within him. He automatically, but discreetly, practiced the breathing exercises taught to him to control the pangs of anxiety.

His first appointment this morning was with none other than occupational health and if they found out about his little fall he could be signed off again for weeks.

Leyland was desperate to be involved in the buzz of work again. Had had been going bonkers stuck in his flat for so long. No cases. No action. No nothing except the dog shit that was daytime T.V. chat shows. He needed to really get his teeth back into the job.

Sure he may be riding a desk for a few weeks, but continue the hard work he had put into getting his leg better and it wouldn't be long.

He could hack that. Just about.

No, best not to mention the fall to anyone. Could have been worse. He would just have to be sharper from then on.

No need to upset the applecart considering he had got that far. The platform.

"Thank you so much for your help Stan," Said Leyland. Curiosity grabbed him.

"Why so long down here? Do you have somewhere? Someone?" he asked boldly.
"I've been taken this route for four years on and off and every day you have been here."
Stan was genuinely a kind hearted man but just as Leyland didn't really want to get into talking about his injuries, Stan didn't want to divulge as to why he had come underground for so long.
"Lots of questions young buddy," he answered with a chuckle.
"I just love putting out that sound," he said, gently shaking his saxophone case.
As if being saved by the bell Leyland's train burst free of the claustrophobic tunnel and came to a halt.
"Take it easy and see you again soon I hope," said Stan offering out his hand.
"I really appreciate your help Stan."
"Good luck today young buddy." And they shook warmly.
Leyland boarded shakily and took a seat. He raised his hand to Stan and the doors closed. Stan raised his pork pie hat slightly in acknowledgement, showing his thinning patch, with a wide smile on his face. The train moved off and Leyland was, finally, on his way. Destination Vauxhall via Pimlico.
He checked his watch. Cutting it fine time wise but should be ok.
No more problems. No more issues and certainly no more stupid tumbles and he should be ok for time. Just.

He relaxed slightly and reclined into his seat. Around a six minute journey. Just relax and breathe for a minute he thought to himself.

Leyland found himself slowly and discreetly scanning the faces in his carriage. Who are they? What stories did they hold within? It fascinated Leyland. It always had. His thoughts turned to Stan and what his story was all about.

He imagined that there were more than a few decent tales underneath that hat. For goodness sake, a Louisiana saxophonist busking on the London underground? How on earth did he get there?

His thought pattern was drifting off on tangents, when it was abruptly shaken by the carriage lurching to a very quick standstill mid tunnel. The lights flickered. Leyland looked around. What the hell could be the problem now?

The lights dipped. Flickered again. The hairs on the back of Leyland's neck sprang up. Flickered again. The lights zipped. And then died. Complete black. No back up lights. Nothing. One second. Two seconds. Three seconds. Nothing. Leyland swallowed. He felt wrong. The air around him had become cold. So cold. Leyland took his phone out for some light. He held it to his eye level. A surge of adrenaline hit him hard. The carriage seemed to be empty. Why would everyone have moved?

His breath was turned to vapour in the cold air that had hit so suddenly. Leyland was just about to get up out of his seat.

Twenty seconds...twenty five seconds. For fucks sake, Leyland thought. His frustration spiked.

The lights flicked on.
"I do hope we get a move on soon."
Leyland virtually jumped out of his socks.
The female voice was right next to him. How the hell did she get there?
"I'm sorry. I didn't mean to startle you," She said.
Leyland fumbled for words.
"I moved over when the lights went out. I got rather scared. I hope you don't mind?"
Surprise turned to annoyance for Leyland. His heart was thumping hard on his ribcage. He'd had more than enough for one morning.
"Do you make a habit of sneaking up on people?" he snapped.
"I mean seriously? Do I look like I'm up for a game of musical chairs?"
Leyland's rant made the females pretty smile drop.
"I'm terribly sorry," she said.
"I was really quite nervous in the dark. You have a protective aura and I felt safer next to you," she carried on.
"I see I could have injured your poor leg. I'm so sorry."
Leyland, once again, breathed deeply and tried to calm.
This lady was very attractive and looked quite genuinely shaken. He had been over the top.
"Hey, I'm sorry too," he offered.
"Delays and stuff make me livid, like you didn't notice," he joked, trying to ease the air.
"I'm Melissa," the lady introduced.
"Melissa. I'm Leyland."

They exchanged a smile. Even though the train wasn't yet moving.

"A protective Aura?" Leyland asked.

"How can you tell?"

"I can see it," Melissa answered.

"Some people can see auras. Like colours," she continued.

"And I have a protective one?"

"Very," answered Melissa firmly.

"What happened to your leg?" she asked.

"Ah well, my protective aura wasn't quite so protective of me. I injured it at work," Leyland answered, still cagey.

"Oh. Not good, Sorry to hear that But you're on the mend though?"

"Very much on the mend," Leyland answered, sounding more confident than he felt.

"Well, you must try and avoid falling over if you're going to keep it that way," Melissa revealed.

"You saw that?" Leyland reddened.

"I did. But I don't think too many people noticed."

"Thanks for helping," Leyland joked.

Melissa smiled at him. She blushed ever so lightly. She swept some of her blonde hair from her eyes. Beautiful blue eyes. Icy and piercing, but so gorgeous.

"So what do you do? Apart from scaring tube passengers?" Leyland asked.

"I was a legal secretary. For a small firm. I work just off Dacre Street"

Ghost Track: Melissa

Her fashion choice certainly backed up that sort of career. Leyland couldn't help but admire her legs covered with skin coloured tights.

A modest navy blue business skirt and white blouse completed her work attire. Her suit jacket was delicately hooked over her arm. Everything about her seemed delicate. Her voice. Her demeanour and her stature.

She was no more than 5 feet 3 tall. Her heels gave her some extra. But not a huge amount.

"Just around the corner from me," Said Leyland.

"Perhaps we could have a coffee one afternoon?" he asked bravely.

Melissa smiled lightly.

"I'd like that, but it would be difficult. Really difficult."

Leyland's face dropped.

"Boyfriend?"

"Let's just say a relationship would be murder." Her smile faded to sadness.

Melissa pulled a business card from the inside pocket of her suit jacket and passed it over to Leyland.

"My mobile number is on there; give me a call if you ever need help."

"Help? With what?"

The train suddenly lurched briefly. Then started to move slowly. The lights flickered again and burst into brightness so intense that he had to cover his eyes.

The train started to move.

"Finally," said Leyland.

He looked at the card and smiled quite involuntary. It hadn't happened for a while.

One fall, one number, he thought. Evens so far today.
The air in the train had warmed again, but Melissa had disappeared.
Leyland felt a huge sense of unease at the encounter and wondered how she moved so quickly. He leant forward and looked up and down the carriage. Was she in trouble? Was she trying to tell him something? He rubbed the bump on the back of his head.
Five minutes to Vauxhall.

Three.

The National Crime agency headquarters were buzzing.
Leyland felt it as soon as he walked back through the doors. That old excitement of doing the job that he loved hit him. He had missed it so badly.
Of course he understood he had a little way to go before he could expect to be back on full duties. But today., well today was a major step forward. Leyland needed this to go well. He needed it badly.
"Good morning D.S. Francis."
The feminine but powerful voice took Leyland by surprise.
He recognised it almost instantly.
"Mrs Ferdinand," he exclaimed nervously as his occupational health officer walked side by side with him.
"You're late this morning, has everything been ok?" she asked, peering over the rim of her glasses in a way that gave Leyland the impression that she had followed him from home and taken notes on his fall.
"Everything is fine...escalator was a bit of a challenge but here in one piece," he answered. Just about he muttered in his mind.
"Let's grab a coffee and we can head straight up and get started," said Ferdinand.
With her beehive type hairstyle and harsh rimmed spectacles Mrs Petunia Ferdinand gave the air of a private school headmistress. Everything about her screamed 'by the book'

Her perfume was heavy and lingered in Leyland's throat. He didn't like it. It was a real traditional scent he thought. Her demeanour and dress sense was conservative to say the least and she had a very big reputation within the Met for a being a first class bullshit detector. Leyland knew that if he wanted back into his squad he was going to have to tread extremely carefully. She had pensioned off more injured Bobbies than he cared to think of.

The canteen was bustling and buzzing. The mixture of early starters and night shift finishers grabbing some breakfast merged with the coffee and toast scent that was a heavenly return for Leyland.

A sudden cheer went up in a corner of the canteen.

"Oi oi hop along!" came a shout.

Leyland knew the voice of one of his team.

Paul Rix. He threw a beaming smile and raised a friendly hand up to the crowd of seven officers. His team. His reason for being there. They were clearly happy to see their oppo back as well. Back on his feet.

"Yeah, thanks for visiting, wankers," threw out Leyland, in mock seriousness. He had just finished the sentence when he felt the X ray eyes of Ferdinand boring into the back of his head. Leyland suddenly clammed up and looked sheepish. He was slightly ashamed that she had heard him swear. Despite his thirty eight years his dad would have still clipped him round the ear for it.

He wasn't completely convinced that the cane wouldn't be meted out to him once in Ferdinand's office as well.

Ghost Track: Melissa

They paid for their beverages and Ferdinand took the lead to her office.

On her desk lay a thick file which Leyland took to be his.

"Take a seat Detective Sergeant," Ferdinand gestured to the chair in front of her desk.

"I apologise for the detour but the wheels of occupational health services simply cannot run unlubricated," she continued.

"As ghastly as the canteen coffee may be." She smirked slightly and looked over the rim of her glasses at Leyland as she sank into her chair.

It was shocking coffee, thought Leyland. Not nearly strong enough.

"So. How does it feel to be back?"

"Weird. Wonderful," answered Leyland, studying her face. She had a look of Joan Sims about her. Leyland remembered fondly the face from the Carry on films they used to watch as a family when he was a child.

"For the past four months I've done nothing but look forward to this day," he continued.

"And now it's here?" jumped in Ferdinand.

"Now it's here I feel like a nervous wreck and wish I'd had an extra day in bed," Leyland replied, chuckling awkwardly in his third rate attempt to cover his anxiety.

"Quite," said Ferdinand stern faced and clearly unimpressed by Leyland's humour.

"Now D.S. Francis, looking at your file and having discussed your case in depth with your counsellors it would seem that you have made reasonable progress in recovering from your physical injuries."

"Another two weeks or so and believe the leg brace may come off, which is splendid news don't you think?"

Leyland paused. Was he supposed to be doing cartwheels at such 'splendid' news?

"It would be considerably more splendid if it was coming off tomorrow. Two weeks is rather a drag," replied Leyland.

"The physical healing process simply cannot be rushed Detective Sergeant."

"And even if it could I think we both know there are more pressing matters to deal with," said Ferdinand sternly, eyes beginning to bulge.

What the hell was she talking about thought Leyland? His 'what the fuck' expression must have been blatantly slapped across his face and allowed Ferdinand to continue.

"Your counsellor has expressed concern regarding your P.T.S.D. following the accident. I have his report here and it would seem that you have been recommended for further sessions," she revealed.

This was news to Leyland and he was stunned.

"I…I felt that the sessions went really well…I got so much out of them. I feel fine. I feel absolutely fine."

Leyland was halted by the raised hand of Ferdinand.

"As well may be the case Detective Sergeant, but we have to take the report seriously. I have to act and commit to the information given."

Leyland knew that. So why was she suddenly patronising him?

He could feel frustration bubbling up within him. He knew he had to contain it. Getting angry would just play further into her hands. Fucking stern bitch he thought.

"My leg has mended well and I feel fine mentally. I'm ready to come back," said Leyland. He drew the words out slowly. Almost sarcastically. Ferdinand pulled her glasses down her nose. There was uncanny precision in her positioning of the glasses when pissed off. She must have practiced for years.

"Detective Sergeant Francis. I have been Occupational Health director for nearly two years." Her look was one of a woman wound up and had Leyland swallowing hard.

"I always act in the best interest of the force and, of course, the individual officers that my department deals with. I trust my experts Detective Sergeant. And the experts say that you are not ready to return to full duties and that you need further help."

Leyland swigged his coffee. He felt the desire to argue burn within him. But he knew that such an act would be futile. No point trying to reason with this bitch. She was renowned for dishing out the hard line. And right then it was his turn to take the hard line square in the backside.

"So it clearly stands to reason that a new counselling and support program be set up for you as a matter of urgency, whilst you return to your position on light duties," Ferdinand announced.

"I cannot and will not allow you to return to active duty on your team as things stand."

Leyland breathed heavily. Very pissed off and slightly shaking with anger.

"I see," he said.

"And is there any sort of timescale on this?" He questioned.

"No timescale Detective Sergeant. It takes as long as it takes I'm afraid," answered Ferdinand slowly pulling her glasses back into position over her eyes.

"Your counsellor will be in touch today and I would strongly suggest a session as soon as possible."

"And Detective Sergeant, as frustrating as it may be perhaps take the opportunity to show your face in some other departments while you're…in limbo shall we say?" she rose and offered her hand to Leyland.

He got up awkwardly with his crutches and lightly shook Ferdinand's hand.

"So how does one get to take a look at how occupational health does its thing?" he questioned slightly sarcastically.

Ferdinand paused and a wry smile appeared on her face.

"Trust me D.S. Francis, you are as close to occupational health as you will ever want to get."

"Ma'am" answered Leyland.

"Your blouse is undone." He turned and headed for the door. Ferdinand busied to do her buttons up, tutting in the process.

"See you soon Detective Sergeant," was her parting shot as Leyland headed out of the clinical office, a face like thunder as he closed the door behind him and started to make his way to the team hub and his desk duties for god knew how long.

He was scanning for familiar and friendly faces as he limped along.

He saw none. Just a throng of officers busy about their various operations. Involved.

Leyland felt a pang of jealousy, sub consciously shaking his head as he re ran the conversation with Ferdinand in his head.

"Bloody hell!" boomed a heavy Liverpudlian accent.

"Seeing you walking in here, well almost walking, madder than bloody Tranmere sunshine. Madder than bloody Tranmere!"

Leyland smiled cheesily and turned to the voice.

"On a Friday night?" Leyland asked.

"On any bloody night! How you doing?" Came the reply from Leyland's closest friend.

Detective Chief Inspector Phil Mercer.

The two friends shook hands warmly.

"So good to see you buddy. What's happening?" Questioned Leyland.

"Oh the usual crap," answered Mercer.

"Missing person. Possible murder. Possible organised crime related so ends up at our door," Mercer answered.

"Same old then?" replied Leyland.

"You got yourself back in business then old son?" Mercer was curious.

"You must be joking. Just came out from Ferdinand's den. Fucking Pit-bull. I'm flying a desk for now," Leyland's face and smile had dropped a touch.

"Hey, don't knock it mate," said Mercer.

"It's not like you're going to be running any marathons soon is it?!" he continued.

"Just take your time. Pop in on us. I can always get you shuffling some paper in murder squad," Mercer jested.

"Wow. What a terribly tempting offer!" laughed Leyland.

"Let me go and catch up with the team," he continued.

"I will definitely pop in though. See how you scousers do the job."

"Anytime you want mate, you know where I am," Mercer replied.

"Really good to see you back Leyland," He added.

"How about a pint in the Weasel later?" Mercer asked quickly.

"Thought you were on the wagon?" Leyland looked puzzled by the offer and was concerned for his old friend.

"I am," said Mercer.

But you're not are you?!" he added.

"The social power of coke eh?" Leyland jested.

"Eh, don't knock until you've…"

"Tried it," Leyland cut in, finishing Mercers favourite saying.

"Still a cheeky git then," Chuckled Mercer.

"As long as you'll always be a short arse," he countered, laughing at the expense of his five foot five friend.

"See you in a bit Phil." Leyland parted with his old friend and carried on with his hobble to greet his witness protection team.

He was excited at the prospect of seeing everyone again. Not quite so thrilled at the prospect of seeing them fly out the door on a job with him having to sit tight scratching his arse though.

Leyland knew that he was going to have to step up his rehabilitation a lot more to get back into his position of team leader. Take the counselling and nod at the right times, smile at the right times and generally kiss arse, he thought.

I can do that for a bit, he agreed with himself.

But only for a bit.

Four.

A tiring, exciting, frustrating, emotional and painful day had moved aside for a chilled and balmy evening in front of the television for Leyland.

He was knocking back a bottle of Budweiser and had swapped his suit and stuffy shirt for a pair of comfortable, loose fitting shorts.

They allowed slightly more airflow around his leg brace which got sweaty and itchy and a downright pain in the arse when it was warm as it had been.

A white 'Foo Fighters' tee shirt completed his ensemble and Leyland Francis was officially in chill mode after his first day back on the job.

He couldn't concentrate fully on the news blaring out of the TV as the day's goings on were whirling and flashing through his mind.

Added to that feeling was the alcohol mixing with the painkillers.

He knew full well he could handle a couple of bottles of Bud on them. Any more than that and he was in trouble and would be sleeping literally where he fell. And he had had enough falls for that day, thank you very much.

The beer was drawing in him into deeper thought. Deeper into his mind's eye. He switched the TV off via remote and leaned back into the sofa. His head semi sinking into its plush form.

Beads of sweat formed on his forehead as Petunia Ferdinand spun through his head. Those glasses. That stern look. They were synonymous with frustration right then for Leyland.

Leyland's thoughts deepened further into the fuzz of his brain. Thinking back. The pain in his leg was edging off nicely. His memory ran and re ran again. The accident.

He breathed slowly and deeply. The sounds came back. Feint at first. But clearer and louder in his mind with every second. The rev of the high powered BMW engine. He could smell the interior of the car again. Freshly valeted that morning. A valet that would turn out to be a complete waste of taxpayers' money. The slam of another car hitting Leyland's side of his vehicle. The deafening and blood curdling screech of tyres on the road. Co-ordination destroying G forces being forced on the body as the car flipped and flipped. And flipped again coming to rest back on its wheels. Shattered glass succumbed to gravity again and hit the upholstery like hailstones. The smell of fuel wafted around on the breeze.

Leyland had, by some miracle, been kept in the car. He turned slowly to his left. His partner, Charlie McGuinness, had been thrown from the vehicle and injured horrendously.

The witness they had been protecting was in the back of the vehicle still. Just. He was twitching. His neck had somehow become slashed. Probably on the jagged edge of the window. A dark stream of crimson spurted from his wound in time with his pulse. Leyland could do nothing. Trapped by his leg under the mangled steering column. He could smell the fuel but he was fading. He looked from his window. The glass no longer there. A sound. Another engine. Revving hard. A door opened. Footsteps. A feeling of brief relief for Leyland as he thought help had arrived.

The footsteps got closer. Sirens in the distance were also getting closer. Leyland prayed they were for him. And then a voice. He couldn't make out what the person was saying. It was a male voice, for sure. A blur of a figure passed his eyes. He couldn't focus. He was losing consciousness. The figure stopped moving. Leyland's world went black.

Leyland's eyes sprang open. His breathing was rapid and sweat was rolling from his forehead down the side of his face tickling his cheek.

The sound of sirens had been from outside his apartment as he snapped out of yet another flashback.

The noise drifted through the open balcony doors with a light whip of the curtains being jostled in the summer evening breeze.

Leyland wiped his brow and tried to calm his breathing, exhaling heavily and semi controlled.

His mobile phone vibrated along the glass topped coffee table. It was Phil Mercer.

"Hey, how you doing?" answered Leyland, suddenly remembering his invitation to the Weasel.

"Alright lad, still in the Weasel. Thought I'd give you a shout. Got some news for you. You been running or something?"

"With this leg? Go on, what news," said Leyland, intrigued but still slightly disorientated.

"If you're interested I can get you attached to my team for a bit," Mercer revealed.

"I've had an informal chat with the Commander and he is willing to give it the green light if you're up for it and happy to use the excuse that I can keep an eye on you," Mercer added.

"An informal chat in the Weasel?" Questioned Leyland.

"You didn't get him pissed did you Phil?"

Mercer chuckled down the line.

"I just thought you could do with a bit of action of sorts rather than shagging that desk of yours for the next few weeks. I hope you don't mind me mentioning it mate?"

"Can I think about it?" asked Leyland.

"I don't mean to seem ungrateful Phil, it's a kind offer, and Ferdinand did say to get some time in other departments. It's just seeing the team again today…well it's…"

"Loyalty?" interrupted Mercer.

"Kind of," replied Leyland.

"More comfort zone than loyalty I suppose," he added.

"Maybe a bit of both."

"Look," said Mercer.

"Get your arse down here for a jar and let's have a chat about it. I just wanted to make sure I hadn't overstepped the mark by checking it out. The opportunity came up quickly," Mercer explained.

"You'll be shadowing me and probably getting out and about a lot."

"We've got a mispers case on right now. Give it some thought. But more importantly get down here and stand a round soft lad!"

Leyland didn't quite know what to say. The thought of working with Phil for a bit was certainly appealing and he was a bit choked up with what his old buddy had done for him. Looking out for him. As ever. What harm could it do short term?

Leyland shifted on the sofa. He owed his mucker a pint at least after his efforts to keep him in the game.

A forgotten memory suddenly nagged at Leyland's sub conscious.

The card. Melissa's card. He limped off to the bedroom with the aid of one crutch and checked the inside pocket of the suit jacket he had on earlier.

The card was still there. Leyland felt its texture. It was smooth but thick. Good quality. He grabbed his mobile and slowly punched the numbers in. A slight knot in his stomach formed. Nerves? Not wanting to look a twat? More like wondering why she disappeared so quickly. It had unsettled him on the tube earlier. Events with Ferdinand had taken his mind from the incident and suddenly he was curious about her again. The call connected and the phone was ringing on the other end.

No answer. Bollocks. He hated doing the message thing.

It continued to ring then clicked over to voicemail. A gorgeous voice, thought Leyland. He could visualise her in his mind's eye. He really wanted to meet for a coffee. He wanted to look over those legs again.

"Hi, it's Leyland from the train this morning." Leyland felt very awkward now.

"Err just wanted to arrange a coffee tomorrow sometime if you're available. I know you said it would be difficult but just thought I would see if that had changed." You sound like a right dick thought Leyland.

"Err give me a call back when you can." Leyland quickly ended the call and under a slight fluster grabbed his wallet, his second crutch and made to head for the Weasel.

The fresh air would do him good. Even if the alcohol wouldn't. It had turned into a gorgeous evening in the capital and Leyland needed out of the apartment.

Just as he stepped into the lift his phone rang. Just once. Leyland checked it.

One missed call. The number was Melissa's. Strange, thought Leyland. But cool. She called back. She must have listened to the message. Maybe she wants to meet up this evening. He wasn't exactly dressed for a hot date. He waited, thinking the phone would ring again. It didn't.

He pushed button G on the lift panel. The doors closed and the descent began. Leyland tapped to return the call. Again it rang and rang and clicked over to voicemail. Leyland ended the call without leaving a message this time. He waited, expecting the phone to ring again.

Maybe they had cross called, trying to get in touch with each other at the same time. The lift slowed to the ground floor. Leyland pocketed the phone and headed out of the lift.

He limped outside into the sunlight of the August early evening and, slightly disappointed about not being able chat to Melissa, succumbed to the call of the Weasel Public House and an evening with Detective Chief Inspector Phil Mercer.

Five.

Phil Mercer opened his eyes.
He very quickly closed them again. The light was merciless as it hit his corneas hard. He grunted.
He was in bed, but he didn't remember at all how he had got there. His head felt like it was being systematically pounded with a sledgehammer. He just about managed to sit up. As soon as he did he felt instant nausea and dashed to the en suite bathroom attached to his bedroom.
His mobile phone rang as he was giving his grand speech to god above, which is who he was pleading with to make the feeling go away.
"Fuck off," he rasped in between retches as the ringtone split his head into two.
He wiped his mouth with his hand. Stumbled to his feet and splashed cold water over his face from the small sink. He slowly moved his line of vision up to the mirror and looked at himself. His heart sank and shame hit him immediately piercing into his guts like a corkscrew.
"You stupid bastard," he whispered to himself. He couldn't look anymore and moved unsteadily into his living room. Another beautifully bright August day was in swing. Mercer grabbed his sunglasses from the table and made to flick the kettle on. He needed a strong brew. God's own hangover cure in his opinion.
He winced and hung his head at the empty scotch bottle he had to move to get to the sugar pot.
He could recall very little about last night at all. All but a brief and very hazy memory of Leyland Francis

entering the Weasel was just about all he had. The rest of his short term memory had been obliterated by an impromptu binge on lager and whiskey and now he was seriously paying for it. Again.

He hadn't hit the bottle quite like that in a long while. He had tried so very hard to keep his drinking on the level. His last lapse was around three months ago. He was finding the fight seriously hard a lot of the time and allowed himself the odd few pints fairly regularly. But he genuinely strayed away from sessions like last nights. As much as he could anyhow. Sessions like that raised questions.

He could explain that one away hopefully without too much fuss just as long as Trudy, his wife, didn't find out at all. And that wouldn't be too difficult to keep quiet given the fact that she was over two hundred miles away back in Liverpool. With the kids.

Mercer wasn't bitter. He wasn't even angry. He didn't blame her for running. God knows he would have done the same if he had been in her position.

Yes, of course it hurt him badly. Damaged him. But she had to put herself and the kids first. All the while he had continued to put the bottle first. If occupational health ever found out he was bingeing again then he would likely be facing the same fate as his friend Leyland. But probably on a much more permanent basis. Assuming he didn't get his arse kicked out of the force completely of course.

His mobile rang again. It was Leyland.

"Hello mate," answered Mercer gingerly with a rough, throaty voice.

"Where are you Phil?" Leyland questioned concern obvious in his voice.

"You were completely rat arsed last night, what the fuck happened to being on the wagon?"

"Fell off mate. It happens. Only a little slip though," replied Mercer.

"A little slip?" Leyland retorted.

"Do you know how many birds went home with you last night? Do you?"

"Birds? What you talking about lad? I'm here on my own," Mercer countered.

"Exactly my point, you haven't got a clue. What time are you going to get in?" Leyland asked.

Mercer winced and the kettle came to the boil and clicked off.

"Give me an hour and I'll be with you," he replied.

"Don't even think about driving in Phil," replied Leyland and ended the call.

Mercer stood and massaged the bridge of his nose. He made the cup of tea. Two tea bags. Extra strong was desperately needed. Extra sugar too.

As much as he had missed Leyland during his rehabilitation, Phil couldn't believe how quickly he had got back into 'old lady' mode as he called it. It was a term of affection for Leyland and Mercer knew he was only worried about him.

As he added a small splash of milk, out of the corner of his eye he caught sight of a pair of black, lacy female knickers hung over the door handle of his spare bedroom.

Mercer winced again, trying to dig deep into the pit of his memory. It gave him nothing.

Ghost Track: Melissa

He approached the bedroom door cautiously. The sound of a light creak of the springs in the spare bed sounded out and Mercer flung the door open.

There in front of him on the bed were two very naked ladies.

"Morning Phil," greeted the first girl. Mercer held the underwear on the end of his finger.

"I'm afraid the party is over girls."

"Oh Phil. That's such a shame. Last night was so much fun." She was a very well-spoken girl; Mercer was quite pissed off that he couldn't remember a thing about what they got up to last night. The second girl stirred.

"Keep us warm Phil."

"It's chilly in here," she tantalised.

Chilly? It's fucking August Mercer thought to himself. He'd certainly outdone himself this time. They were good looking girls. Mercer closed the door behind him.

"Were you as bad an influence on me last night?" he asked, slipping in between them.

Leyland Francis was getting pissed off waiting for Mercer to haul his hungover backside into action.

He was nursing a bit of a heavy head himself in truth.

The mixture of alcohol and his pain killers had him waking up earlier with a very fuzzy feeling. He also thought he might stand a chance of bumping into Melissa on the tube journey again but foolishly realised that he managed to get on his intended train that morning which was ten minutes earlier than the one he took yesterday. And at that moment in time he found himself hanging around Mercers investigation hub like a spare prick at a wedding. Waiting.

He said he would be an hour. Nearly two had passed. Leyland pulled out his mobile.

His leg was aching and that wasn't helping his mood at all either. He had just finished dialling Mercers number when he heard the familiar scouse accent. Leyland spun as smoothly as he could on crutches and caught a grinning Mercer bounding through the doors.

"Morning Goldilocks," Mercer aimed at Leyland, whose expression must have been very obvious.

"Alright alright, don't look like that. I got held up." Mercer defended himself. Not that he could really. He was more than an hour later than he said he would be due to his liaison with Shana and the lovely red headed Maria. At least he would remember that session because last night's shenanigans were nowhere to be found in his memory.

Leyland moved over to Mercer and gently pulled on his arm.

"You O.K.?" Leyland asked, straight faced.

"Never better, why?" Mercer replied.

"Falling off the wagon and all that. Just wondered why, what with Trudy and the kids"

"She left me remember, and things got a bit out of hand last night but nothing to worry about at all buddy," Mercer added flashing a trademark 'Trust me' smile.

"How's your head anyway? You weren't exactly sitting on your hands last night," chuckled Mercer.

Ghost Track: Melissa

"Me? I'm fine and ready to shadow the master," Leyland jested.

"Well we have a briefing in half an hour, so let me show you around and introduce you to the team." Mercer seemed more excited than Leyland.

"I really do appreciate you doing this for me Phil," Said Leyland quietly. As he did so he saw out of the corner of his eye Petunia Ferdinand watching him. Just standing there and watching him. As Leyland looked over to her she looked at her phone quickly and carried on walking. But she was definitely fixed on him before that. Leyland felt briefly uncomfortable.

"You'll be doing me a big favour to be honest fella," Said Mercer.

"An extra pair of eyes on things, someone trustworthy. I appreciate you coming over for a bit," He added.

Leyland had, for now, brushed off the thing with Ferdinand and was now shaking hands and patting backs.

He felt a huge amount of respect and pride for his friend. He had built up a superb team, had risen through the ranks and consistently achieved phenomenal detection and success rates. Leyland guessed that's why Mercer held a fair amount of clout with the Comnander regarding certain decisions, including Leyland's attachment to his squad. Those closed door discussions usually involved copious amounts of alcohol as well. And that's where as immensely proud of Phil Mercer he was, he was as equally worried for him too.

Phil Mercer was always one step ahead, full of confidence and full of scouse bravado and humour. He had a wonderful wife supporting him and two gorgeous sons.

Trudy Mercer had struggled initially to settle in London with the boys, but she put up for the sake of Phil who was starting to really go places in the Met.

The drinking culture started to catch up with him though. Shifts ran into days and as much as Trudy loved him with all of her heart she simply couldn't handle the prolonged periods of drunkenness, the hangovers, the temper flare ups, the fights and the downright hell of what he had turned into.

A period of rehab for Mercer (forced upon him with the threat of dismissal from the force hanging over him) coupled with revelations of his womanising put the final nails into the coffin of their marriage and of their time together in London.

Trudy hotfooted back to Liverpool to be near her mum, taking the boys with her.

Even then she had left the door open for Phil. Even after all that shit.

There were conditions attached of course. They could make a go of it. But he had to go back to Liverpool. For starters. Phil, well he never said no. He just kind of drifted for a while. He hid the extent of his drinking although he felt he had it well under control. Nights like last night, well they were fairly few and far between if the truth be told these days. But when they happened, boy did he go for it.

It had caused friction outside of his family circle as well. Commander Rawlins was aware of this. He didn't get to where he was by being thick, that's for sure, but Mercers success rate meant that he had to be kept around.

Certainly not at any cost. There were always warnings, stark warnings, if Mercer ever came close to overstepping any marks. And Mercer always heeded those warnings, conscious of the fact that the consequences of ignoring them could mean Petunia Ferdinand standing over him one day with his bollocks in her hand, laughing at him. He certainly didn't want that happening. With her reputation once would be enough, and given that they had clashed a few times in the past over her treatment of his officers, Mercer knew full well that she wouldn't hold back if she got the chance to take him down.

So he was careful. Careful enough to make sure the opportunity didn't arise.

The briefing was due to start in about twenty minutes and once the introductions had been completed Mercer and Leyland headed for the refreshment area of the hub and poured fresh coffee.

"Nice team Phil," commented Leyland.

"Where and how do you plan on fitting me in? Looks like all the angles are covered. How are you going to make use of a bit of dead wood like me?" Leyland chuckled the 'dead wood' bit out. But he was being semi-serious.

"Well," began Mercers explanation.

"Firstly I can keep an eye on you and make sure Ferdinand backs off a bit. She seems rather keen on tracking your movement's lad and that's not a good thing," Mercer continued.

"Fuck," exclaimed Leyland.

"I saw her watching earlier"

"I did give her a bit of shit in our meeting," Leyland added.

"Bad move buddy," said Mercer, adding three sugars to his coffee.

"She'll trim as much as she can from the wage and pension budget through officers not quite pulling their weight, injuries or no injuries. She's been doing it from day one of getting the job," he added.

"Secondly, I think you'd benefit from seeing what goes on in this team. You're a good friend and an excellent copper," Mercer continued.

"You've had a shit run of luck recently and I know what it can be like when that happens."

"I don't need sympathy Phil; I don't need favours either although I appreciate what you've done. I want to be here on my own merits," said Leyland.

"Look fella, you looked after me as best you could when Trudy left. And you're still doing that now."

"It's what good friends do," said Leyland.

"Exactly. Then let me do this for you Leyland. Besides. I trust you to give it to me straight if needs be."

"I can guarantee that," answered Leyland.

"Boss!" a shout came from the office area.

A colleague was holding a telephone handset in the air.

Mercer strode over and took the call. His face dropped. It clearly wasn't good news.

"Briefing starts in two minutes," bellowed Mercer to everyone within the hub.

Ghost Track: Melissa

"What's happened Phil?" questioned Leyland.
"Our missing person has just been found."
"Good stuff. Why so unhappy then?" Leyland asked.
"Our missing person has just been found murdered," said Mercer stone faced.
He grabbed his coffee and marched to the front of the briefing room. Even at five foot five he cut an authoritative stance helped by his number 2 cut all over. Liverpool FC tie tucked into his shirt.
"Right, listen in everyone," shouted Mercer. He paused.
"OK settle down," he lowered his voice a notch.
"OK. As of two minutes ago a body matching the description of our mispers has been discovered."
There was dead silence in the room.
"Without official confirmation or identification we cannot say one hundred percent if this is our female. But the description given to me means we should expect the worse and prepare for this investigation to switch to a murder investigation."
Heads dropped.
"Sorry it's not better news people, but not entirely unexpected as we have all experienced before."
"Let's keep all channels open still, by the book as always until we have absolute confirmation, OK?" asked Mercer.
His team, subdued by the news nodded quietly and solemnly.
"Right, let's keep going. Kirsty, Steve I need you both to speak to the Marshall family and update them on developments."

The team streamed back into action but the atmosphere in the hub had clearly changed and there were more than a few despondent looks by officers. This was never the news a team wanted to hear when searching for a missing person.

The name jogged Leyland's memory. He suddenly felt slightly embarrassed that he hadn't as yet taken any time to find out about any details of the case going on.

Mercer was busying himself with some phone calls and so Leyland took the opportunity to rectify his embarrassment.

"Phil, OK if I catch up in there?" Leyland was pointing to the main investigation room. Full of pictures on the wall and a massive whiteboard with essential information on it would help Leyland get up to speed on things.

"Fill your boots mate," replied Mercer briefly holding his hand over the telephone mouthpiece.

Leyland grabbed his mug of coffee and wandered over to the room.

Upon opening the door he was faced with a multitude of maps, photos, notes and symbols placed on the massive whiteboard that stretched along the front wall of the room.

The name on the board didn't quite register with Leyland immediately.

'Melissa Marshall'

The name bounced around his still slightly fuzzy head for a few seconds.

Then he focused more on the photographs and limped slowly closer to them.

Ghost Track: Melissa

His stomach hit his feet like a broken lift.

The blonde hair. The piercing blue eyes. He knew the face. And he connected the name. Melissa Marshall, his tube lady, had been missing for three days and had likely been found dead. Leyland's head was going crazy. He was desperately trying to process all of the emotions and information but his head couldn't connect it all properly. How? Why? When? He had seen her. Spoken to her. He had her business card in his wallet. His legs trembled and his grip on the coffee mug was lost sending it falling to the floor. It hit the carpet and broke into five pieces, spraying dark liquid in the immediate vicinity. Leyland tried to hold onto a desk next to him but it was to no avail. He was feeling out trying to gather his balance desperately. A cold sweat had formed over his forehead and his legs gave out on him. The fall pulled on his injured leg and Leyland let out an involuntary howl of pain. A few of the officers nearby must have heard him and rushed in to help. The found Leyland in a crumpled mess on the floor splattered with coffee. Leyland retched. He wanted to puke but nothing came out, trying so hard to control himself. Mercer rushed in, alerted to the commotion and knelt next to Leyland.

"What is it mate? Is it your leg?" he questioned quickly.

Just get me up, get me to the gents," Leyland rasped, wincing as pain rushed up his leg like an electric shock. He could feel the nausea winning against him.

"Quickly, please," he barked.

"Help me here guys," ordered Mercer. Three of his team moved in with Mercer and helped Leyland get to his feet and supported him until he got his crutches in position to hold his weight.

"Leyland, what the hell happened?" Mercer questioned.

"Just give me a few minutes," Leyland replied, moving out of the hub as fast as his crutches, and the pain, would let him. As he turned the corner out of the hub area he nearly collided with Petunia Ferdinand.

"Sorry ma'am," he apologised as he dashed off and into the toilets.

Ferdinand fixed her stare on the door long after he had disappeared. She turned, narrowed her eyes and marched into Mercer's briefing room.

"What's wrong with D.S. Francis?" she demanded.

"Coming down with a bug I think Petunia. Nothing for occupational health to worry about," Mercer answered. Barely shielding his contempt for the woman.

She scribbled something in her notebook, looked down her nose at Mercer and walked out.

Phil Mercer crossed the corridor to the toilets, seeking out Leyland. He could hear someone vomiting and he knew who it was. Mercer stood to one side of the cubicle. Leyland hadn't been quick enough to close the door.

"So. What's this all about buddy?" Mercer questioned his friend.

Leyland was spitting into the toilet and grabbed some tissue.

"Must be the booze and painkillers last night," replied Leyland feebly.

He turned and faced Mercer while still on the floor.

"Then stay off the bloody booze then," said Mercer. He said it so stone-faced to begin with that Leyland believed what he was trying to offer as advice. Then the familiar grin appeared.

"But personally I'd lay off the painkillers if it's affecting your drinking pal," he chuckled.

"Get yourself cleaned up properly. Your number one fan is asking questions about you," Mercer added.

"Ferdinand?" asked Leyland.

"Who else?" Mercer answered.

"Get some fresh air, you're going to need it where we are heading next," he added.

"Not going to the pub again. Not with you," Leyland wailed.

Mercer chuckled deeply.

"We're going to see the body and where it was found," he revealed.

"I don't want you embarrassing me when we're there by throwing up. People will think I've gone soft bringing you onto the team!"

"Oh god," exclaimed Leyland.

"Do we have to?"

"We do. And I need you with me," Mercer answered.

"However rough you're feeling."

"OK boss," answered Leyland

"But do me a favour though," he asked.

"Shoot," said Mercer.

"Give me a full update on the case so far. I need the full heads up if I'm going to be of any use to you."

"You need to stop falling over if you're going to be of any use to me," joked Mercer.

"Get sorted out and meet me in my office," he added, slapping Leyland on his shoulder.

As Mercer walked out Leyland struggled to his feet and gingerly moved over to a basin. He washed his hands and rinsed his face. The feel of the cold sweat was sticking to him and he wanted rid of the taint.

His head felt slightly clearer but a barrage of questions were entering his head. Could he have been the last person to see her alive? How did she die? They said possibly murdered. Could he be deemed a suspect? Should he say anything? No! No way! He was in the Weasel for most of the night with Mercer. He had seen her on the tube that morning. No way could he be in the frame…but…no. Slow down. Slow down. Leyland breathed deeply. He needed facts. The first fact was that if he mentioned in any way that he had seen Melissa Marshall then he could kiss his attachment to Mercer's team goodbye most likely. Maybe his career.

He dried his face and hands on some paper towels. Pale and dark eyed Leyland headed for Mercer's office.

As he entered Mercer was waiting for him.

"So," said Leyland.

"What's the story so far?" He sat and produced his notebook and pen ready to take notes.

Mercer pulled a cigarette out of his packet and lit. He stood and opened his office window to allow the smell an escape.

"Right, well four days ago a report was received by local uniformed regarding the sudden disappearance of Melissa Marshall."

Mercer pushed a photograph of Melissa across the desk to Leyland. He didn't touch it. He stared down at it. At her eyes. He swallowed. Mercer continued.

"Report was filed by her sister. She touched on the possibility of her life being in danger from Russian organised crime elements. That got flagged up and passed to us here at NCA, naturally."

Leyland was scribbling intensively.

"Checks with friends and employer have thrown up very little as yet. And strangely the sister has been uncontactable since making the initial report."

"So the sister is missing as well?" questioned Leyland, raising his eyebrows.

"Uncontactable buddy, not missing as such."

"So the mafia claims seem to be unfounded?" Leyland asked.

"Our initial investigations threw up nothing to suggest that she hadn't just taken off for a while," said Mercer.

"There were one or two nervous employees at her place of work, but nothing to suggest any wrongdoing," he added.

"The discovery of a body in suspicious circumstances slightly changes the game plan to be honest."

"It certainly does," agreed Leyland.

"No history of depression or illness at all?"

"Nothing flagged up from GP records."

Leyland scribbled some more.

"Where was this body discovered?"

"In woodland near Purfleet," answered Mercer.
"Initial reports from the scene suggest fully clothed as well. Found by a dog walker," he added.
"Local pervs and nonces been shaken down as yet?"
"The usual's either know nothing or have alibis. We're still following up a few of those of course."
"Of course," chipped in Leyland, not taking his eyes of his notebook.
"I guess we'd better go and check this body out then hadn't we?" Leyland rose from his chair and snapped his notebook shut.

Mercer noticed a slight change in Leyland's attitude. He stayed tight lipped for now. There seemed to be a shift up in gear from him.

That was true of course. Leyland wanted answers. Real answers. He had seen Melissa in the time period when she was supposed to be missing. It was an unusual encounter as well. Very unusual.

He would keep that under his hat for now but he knew full well he would have to confide the truth in his friend soon enough.

Maybe it's because he finally was able to get his teeth into something after so sitting on his hands at home, thought Mercer who grabbed his car keys from his top drawer.

"Let's roll" Said Mercer, after he had flicked his ciggie out of the office window.

Leyland tutted and followed closely. His leg was still throbbing after the fall but he was getting seriously pissed off with his crutches. His temper was telling him to ditch them. There and then. His reasonable

Ghost Track: Melissa

side and the slight electric pain in his leg was telling him to hang onto them for a tad longer.

Mercer was barking orders at two of his officers to continue trying to find the sister as they headed to the car park. To see the body of Melissa Marshall.

In her office Petunia Ferdinand was staring out of the window out into the bright blue August day. She was observing the car park and saw the figures of Leyland and Mercer. She picked up the telephone handset from her desk and dialled.

"It's me."

"Has Detective Sergeant Leyland Francis had his counselling sessions set back up yet?" She asked.

The reply must have been in the negative. Ferdinand's eyes narrowed.

"Well that's not good enough."

"I want it dealt with within twenty four hours. Do you understand?"

An answer. Probably affirmative.

"Good." Said Ferdinand. She ended the call.

"I'll take you both down," she said to herself as she looked out of the window again to see Mercer's car gunning out of the car park.

"Just you wait and see what I've got lined up for you."

Six.

Phil Mercer was driving the black Audi A4 fast and hard. They had about a half an hour journey at that rate.
"The body was found at about half seven this morning by a female dog walker," Mercer initiated conversation.
"Found in woodland near to Mar Dyke in Purfleet," he added.
Once again, in the passenger seat, Leyland was attempting to scribble notes. Not quite so easy when your partner was throwing the car around at over eighty miles per hour.
"Forensics are on scene, the body is still in situ."
Leyland's throat dried. He was becoming nervous again and felt a tinge of the nausea that had affected him earlier. He was just trying very hard to focus on the job in hand and prayed that the feelings would subside. The questions in his head would have to wait. Especially the biggest questions of all, the two he was really struggling with. 'Have I lost my mind; and 'Will I end up as a murder suspect.'
Hopefully there would be some sort of explanation regarding his experience on the tube train. He didn't know what, but right then was close to praying. And religion didn't come easy to Leyland.
Mercer's voice started to fade. Leyland was slipping deeper and deeper into thought. Back to yesterday morning. The carriage lights. The temperature. The fall even. Strange goings on, but not entirely unexplainable.

Ghost Track: Melissa

Ferdinand was another worry as well.

If she caught wind of any of that stuff then he could kiss his career goodbye. And quite possibly his freedom. And right then Leyland did not fancy the prospect of being locked away in an institution.

His thought process turned to the rational.

How could Melissa Marshall have given him a business card if she was missing or possibly dead? How could she have called his mobile phone? Simple, thought Leyland. A dead person could not have. If the body was that of the Melissa Marshall that had been missing then it would have been fresh and the murder would have been sometime in the last twelve hours or so. If that was proven the case then Leyland would be clear to reveal the fact that she had made contact with him in the hours leading up to her death. But it was all very innocent. He would be in the clear, no problem at all. He breathed a bit easier after running the facts through his mind.

"McCall and Scott are heading to Marshalls employer again later. See if news of a body turning up jangles any more nerves," said Mercer.

"Although I'm not holding my breath on that score," he added.

"Where did she work?" asked Leyland.

"A law firm. Small but with some fairly heavy hitters on the team, Dealt with a lot of corporate clients. So we are treading fairly carefully at the moment in that area."

"Whereabouts was the firm?" Leyland continued. He had a horrible deep feeling where this could be going.

"Philips and West," said Mercer.

"Dacre Street?" Asked Leyland.//
"Precisely. Just around the corner." Mercer and Leyland said it in union.
"Fuck fuck fuck!" Muttered Leyland under his breath. He could feel the cold sweat hitting him again.
"Stick the air con on," he requested and Mercer obliged with the flick of a switch.
"How you feeling now?" asked Mercer.
"Bit ropey mate, but a lot better," he lied.
"And it's only Tuesday," Mercer joked.
"Madder than Tranmere!" he added.
Leyland's mobile phone rang. They were about halfway through the journey and Leyland answered.
"Occupational Health services D.S. Francis. Just wanted to chat and set up your counselling sessions."
"Oh right, well I'm tied up right now," answered Leyland, quite honestly.
"Ah I see. Can I call you back at some point later today? Dr Ferdinand was most insistent that we get together urgently."
"I bet she was," Leyland murmured.
He started to fiddle with his tie and could feel anger rising inside him at her interference.
"Call me back in say two hours and we can arrange."
He was pissed off but he knew he had to play ball and tick the boxes.
"I will do just that then Detective Sergeant," and the call was terminated.
"Prick," muttered Leyland.
"Who is?" asked Mercer.
"Occupational health. On the hassle already," Leyland added.

Ghost Track: Melissa

"Don't sweat it buddy, just play good dog and stick your tongue out and nod," advised Mercer.

"Don't kick back against the system, you know what I mean?"

Leyland didn't speak. He stared out of the window and watched the traffic and trees blurring past. He felt like he was losing control and he had only been back for twenty four hours.

These kind of events were unprecedented in Leyland's life. They would be in anyone's life. Missing persons reaching out and all that.

His leg was still throbbing a bit. He'd give anything to be rid of the bloody strapping he had to keep on at the moment.

His next physio appointment was Friday and he desperately wanted some good news from that.

He turned and looked at Mercer. He was in his element. Chewing on a piece of gum, his eyes darting between the road and the rear view mirror. Constantly scanning the journey path expertly whilst driving at high speed.

They would be at the scene within the next five minutes and Leyland needed to prepare himself psychologically for what he may be about to see.

"The crash," said Mercer, quite out of the blue.

"You always said to me that you felt there was more to it than being an accident."

"That's right Phil? You've always known that," replied Leyland, slightly taken aback by the mention of it.

"Why did you never demand that the investigation be reopened? As the only surviving person," asked Mercer again.

"Apparently it couldn't be justified. And I wasn't the only survivor, was I. No new evidence had come to light in any way," Said Leyland.

"Even though the driver of the other vehicle was never found?"

"That was never a suggestion of foul play in the enquiry. Just a very unlucky case of a hit and run with a stolen car according to the coroner. The driver was never found. Probably never will be Phil. The search has probably stopped to be honest by now. What does a chap like me do about that?"

Leyland looked at Mercer.

"The fact that it becomes clearer every time I dream, that someone got out of another car and made sure our witness was dead could never be taken seriously could it?" Leyland was getting angry again.

"Because of a lack of proof. Lack of witnesses," he continued.

"Ever think about doing a bit of digging around while you were at a loose end?" asked Mercer.

"Wouldn't you? If some fucker kills your partner and the witness you're moving and damn near kills you too?" Answered Leyland.

"If it wasn't for the fact that my leg was trashed and it would cause ripples with Ferdinand I would have been very tempted. Sensibility took over I guess."

"Well, you know if you ever do, give me a shout," Said Mercer.

"Always follow the gut instinct," he added.

"Not enough coppers coming through the ranks know how to do that. But for people like you and me, well it's essential. It's how we survive. How we thrive. How we make it to where we are."

"Whilst you know I would generally agree with you about that, I think we should concentrate on the job in hand," Said Leyland.

"Tell me what we know about the sister," he asked with his notebook poised.

"Well, she made the initial report about Melissa Marshall being missing."

"Despite suggesting that she may have been kidnapped or there were suspicious circumstances about the disappearance she wouldn't be drawn on what those circumstances could be, or provide any proof."

And the sister has been uncontactable since that initial report?" asked Leyland.

"That's right."

"Felicity Marshall. She has connections to a few tabloids and was working freelance as an investigative journalist," informed Mercer.

"The consensus of opinion from info gained by the team is that she may well have gone underground to look for her sister herself."

Leyland was scribbling. He wondered what the sister looked like.

The Audi pulled into Mar Dyke where the scene had been sealed off with Police tape. The forensic tent was clearly visible between some trees just on the outskirts of the wooded area.

Leyland and Mercer got out of the car. Leyland was still on two crutches and anticipated tricky terrain on the scene.

Mercer was five steps ahead of Leyland. His Liverpool Football Club tie was flapping in the summer breeze. The smell of low tide was thick in the sticky air this close to the Thames.

Mar Dyke was what passed for a beauty spot in this neck of the woods and was probably the biggest cluster of trees (hardly a woodland at all) before reaching the Kent border.

The two officers ducked under the blue and white tape.

The step forward of one of the uniformed officers guarding the scene prompted Mercer to show his warrant card, and he backed off.

They approached the tent and Leyland felt a wave of apprehension wash over him. His mouth dried and, although trying to keep as cool as possible, sweat beads began to form on his forehead and top lip. And it certainly wasn't toasty August causing it.

Mercer managed to sidestep some dog shit just in time. He marched toward a white overalled forensic officer.

"Morning. What have we got then?"

"Good morning D.I. Mercer," said the officer obviously recognising one of the most successful murder squad detectives in the last thirty years.

"Well this is a tricky one," he said.

"Time of death?" asked Mercer, walking toward the tent entrance.

"Approximately seventy two to seventy eight hours ago."

Leyland's legs started to tremble.

He touched his tie knot gently, breathed deeply. The three officers entered the tent, Leyland at the rear of the group.

There on the grass lay the body of Melissa Marshall.

"She was found in this sort of foetal position initially."

"That made any injuries quite difficult to detect visually, but upon closer inspection the victim appeared to have sustained three wounds. I would say they are bullet wounds."

Leyland was fighting back bile as the smell of early decomposition hit his nostrils. It wasn't surprising at this time if year.

Mercer moved to look more closely at the body. Leyland got his first proper look. To his initial surprise she was fully clothed. He then remembered it being mentioned in the briefing but it seemed strange to see. He scanned the body up toward the head. He saw a mass of blonde hair. Then the face. Pale. Eyes closed. Almost angelic. He exhaled heavily and loudly. Mercer twisted his head and gave Leyland a look. Leyland tried hard to control his breathing and his stomach contents.

"Detective Sergeant," said Mercer.

"Notice anything unusual about this scene, giving the fact that the victim may have been shot three times?"

Leyland was struggling to stop his head spinning. The heat in the tent was reaching an unbearable level.

"Leyland? Well?" Mercer asked again.

Leyland scanned. He expected a naked black and blue body with blood everywhere. Maybe even guts. But there was none of the above at this scene.

"Three bullet wounds," said Mercer.

"No blood in the vicinity," Leyland managed to blurt.

"Meaning?" asked Mercer.

"She wasn't killed here," answered Leyland.

"Good," said Mercer.

"So reported missing four days ago and probably killed within hours of that," Mercer added.

The forensic officer jumped in.

"Fully clothed obviously. No sign of sexual assault. Underwear intact. Personal effects have been booked in already. That amounted to no more than a bracelet."

"No handbag? No mobile phone? Purse?" Asked Mercer.

"Nothing at all like that found."

"The local area has been combed with no sign of any objects."

"OK," replied Mercer.

"Get her back for post mortem as soon as possible please, especially for ballistics."

Mercer and the forensic officer left the tent. Leyland heard Mercers mobile go off and he began chatting away on it.

Leyland was in the forensic tent and on his own.

He lowered himself down slowly to sit on the grass. He looked at Melissa. Chin on his knees he started rocking slightly. Tears rolled down his cheeks. He couldn't control it anymore. That beautiful woman on the tube train. That smile. The card. The eyes. How?

How could that have happened when she was dead? How?

He held his head in his hands, trying not to let his sobs escape the tent.

"I'm not fucking mad," he whispered to himself.

"Why reach out to me? Why?" he questioned.

The sound of the tent door flapping in the breeze and the summer birds singing suddenly brought Leyland into focus. He dried his eyes. Paused for a moment. He touched Melissa's hand. Gently. A calm seemed to wash over him.

"I will find out," he said.

"I promise I will find out what happened to you."

He rose from his seated position. Took one final look and turned to leave the tent. Mercer was still on his phone. Leyland breathed in fresher air. Deep refreshing breaths. He was deeply confused but in the midst of the hell storm in his head he felt a new determination. He felt an overwhelming sense of purpose. There was a reason for this happening. He didn't know what the hell that reason was or why this was happening to him, but by god he wasn't going to stop until he had found out.

He had an urge for a stiff drink. And he needed it quickly. Leyland wasn't really an advocate for on duty boozing but under the circumstances he was damn sure Mercer would cut him a little slack.

Mercer had finished his call and his face was like thunder.

"C'mon. We need to get to the Weasel," ordered Mercer.

"What's up Phil?" Leyland asked, concerned for his buddy but a little happy that he was too side-tracked to notice that he had been crying.

"Nothing. Let's just get a drink shall we? You've certainly earned it. And you look like you need it."

Sounded good to Leyland. But something had got up his friends nose and he wanted to know what it was.

They were both back in the Audi and heading for the pub.

"It's Trudy" Mercer said out of the blue.

"OK. What's happened?" Asked Leyland with concern.

"Her and the boys are alright aren't they?"

"Oh yeah," Mercer answered.

"Bloody brilliant."

He paused and took one hand off the steering wheel to loosen his tie.

"She's moving her new fella in." Mercer was visibly hurting. He punched the steering wheel.

"Oh Christ Phil...I'm sorry mate. I never knew that was on the cards."

"Neither did I," answered Mercer.

"I never thought she'd do it," he carried on.

"I know I deserve it. She deserved better. She always did. But I never thought it would really happen."

Leyland didn't know what to say.

"Well. I vote, for once against my usual better judgement, that we get pissed," suggested Leyland.

"Fucking fabulous idea young man!" replied Mercer.

"And after that, you and I, we solve this murder," Mercer added.

Ghost Track: Melissa

"Oh count me well and truly in on that plan my very good friend. Count me in."

Seven.

The voice in the head was trying to reason.
Upper body only. No messing around with the leg. Upper body. Rowing machine maybe for cardio? Treadmill is out of the question.
'I can feel it coming in the air tonight' pumped into Leyland's ears and his workout began.
His arms burned as he lifted weight after weight. Repetition after repetition.
'And I've been waiting for this moment for all my life'
He had stuck to the Vodka yesterday. It always meant minimal hangover the next morning. And he had managed to squeeze quite a decent sleep in between the thinking about and picturing the body.
The Nonpoint version of the Phil Collins classic was firing him up just like it used to.
Time to get some fitness back. Time to take back control. Leyland had uncovered a fresh determination in himself. Seeing the body of Melissa Marshall had affected him profoundly. But he knew full well that he had to play smart. His appointment with the counsellor had been set for eleven o'clock and he needed to be focused and well prepared. No slip ups.
His confidence in his leg had slightly improved. After his gibbering journey on the underground on Monday he needed to see some sort of positive upturn.
Maybe the vodka from last night had numbed the pain. Time would tell. He felt like he was sweating out the spirit at right then.

Ghost Track: Melissa

He hadn't called Phil Mercer this morning. Leyland had managed to get him home in one piece but he was in a shit state. The news from Trudy had hit him harder than his pride would ever have allowed him to show. Leyland hoped and prayed that it wouldn't be something that Petunia Ferdinand would pick up on and use against him. He had to be very careful with the level of drinking under normal circumstances, let alone something like that.

Any obvious slipping of standards in that department would have a very adverse effect on Mercer's career.

The endorphins were flying around Leyland's body and he could feel the addictive effect of the gym returning to him.

He hadn't been able to work out like this for a long time. He missed it and he had needed it. Badly.

Phil Mercer was also up and about and getting busy.

He was pulling on a cigarette as he made his way from his car.

Several other members of his team were waiting for him on the pavement outside a large old Victorian house which had been converted into flats.

In his hand Mercer held a search warrant.

That morning they would be carrying out an extensive search of Melissa Marshalls flat. The curtains of the ground floor flat were twitching already.

Mercer undid his top button. Liverpool FC tie on again, which he loosened only slightly. Scotch was knocking on his temple again but he was handling it. As he always had a million times before.

Mercer he took the lead up a set of six stone steps to the main front door. He rapped on it twice with good force. Just in case anyone was still in bed.

At first nothing. Then the sound of a chain being taken off the door. It opened slowly and slightly with a creak.

A short elderly lady stood looking through a gap of about six inches.

"Yes?" She asked.

"Police Ma'am," answered Mercer, flashing his warrant card and a grin.

"We're here to search flat three. I have the relevant warrant here." Mercer handed them over to the old lady. She took them tentatively from him, hand shaking.

"Ooh," she exclaimed seriously. "You had better come in then." She opened the door and the team shuffled in off the street into the dark hallway of the house.

"Which flat do you live in Ma'am?" asked Mercer.

"I'm in number one. I'm the landlady," she answered.

"Do you have access to flat three at all?"

The old lady pulled an annoyed face.

"Of course I do. I'm the landlady," She reiterated adding a tut and rolling her eyes as if Mercer was talking French or something.

"Can we have access please Ma'am?" Mercer kept his manners strictly old school.

"Be better than kicking the door down you see."

The landlady tutted again at Mercer and gave him a stern narrow eyed look before she shuffled off to get the key.

He couldn't help but crack a smirk at his team, who were all trying hard to suppress their giggles.

The landlady shuffled back slowly and handed the key to Mercer.

"Thank you Ma'am. Very kind."

"And you all check your shoes," the landlady aimed at the rest of the team, jabbing her finger in their direction.

"I don't want mud walked up my stairs."

Mercer stared in disbelief. At the command of a seventy four year old lady one of the hardest and most experienced murder squads in the country were collectively checking the bottom of their shoes.

All clear, they clambered up the stairs past a landing and up another flight to the door of flat three.

Mercer engaged the key in the lock and pushed the door open. The team entered.

"Right!" Said Mercer. "Yous two take the bedroom. You and you the kitchen. Mac you and me take the lounge," he barked drafting his team into pairs. He continued.

"As we know the body was found with virtually zero personal items with it."

"Pay particularly close attention for any phones, diaries, laptops or notebooks. Anything that might give an indication of movements or any meetings."

The team got down to work.

This had to be meticulous. Just before Mercer got stuck into the search with Mac he sent off a text message. To Leyland.

'Good luck this morning buddy. Thanks for last night.'

In the gym Leyland was well in the zone. His phone vibrated and he broke off momentarily to check the message. From Mercer. He guzzled some water and decided that was enough on the upper body for a bit.

Time for some cardio work.

He towelled himself down as sweat was running from him in a torrent. Months of very little by way of exercise had taken its toll. It was certainly going to take a lot of hard work to get his operational fitness back. And Leyland was always one to go above and beyond and prided himself on keeping fitter than the job required. That wasn't being big headed, it was just how he liked to do things. He may well have been labelled as borderline OCD during his counselling sessions regarding his appearance. He did nearly flip out when he fell over on the underground and thought he had dirtied his suit.

He limped over to a vacant rowing machine, sat in position and took a grip of the handles.

Unsure at first, Leyland pulled very very cautiously. The technique required some bending of the knees but thankfully didn't affect Leyland's injury area apart from a bit of pressure when he pulled.

Slight pain but he could certainly handle it.

Gently he continued the exercise very slowly increasing his speed. Into his ears poured more music and his rate increased. His leg hurt but it was not a terribly unbearable pain. It was more of an unshackling type of pain for Leyland. It made him feel euphoric. He could feel the rarest taste of freedom from his injuries and he was drinking it in.

Ghost Track: Melissa

The search was in full swing at Flat three and a number of items had been located quite easily, much to the surprise of Phil Mercer. Those items were being placed into evidence bags and clearly labelled. A mobile phone. A handbag. A diary and a few other less significant possessions.

"That phone needs to be fast tracked to the techs. I want it cracked for any calls or messages on it. As soon as possible."

"Got it boss" answered McCall.

He grabbed the phone in its bag along with some other items and took them down to the car and headed back to the headquarters.

After the morning meeting that had preceded the search of Melissa's flat it had been discussed that the previous days visit to her employers had thrown up some suspicious elements with regards to the behaviour of one Mark Montague. A junior partner at the firm. He had become noticeably agitated and nervous upon being informally questioned about Melissa's disappearance.

Background checks had shown that Melissa had not fallen into debt. She had no criminal record to speak of. No indication of any drug abuse or addiction at all. Given the fact that they had turned her flat upside down and hadn't found so much as an empty cider can, Mercer felt it safe to assume that Miss Marshall wasn't the sort of person who was abusing alcohol.

Some unusual finds within the flat were an empty laptop case next to a plugged in USB lead.

A computer monitor and mouse were also found on a desk in the bedroom but no tower unit was present. Yet there were leads in situ for one.

The next stage at the flats was to interview the landlady and the occupant of flat two.

Mercer had done the sums and given the fact that Melissa had been dead for about three days she would have been taken around Saturday at some point. He took a female officer with him to speak to Mrs Rosamund as she seemed a bit frail.

As soon as the search had been exhausted and the team had left the flats for headquarters Mercer and D.C. Roxanne Lilywhite (Blondie as Mercer affectionately called her) knocked on Mrs Rosamund's door.

She opened up slowly and took the key for flat three from Mercer.

"Do you mind if we come in for a quick chat Mrs Rosamund?" asked Mercer.

"Why do you want to talk to me?" She asked with a look of complete surprise. Almost disgust.

"Just a few questions about the young lady from number three," Mercer answered. "Won't take too long ma'am. Any chance of a nice cup of tea at all?"

Mercer walked into the flat closely followed by Lilywhite who smiled sweetly at the old lady.

Mrs Rosamund tutted and shuffled off into the kitchen to put the kettle on.

"How long had Melissa been living at number three?"

"She had been here for nearly a year. She was never any trouble for me. Always polite. Always helpful.

Lovely manners. Rent was never late," answered Mrs Rosamund.

"Do you remember any boyfriends or acquaintances that might have visited at all recently?"

"No," answered Mrs Rosamund straight away. "Well, there was only the chap that used to pick her up and drop her from work. But he never came in." She was shakily filling an old teapot with the water from the boiled kettle.

"Can you describe the gentleman at all?" questioned Mercer. Lilywhite was poised with her notebook and pen.

Mrs Rosamund looked sheepish.

"Oh I don't really know," she answered. "I only saw him through the window. Young chappy with dark hair," she said.

"And you wouldn't know his name by any chance?"

"Oh no dear. Certainly not." Mrs Rosamund was slowly bringing two cups and saucers of tea into the living room.

A lot of the tea was ending up in the saucer soggying the digestive biscuit perched on the side.

"I just keep myself to myself here."

Mercer rubbed at his chin.

"Who lives in flat number two?" chipped in Lilywhite.

"Mr Carmouche lives in flat two. He's an American and very helpful as well."

"Is Mr Carmouche home at the moment do you know?"

"No no. He is never in until about half nine," She paused looking up at the ceiling. "He is a very busy man you know, He stays away overnight sometimes."

"We will need to speak to Mr Carmouche at some point soon. Just to check on anything he may have seen or heard at the weekend," informed Mercer.

"I'm sure he was out a lot," Said Mrs Rosamund. She seemed lonely. Scared even. But at least she had someone within the house with her.

"Well, if you can think of anything else that may be of interest to us please give us a call. Could you give a card to Mr Carmouche for me?" Mercer stepped over and handed a card to the frail old lady.

"We're only a phone call away," he added, feeling a little bit sorry for her. He drained his tea. It was a proper old school brew. The best he had tasted for quite a long time. He took the biscuit with him. Lilywhite hadn't touched hers.

"Take care ma'am. Thank you for the tea," Mercer chirped as they headed for the door. Mrs Rosamund smiled.

"I'm sorry I didn't see anyone go upstairs," she muttered.

Mercer was stunned and threw a look at Lilywhite that said 'what the fuck?'

He thought briefly, and then gestured for Lilywhite to head out of the door.

"No problem Ma'am," replied Mercer.

He heard at least two chains being engaged on the door behind them. On his way out of the flat he had observed at least four on the door frame. Three of them looked very bright and shiny as if they were new and recently fitted.

"Blondie. I want an unmarked watching this place around the clock."

Lilywhite was confused. "Guv?"

"That woman was scared. And who asked her if anyone went upstairs?" Mercer added.

"Confusion maybe," answered Lilywhite.

"Maybe. But three new chains on the door? When the old one may well have sufficed. Bit much? Especially with a male living upstairs." Mercer continued. "Am I being paranoid do you think Lilywhite?"

"I don't think so boss. It didn't feel particularly right in that flat."

"Get the watch sorted out as soon as," Mercer ordered.

"And not a uniformed unit either," He barked at Lilywhite who peeled off to her car, throwing him a smile and a thumbs up.

Mercer sparked up a cigarette and drew hard on it.

Leyland Francis had finished his workout. He was feeling immense. Almost invincible.

The water from the power shower hit him and cascaded off his sweat covered shoulders and neck. It felt glorious.

He had one hour before his counselling session. Where he was feeling nerves before, he was now feeling nothing less than confident. He massaged shower gel into his hair and body. Bring it on. Bring it on.

He kept repeating that in his mind. He was ready to take on and prove to occupational health, especially to Ferdinand, that he was ready. Despite possibly having spoken to a dead girl, which he wasn't going to bring up at the session, he was going to prove that he was worthy of taking his place back in command of his team.

After taking care of business with his pal Mercer of course. He had made a promise to him. And despite the unusual, albeit fucked up, circumstances in which he found himself making that promise, he was going to see it through.

He considered as reasonably as he could as to how a 'ghost' could have communicated with him in the way that Melissa Marshall had on that Monday. She had possibly been dead for two days before that. He wanted to broach the matter with Mercer, but didn't have the first clue where to start.

He stood under the hot powerful water in a world of his own. Was it because of the accident? Was it P.T.S.D? Had the severe concussion messed with his brain chemistry enabling him to see dead people? Or think he was seeing dead people? If it hadn't been for these experiences he would have scoffed at such suggestions generally.

Laughed. Called the person a crackpot for even thinking that such things could ever take place. But take place they did. And to him.

Maybe it was the fall on the underground. He had bumped his head. Hard. Maybe it was as a result of that? But if so then how did he manage to be in possession of her business card? And how did she ring his mobile phone?

These were tangible objects and events that proved it certainly wasn't all completely in his head. They bought the very possibility of fantasy into reality. He had held the card. Touched it. Smelt it even. It was real. And she had given it to him.

Why would she do that? Why single him out? Maybe there were others that could claim similar encounters? Maybe he wasn't the only one. Maybe he had tapped into some sort of energy or power from somewhere.

He was going round and round in circles again in his head. He needed to focus properly. It was Ok questioning everything like that but it would end up driving him crazy if he didn't control himself. He switched off the shower and inhaled deeply. He started drying off and sat on the bench next to the cubicle and paid attention to his lower right leg.

Bright pink scars intercrossed the back of his calf with a rough two inch square chunk about half an inch deep missing.

Leyland winced as he ran his hand over the wounds. One thick scar led around to the front of the shin and trailed off just under the knee. The pain of the three operations had faded to a degree. The pain of losing a close colleague had not faded quite so easily. That, coupled with losing the witness they were moving, had affected Leyland very deeply in the early weeks of his recovery.

The main issue that caused him the guilt was the one of him being the only one who survived.

He couldn't look any one of Pete McGuinness's family in the eye. The injuries he had sustained were horrendous. He had been thrown from the car and had died almost instantly.

The witness was being moved by Leyland and McGuinness into protective custody after a specific and immediate threat to his safety had been identified. The plan was to deliver him into a witness protection programme. In the ensuing investigations and inquests the witness was identified only as 'Witness A' but to Leyland Francis he was so much more than just a letter in the public domain. Witness Alpha was one of the bravest people Leyland had known in such a short space of time.

Curtis Smith had agreed to carry out testimonial against a Russian organised crime boss.

The Russian in question was on trial for being the kingpin of a major money laundering operation.

The NCA had spent millions of pounds in resources in the attempt to bring him to justice. Three years and thousands of man hours had bought the agency close, but never to the point where they could get their 'money shot' on the front of the national newspapers of the kingpin in handcuffs.

That was until Smith defected and offered major evidence on the laundering operation in return for immunity and protection. It was the coup that the agency had been praying for.

Leyland's team had been tasked with protecting him during the transportation to court and afterwards to his new life as a different person. He would have been given a new face as well. Anything to keep him safe and alive after turning on one of the most influential and brutal crime bosses of the century.

Leyland himself was behind the wheel when the move was finally authorised. As team leader he wouldn't let anyone else put themselves in that position. McGuinness bravely convinced Leyland that he would need some back up and booked himself into the passenger seat. A decision that left his eight year old son without his dad. That pain, more than the pain of the operations and the injuries, that pain stabbed at Leyland's heart and he felt that it probably would for the rest of his days.

The telephone on Dr Martinez's desk rang.

"Hello?"

"Dr Martinez, Petunia Ferdinand again."

"I have D.S. Francis due at eleven, within twenty four hours just like you ordered," Martinez snapped.

"Dr Martinez, I need you to probe this officer probably a bit more aggressively than you may had planned or would normally. I need a reaction from D.S. Francis."

"It's not generally my style Petunia," replied Martinez.

On the other end of the telephone, unbeknown to Martinez, Ferdinand had lowered her glasses.

"Dr Martinez, Detective Sergeant Francis represents what is not required on this force. He has tried to pull the wool over all our eyes regarding his mental condition and I need you to prove that fact by getting under his skin. Is that clear?"

"As much as I would hate to disrespect your expertise," countered Martinez. "Wouldn't it be a better use of resources if we actually try and help this officer? Is that not what we are here for?"

"Dr Martinez, you're not there to offer opinion on the effective use of occupational health department resources. You are there to follow my instructions to the letter. Do you understand what I'm saying Dr?"

There was a pause. Martinez knew from experience that resistance was futile. Especially with her at the helm.

"I Understand fully Petunia," he answered.

"Good because any misunderstanding could well be to the detriment to your career Dr. so when Francis shows his face, play rough. O.K.?"

Ferdinand didn't wait for another answer. She ended the call.

Martinez sat in a brief stunned silence. He had Leyland's file in front of him which contained pages upon pages of information on the officer, his career and his injuries, all giving the doctor a very good chance of getting the demanded reaction that Ferdinand wanted. The question for Martinez was not where to start, but where to stop.

Sitting fairly low down in her classic Jaguar XJS Petunia Ferdinand watched and waited. She was parked about thirty yards away from the entrance of Talbot's gym. Waiting. Waiting for Leyland Francis to leave. She had followed him from his flat that morning sensing an opportunity to discredit his claim that his physical difficulties were improving.

In her mind there was no better way than seeing how his training session had cut him down.

She glanced into the rear view mirror and dabbed her index finger lightly over her lips, smoothing her lipstick gently. Perfect she thought.

Her mobile phone was on the dashboard and she grabbed it and checked her messages. Only one received.

'How's it going on stakeout?'

Ferdinand pulled a very thin smile. She tapped on the touch screen *'Patience is a virtue. As you know I always get the right result. Ready to step up?'* and pressed send.

'Always ready' came the swift reply.

'Then make sure you are ready for Friday night. Don't let me down with what I want' typed Ferdinand and sent.

Another quick comeback *'Have I yet?'*

She wasn't getting into text tennis and deleted the received and sent messages. As she placed the phone back on the dash she caught the figure of Leyland heading out of the gym. She thought he seemed to be limping quite badly, which was good in her view, but he was only using one crutch which she viewed as a negative for her purposes.

She let him move up the street a bit more before leaving her car. She marched into the gym with the air of the occupants being ten times lower than her own excreta. Her face could not have shown more contempt if she had a million pounds riding on it.

She had her warrant card ready for the approach to the reception desk.

"Good morning," she said to the meathead in a vest at the desk. He looked slightly unsure as to how to react to her when she flashed her card at him.

"Don't worry I'm not here to seize your steroids. I need access to your C.C.T.V. from the last couple of hours," Ferdinand demanded.

"This person," she held up a photo of Leyland. "Was in here very very recently," Meathead nodded affirmatively.

"I need to see where he was training, what he was doing and how he handled it and I need to see that footage now."

Meathead looked very unsure and was hesitant. But this was the Police. She sensed his uncertainty.

"We can do it quietly," said Ferdinand "Or we can go very official, and by official I mean you'll be locking your doors for a week." She stared at him very sternly.

"It's up to you," she added.

Meathead grabbed a bunch of keys from the reception desk and gestured to an office behind them. "In here," he grunted, unlocking the door. And they both walked into the office.

Ferdinand found it amusing that he could only seem to walk like he had bags of flour under his arms. Meathead squeezed into a chair at the computer station and tapped into the cameras on site. There was an extensive range, just what Ferdinand had hoped for.

"Thank you, if you could leave me for ten minutes," she requested, with the tone more associated with an order. Meathead shrugged and struggled out of the chair and made to leave the office.

"Pull the door too," Ferdinand added as he walked out. She got to work on her ongoing vendetta against Detective Sergeant Leyland Francis.

Leyland was waiting to be called into Dr Martinez' office and was feeling tight after his workout.

It was a satisfying session but he was feeling the tiring effects of it at that point. He checked his phone as he took a sip of water from a bottle. He had a voice message from an earlier missed call. It was from his dad. Leyland hadn't spoken to him for a while and felt a little bad. No doubt he would be getting the guilt trip in the message and sure enough as the voicemail played out Leyland's father ran through who he was, where he lived and his telephone number. All with a heavy dollop of Arthur Francis sarcasm. He had done it a million times; it was his own quirky sense of humour. Being an ex-military man Arthur was so very proud of his son making the progress in his career that he had. It was from the military career and the training that his father had received that Leyland believed his own obsession of neatness had come from. He would visit soon, for sure. He had promised he would visit more since mum passed away.

"Mr Francis," called Dr Martinez, snapping Leyland out of his train of thought.

Leyland rose from his seat in the clinical waiting room.

"I'm Dr. Martinez," he introduced.

"Good to meet you," acknowledged Leyland offering his hand. The two men shook and made their way into the cosy yet functional office.

Leyland was feeling his nerves a little bit but his battle plan was as clear in his mind, as it had ever been, and the advice of Phil Mercer was resonating in his head. 'Just play good dog'

"Take a seat," offered the doctor.

"So, how have things been?" A standard procedure kick off to a session. Martinez settled into his seat and opened the file on his desk. Leyland's file. The first page was a handwritten list of questions and side notes.

"Things have been good. Although I've only been back, if that's the correct term, for a few days."

"Would you not be happy using that term Leyland? You don't mind me referring to you as Leyland do you? Rather than your rank?" Martinez awaited an answer.

"Leyland is fine," he answered. Martinez cut in again.

"Have you been frustrated by not being allowed back on full duties yet?"

Leyland paused. Considered.

"Frustrated? Certainly. But that in no way means I would not heed the advice afforded to me." Good eye contact. Fairly relaxed.

"That's good to hear. I don't mean to sound uncaring but the physical aspects of healing aren't particularly my speciality," Martinez continued. "More the emotional and mental damage"

"I didn't think you were here to take my temperature," Leyland joked.

Martinez looked up from his notes. Stone faced.

"Quite," he said harshly.

"Tell me, how have the after effects of the death of D.C. McGuinness and Witness A been dealt with by you Leyland?" Straight to the heart.

The question took Leyland slightly by surprise. His heart rate increased slightly.

"Well, Dr Martinez, having been guided through a number of techniques to deal with, and ultimately heal, any anxiety, guilt or grief, I feel that I have dealt with all of those issues very well indeed," answered Leyland. His palms had started to sweat slightly.

"I did after all get out of bed and dress myself this morning," he added for good measure.

Martinez couldn't help feeling like a complete bastard. He looked at the picture of his wife and two gorgeous children on his desk. But with Ferdinand leaning on him heavily he had to seize on the one word Leyland had just come out with. Guilt.

"Do you feel guilty about the deaths Leyland? Do you feel responsible?"

Leyland stared hard at Martinez for a few seconds.

"Of course I feel guilt."

"Two people died in my care. Under my command, in my custody. Do I feel it was my fault? No. I had no control over the incident and, as I'm sure that big file there will tell you, I was cleared by the enquiry of any fault. I had no way of avoiding the collision."

"Ah yes the fateful stolen Mercedes," said Martinez.

"The mystery hit and run driver never located." Martinez sneered as he read from the file.

"You're point?" Snapped Leyland. Martinez was getting somewhere.

"Did you ever feel vengeful? Want to find this person? Make them pay?"

"After all in your earlier counselling sessions you stated that you felt the investigation had let you down." Martinez pressed on.

"Not a particularly good view of the Police service that provide you with a good wage was it Detective Sergeant?"

"Of course I felt vengeful. Bitter even. I was curious as to how I would feel if I ever had the chance to face the perpetrator," Leyland explained.

"I meant no harm in my comments. In confidence. I did feel let down. Anyone would have. But I have confidence and respect for the force I serve and I know that they would have exhausted all avenues."

"Ever consider investigating yourself? Go solo?" Asked Martinez.

"No! Never," snapped Leyland again, desperately trying to keep his mouth under control.

"Are you a maverick Leyland?"

"Would you disregard formal procedure for revenge?"

What the hell was his problem, Leyland thought. He had walked into a buzz saw job.

"I follow the rules and procedures Doctor."

"I do the job to the best of my ability" Leyland added.

"When did you last have a nightmare?" asked Martinez.

"A small one. Two days ago," Leyland answered honestly on that one.

Martinez paused, looking down at the thick file. He closed it.

"And the last time you had to rely on your painkillers?"

"I thought you weren't concerned with the physical side of things" Retorted Leyland.

"Are you addicted to them?"

"In no way shape or form."

"What about alcohol? Are you drinking?" The good doctor questioned again.

Leyland held up his half full bottle of water.

"This is my tipple," he answered, smirking with his temper back under control.

Martinez could see he wasn't going to break Leyland to the point that he needed. Nor did he really have the stomach to go any further with his line of questioning toward a vulnerable officer.

He didn't do this job to make officers in need of help, like Leyland, think that they couldn't turn to him if the shit hit the fan emotionally for them.

He gently massaged the bridge of his nose.

Not the first time was he regretting very deeply being beaten to the Occupational Health Director job by Ferdinand. These were the consequences.

"Do you feel that you may have inadvertently made enemies Leyland?" Softer and much more friendly this time.

"As a Police officer for many years Doctor, I have naturally made enemies. Out there on the street. But you know what the worst kind of enemy is? The enemy within your own ranks. An enemy you didn't deserve, If you get what I mean Doctor?"

Martinez smiled. A good man made to do a bad thing.

"I fear I do get what you mean Leyland," he answered.

"And I fear that an 'enemy within' as you so put it has coerced me to act terribly. Forgive me?"

Leyland paused for a few seconds. Shocked. It could only be Ferdinand. She was getting to guys like this? She was way out of control. But why? He swigged from his water bottle. His throat dry. Why? He racked his brains.

"Dare I ask who that may be?"

"I think you may already be aware given your detective credentials," Martinez answered.

"Ferdinand perhaps?" Offered Leyland.

Martinez smiled slightly.

"I don't know what you may have or have not said or done to have her taking such an interest in you," He revealed. "But watch every step you take Leyland. She will try and lean on or blackmail or bully anyone to get the result she wants."

"And how would a person like me possibly reverse her fortunes in that department?" Questioned Leyland.

"I really don't think I'm the person to suggest," said Martinez.

"But I am the person to suggest that you should look between the lines. What may not be obvious? What may be very well hidden? Follow your nose," Martinez continued. "Just be very careful if that's a road you choose to take," he warned seriously.

"Please don't let this session put you off getting in touch should you ever need any help Leyland. I'm sorry. Shall we start again?"

Leyland smiled at Martinez warmly. He seemed like a good guy after all. He got up and extended his hand to the doctor over the desk. Martinez shook firmly.

"Let's say you owe me one," Leyland offered.

"Be ready if the tide turns Doctor. I may well call upon your services," Leyland parted with.

He stepped out into the sunlight, breathed deeply, and his phone chimed. It was Mercer.

"Hello mate," He greeted.

"Buddy, briefing at the hub in half an hour," Mercer informed.

"And we need to interview the resident at Flat two afterwards, so get here asap."

"I'm on my way," Answered Leyland simply.

"How did the appointment go?" Mercer asked.

"Interesting. Let's just say that Ferdinand is sticking her fingers in a few too many pies for my liking."

"More trouble?"

"Yep, and an ally. Will tell you more when I get there. See you in a bit." Leyland ended the call.

He made for the nearest tube station but decided he didn't want to push his luck and hailed a taxi and headed for N.C.A. headquarters.

Eight.

Within the investigation briefing room there was the usual buzz.

The general consensus of opinion was that although they felt no closer to arrests, a massive amount of progress had been made within the investigation.

Leyland had managed to grab a large latte from Starbucks on his way in thus avoiding the canteen dishwater.

Mercer was preparing his info for the briefing and he had Roxanne Lilywhite setting up a laptop to link up with the interactive whiteboard behind them.

Mercer gave Leyland a thumbs up as he spotted him taking a seat and preparing his note book.

Leyland scanned the many characters in the room of his temporary home.

This was obviously a full team briefing. A sudden mesmerised silence came over the room. Leyland looked over his shoulder. The Commander had entered the room. He took a seat at the back of the room and removed his hat. Mercer looked up from his business on the laptop, his familiar Liverpool FC tie hanging down. Lilywhite took over and tapped a few buttons, whispered some instructions to Mercer and the briefing was pretty much good to go.

"O.K. ladies and gentleman settle down please and listen in," Shouted Mercer, catching everyone's attention.

He tapped the first key on the laptop and the required information was projected onto the screen on the wall.

"O.K. Melissa Marshall's time of death has been placed at some time between Sixteen hundred hours and twenty two hundred hours on Saturday. Cause of death has been established as a bullet wound to the heart. Two further bullet wounds to the chest and left breast were also found." Mercer paused and scanned the room.

"The victim was found fully clothed. No sign of sexual assault. No signs linked to a struggle or fight were found either," Another pause.

"A search of Marshall's flat found a mobile phone, a handbag, a purse and a diary. We are awaiting results from tech regarding the phone."

Leyland shifted uncomfortably at the mention of the phone. Was that the one she called him from?

"The diary threw up nothing other than a couple of names that were in it. Mark Montague and Felicity Marshall." Mercer tapped another button on the laptop.

Leyland was scribbling away into his notebook. He near enough had his tongue poking out with the amount of concentration he was putting into it.

"We have spoken to Mrs Rosamund, Marshalls landlady, we are taking a statement from the resident of the other flat, a Mr Stan Carmouche, after this briefing."

Two pictures flicked up on the screen. Leyland looked up and double took. There on the screen was a photograph of none other than the man who had helped him when he fell over on the tube. Stan. Stan the Louisiana saxophone player.

"No information relating to Melissa's disappearance could be gained from Mrs Rosamund. We will be speaking to Mr Carmouche this morning. Interestingly the landlady seemed scared when informally spoken to. She appeared to have stepped up her personal security in her flat somewhat extensively," Mercer continued. "Couple that with a check on Melissa's home insurance schedule and it would seem that a laptop and personal computer tower are missing from the flat. They are not at her place of work. This makes the possibility that Melissa Marshall was abducted and subsequently murdered because of some information that may have been contained on those devices. Until they are located we must treat that as possible motive." Mercer looked around at the sea of serious faces.

"Going forward from this moment I want a full top to bottom search of her workplace carried out. Warrant is pending given the nature of their business and should be ready within the hour. We thought belt and braces would be the only way to go on that."

"I want statements from all work colleagues no matter how far down the food chain they are. Probe for any reasons, however ridiculous, there could be for her being killed in that way." A pause.

"Any questions?" He asked.

Leyland had a curiosity.

"Has there been any further contact from the sister at all?"

"None whatsoever," Mercer answered. "She is a freelance investigative journalist and the suggestion is that her work may have taken her overseas."

"Even though her sister was missing?" Leyland looked puzzled.

"It would seem so D.S. Francis."

"The bullets taken from the body are with ballistics who will cross reference with Interpol and National databases for any matches to previous hits. As we all know this can take some time. You all have your assignment instructions so let's pull our socks up and get out there and get a result for this young lady." Mercer ended the briefing with a trademark "Let's roll."

Leyland needed to bend Mercers ear about Stan.

"Phil, the guy from flat two. I know of him," he revealed.

"How so?" Asked a slightly perplexed Mercer.

"He helped me on the underground a couple of days ago."

"Well haven't I always warned you about men you meet on the underground?"

Leyland smiled. "He seemed a really genuine and nice guy. I'm sure he would help if he saw or knew anything. Might help with a slightly familiar face there as well."

"Absolutely" Agreed Mercer. "Be heading off in five minutes. Be ready!"

Leyland limped off to the toilets.

Commander Rawlins approached Mercer.

"Good briefing Phil. What's your gut telling you on this one?"

"Well Sir, it's a murder that points toward I would say a discovery of some sort of sensitive information."

Amongst the buzz of the investigation team stepping up a gear Rawlins put his hand on Mercer's shoulder and moved in closer.

You know I have every faith in you Phil, but the press seem to be climbing all over this. You know I'd never ordinarily push but it would be nice to throw the dogs a bone to shut them up for a bit." The two men locked eye contact. Rawlins had a smile but his eyes were all business.

"You know what these fucking vultures can be like."

If the Commander was leaning on him, it was because the chief was getting some crap from further up. Pure and simple. Mercer nodded knowingly.

"Look, sir, the last twelve hours have produced a lot of leads to a degree. It'll be how we approach those leads that will give results. I wouldn't be at all surprised that in another twelve hours we'll have a bloody great bone to throw to your vultures," said Mercer, applying a small tablespoon of Billy bullshit. Had to be done sometimes when the Commander came sniffing.

"Also Phil, it has come to my attention that Ferdinand has been sniffing round young D.S. Francis. And she also thinks you are back on the bottle. Any truth in that? And is Francis up to deflecting her?"

"No truth in that at all." Mercer shook his head and rolled his eyes. "I've had my slip ups. She is getting out of control Jack. Way out of control. Francis can handle her but she is making it personal for some reason."

Rawlins smiled. "I've got your back Phil. But I just like to hear these things from the horse's mouth so to speak. I have always said she will hang herself one day. All she needs is enough rope and to seriously piss off the wrong person. What concerns me is who she might try and take with her Phil. Try not to be around if and when the time comes. If you are make sure you're clean," warned Rawlins.

Mercer shrugged, and flashed a grin. "You know me Jack. Always at least one step ahead."

"And what about Francis?"

"I'll be looking out for him just like you look out for me Jack. Don't worry."

"Keep things tight Phil. See you soon." The two officers shook hands and Commander Rawlins wandered back to the thin air of the tenth floor.

Mercer barked at Leyland.

"C'mon soft lad, let's roll."

"Keep your hair on," jested Leyland.

"Boss!" Came the shout from the door to the briefing room. It was D.C. Scott. She had a bundle of papers in her hand and was gesturing to Mercer.

Mercer strolled over to her.

"Marshalls mobile was cracked finally," She informed.

"These are the logs. Text messages, voice messages and calls in and out to the phone. All listed in date order."

"Superb!" Mercer beamed. "Just what we have been waiting on. Any news on email accounts and the like?"

"Proving tricky to crack the password encryption boss."

"O.K. good stuff Scotty. I guess we should start trawling this little lot then."

"D.S. Francis," Mercer called over to the waiting Leyland who moved toward Mercer looking curious.

"Can you handle flat two on your own?" Mercer questioned.

"I should think so, why?"

"Scottie and I are going to sift through this little lot." Mercer waved the wad of A4 to Leyland.

"No worries. Will grab a cab there. Have fun with your paper," Leyland joked.

"I spoke on the phone with him briefly earlier so he knows we are coming to speak to him. He said he would make himself available so squeeze as much out as you can," Mercer informed.

"See you in a bit," Leyland parted with and headed off to hail a cab

Leyland made his way through the corridors and out into the August brightness. It took him all of fifteen seconds to flag down a passing cab and make start the ten minute journey to Churchill Place.

In the back of the cab he took the opportunity to give his leg a quick rub. It was feeling a bit tight again and he didn't want it cramping up. especially not when he was interviewing Stan.

He reflected on the fact that his gym session had gone pretty well and he was pleased that he was closer to returning to full physical capabilities. Screw what Ferdinand and her cronies thought. It wouldn't be long before he could damn well prove it. He knew it was one thing to sit and try and tell how he was fine and could do his job. It was certainly another to make them stand up and see that he could actually prove the fact. Prove them very wrong.

Leyland was close to that point and was itching to rub their noses in it. Especially Ferdinand.

The taxi pulled in just outside Churchill Place. Leyland paid and decamped, and viewed the Victorian frontage of the building as he made his way up the steps to the front door. He pressed the button on the intercom marked flat two.

"Hello?" Came the muffled voice.

"Mr Carmouche it's the Police. I'm here to ask you a few questions."

"Push the door officer," replied Stan and a buzz allowed the lock to disengage and Leyland walked in.

He struggled slightly with the stairs up to flat two and a very strong, almost overwhelming, feeling came over him when he considered that Melissa had live just upstairs. Had climbed these very stairs.

He dealt with these feelings by justifying to some degree that they were beyond his control. he didn't ask for any of this to happen to him and he certainly wasn't going to second guess any of the goings on. he was going to do his job well. Any help that might come from supernatural areas would be gratefully received but by no means were essential to him.

Stan was at is door waiting to greet the Police officer coming to see him. His face broke into a massive smile as soon as he set eyes on Leyland working his way to the landing.

"Well now see here," he boomed.

"Seeing you still upright warms an old man's heart."

Leyland himself wasn't too surprised as he already knew who he was coming to question. But the greeting was nice and he raised a big grin upon seeing the saxophonist again.

Leyland made it to the door and the two men exchanged the warmest of handshakes.

"Really good to see you again Stan," greeted Leyland.

"You too buddy, you too. how has life been treating you since your little tumble, huh?" Asked Stan, ushering Leyland into the flat.

"Oh, up and down. But not in a falling down sort of way which is good. How about you? How's the Sax?"

"Smooth as ever buddy. Smooth as ever," chuckled Stan. "You want a coffee?"

"I would love one Stan, but please understand I'm here on official Police business" Said Leyland stepping up the seriousness a level.

"About the poor girl upstairs?" Stan asked.

"Yes. Melissa Marshall."

"Oh yeah, I spoke to that other guy on the phone," offered Stan.

"Yes, Detective Chief Inspector Mercer. My superior."

"I liked him. He's just like me with that accent. He ain't from round here either," joked Stan.

Leyland smiled. Phil had left his impression on the man from Louisiana.

"As much as I wished I could help, I was away for the weekend when she went missing. I only got back late last night and Mrs Rosamund downstairs filled me in on some of the details."

Leyland was scribbling in his notebook.

"Stan, Mrs Rosamund. How has she seemed to you since this all happened?"

Stan considered for a moment.

"She's been shaken up. Hell, she's an old lady and scared. Who wouldn't be after all that going on." Stan walked over to the Beech wood table that Leyland was sitting at.

"Have you noticed the extra chains on her door?" Leyland probed.

"I heard her trying to take the damn things off when I knocked to say I was back."

"I damn near grew a beard waiting," Stan joked lightly. His smile dropped a bit.

"I do worry about Mrs Rosamund. She ain't got no family around anymore. So I look out for her where I can." Stan sipped his coffee and pulled out a packet of Benson and Hedges cigarettes from under his pork pie hat. "Do you mind buddy?" Stan asked.

"Oh, of course not," replied Leyland feeling a touch awkward.

"It's your flat Stan," he joked taking in a sip of coffee. It was strong but very flavoursome. a hint of bitterness. Delicious.

Stan lit up his smoke and dragged heavily. Leyland's sense of comfort had increased with the big guys hospitality and frankness. No bullshit. Just facts.

"Stan, my colleague who called earlier."

"Phil?" Cut in Stan.

"Yes Phil. He seemed to have a very strong feeling that Mrs Rosamund was scared for possibly a direct reason. That maybe she had seen something but didn't

want to say." Leyland put it out there. Sipped his coffee again and continued.
"I would hate to think of her lying awake at night feeling scared. Especially when we could help."
Stan considered his thoughts for a moment and nodded lightly but positively.
"I understand your concern buddy," he answered.
"I trust Phil Mercer one hundred percent Stan. He's not just my colleague. He is a good friend of mine too. His instinct is second to none. He wouldn't think such a thing if he didn't feel very strongly about it."
Leyland paused. Stan was rubbing his chin.
"She is very fond of you Stan. How would you feel about perhaps speaking to her for us?"
Stan was thinking. He looked Leyland right in the eye.
"I like you guys," he revealed. "And if you're tight like you say, then sure I'll try and help."
Stan inhaled some more smoke.
"I'm having dinner downstairs this evening. I'll approach the issue then."
"That would be brilliant. Thank you Mr Carmouche," said Leyland, excited at the progress.
Stan pulled a face.
"Mr Carmouche?" He laughed. "Hell I've not been called that for a long while. You call me Stan buddy, otherwise this old fool is gonna feel awkward," Stan jested.
Leyland drained his coffee and stood up. He took a slow wander and took in the many photographs on display in Stan's cosy abode.
"You're an ex-military man then Stan?"

"Twenty five years in the United States Marine Corps young buddy." Stan revealed. Pride in his voice was evident and warm.

Leyland spotted two objects on ribbons pushed to the back of Sans sideboard. Purple hearts.

"Were you in Vietnam?"

"Sure was," confirmed Stan. "That's where I won those two little things there." He pointed to the medals.

His smile seemed to drop as the memories of his various tours of duty ran through his mind.

"Sure wasn't the best place to be a lot of times." He said softly.

"My dad was in the Army," revealed Leyland. "In the Falklands."

"He always said to me that no matter the horrors or how shitty the situation ever got, you always had this kind of warmth knowing that you had brothers around you. In the shit together."

Stan nodded his agreement.

"No truer word spoken than that from a man as wise as an old warrior," said Stan.

Leyland noticed the saxophone case on the floor.

"Where did you find time to learn to play?" He asked pointing to the instrument.

"Ahhh yeah. Mr sax." Said Stan, his big beam returned.

"Well I have to admit I was into the music from a such a young age," he reminisced.

"My daddy was in a blues band and if I behaved, which wasn't often you understand, every now and then he'd take me along to a performance. I was hooked when I saw how they played and the fun they had. I'd sit there watching with a bowl of Gumbo and a coke. I was never ever happier than being there during those times. Never." Stan sparked another cigarette.

"From there on I was hooked and badgered daddy for weeks upon weeks to teach me how to play. Finally he couldn't take no more and he gave in and started me on the path." Stan was looking wistfully at a black and white photo of a man who looked very much similar to him. Leyland made the assumption that it was Stan's dad.

"Hasn't been a day gone by in the last fourteen years where I haven't played."

"Is that since you finished your service?" Leyland asked.

"Not quite," answered Stan. "You see this picture right here" He pointed to one on the shelf, slightly obscured by another frame. Stan and another stood beside a helicopter.

"I worked with this guy for over twenty years after Vietnam."

"Doing what?" Asked Leyland, like a small boy being held under the old man's story telling skills. This guy was interesting and mysterious. Leyland liked his company.

"Working for the C.I.A." Answered Stan in a very matter of fact manner.

Leyland's jaw nearly hit the carpet. "The C.I.A? As in THE C.I.A?"

"The one and only," confirmed Stan.

"You must have seen some real sites. I mean were you undercover? Where did you operate?" Babbled Leyland excitedly almost in disbelief that this guy, this guy who busks with a saxophone on the tube, was in the C.I.A. for twenty years.

"Let's just say that old Stan learnt a few tricks over the years." He winked and turned around to collect the empty mugs.

"You got a number I can reach you on?" Stan asked. "After I've spoken to Mrs Rosamund I can give you an update."

"That would be brilliant," said Leyland and he pulled one of his cards from his wallet and placed it on the dining table.

The two men shook hands and Stan gently tapped Leyland's shoulder in a gesture of respect. And hopefully trust.

"I really hope you catch who did what they did to Melissa. She was a nice girl. Such a damn shame."

"If I have anything to do with it, it won't be long," suggested Leyland as he moved toward the front door. "Speak soon Stan," Leyland parted with and headed out of the old house.

In the confines of the investigation hub Phil Mercer was flicking through the pages of information relating to Melissa's mobile phone. He was about halfway through the pile. Nothing unusual found so far. Usual stuff. Work. Sister. Chinese takeaway. The tech forensics had done a sterling job by retrieving messages and call logs and noting who the numbers belonged to and any other relevant information. And they'd done it quickly.

Mercer continued to scan and flick. Something caught his eye very quickly. A mobile telephone number. The date. The time. No name next to the description. Just the number. But it rang a bell in Mercers head.

It was from someone he knew. Mercer had a sick feeling. He vaguely recognised the number, but only vaguely.

He took his phone out of his pocket and started to flick through numbers on it.

It didn't take long for his fears to be realised.

He placed his phone on his desk and his head in his hands.

Anyone but him. What the fuck was going on?

"You O.K. boss?" D.C. Scott asked.

"Got any Scotch on you?" Mercer replied shaking his head.

"Err I'm afraid not boss!" Scott replied, confused. Concerned.

"Could you grab me a strong coffee from downstairs." Mercer slipped a fiver across the desk.

"Grab yourself one as well," he added. Scott wandered off, still a bit unsure as to the issue.

Mercer picked his mobile up and dialled.

Lightly bouncing down the stone steps outside the old Victorian house Leyland felt a sense of progress. He was looking out for a cab when his phone rang out. It was Mercer.

"Hello mate," Leyland greeted. "Made contact with Stan Carmouche who is going to have a chat with the landlady this evening regarding any comings and goings."

Ghost Track: Melissa

"That's brilliant," replied Mercer. "Now I need you back here straight away," he ordered. He was Stern. Clearly very serious. Something was wrong thought Leyland.

"Everything O.K. Phil?" Leyland queried.

"Just get back here now," answered Mercer and terminated the call.

Strange, thought Leyland. Maybe it was Trudy pissing him off again.

Leyland waved down a passing cab and jumped in. As they pulled away Leyland mobile rang again.

"D.S. Francis, it's McCall. I'm on watch outside Marshalls flat, and I've just seen you leave."

"That's right just a second ago," Leyland replied.

"Just thought you might like to know that Petunia Ferdinand was watching as well. She is following you."

Leyland turned around slowly and looked out of the rear window of the cab. Sure enough there was the familiar Jaguar three cars back from them.

Leyland breathed in and considered for one moment if he should tell the driver to try and lose her, and then the sick feeling of being in a speeding car hit him. The impact of the accident flashed through his mind and he realised it wasn't worth risking the drivers life just to give her the slip. Not worth it at all.

He took deep breaths and tried to reason in his mind why the hell she would be tailing him.

He thought back to his session with Martinez. What was all that 'Between the lines' stuff about? Did Martinez have some sort of belief that Leyland could take her on?

And even if he wanted to, did he really have the time or the mental strength to go toe to toe with her at the same time as working out why ghosts were casually handing him business cards?

Probably not, he concluded very quickly. Whatever her problem was, it was going to have to wait until he, Mercer and the rest of the team had got to the bottom of Melissa's murder.

Leyland had more reason than most to want to solve it quickly. He was personally invested. He had been touched by her appearance on the tube. He needed to know how or why. At the very least to have something to cling to and be able to look at further.

"Let the bitch follow," he said into the phone.

"I'm only going back to HQ so if she wants to piss her time away then let her. Thanks for the heads up though buddy."

Phil Mercer was pissed off. It took a lot to do that to a man who prided himself on his 'wicked scouse sense of humour'

He was proud of his accent and proud of his roots. He was proud to do the job that he did to the absolute best of his ability. He expected the very same standards from those he worked with as well.

The team he had built around him was testament to those ethics.

It had taken a while to weed out the bullshitters and the wannabes. The brown nosers and glory hunters. They had no place or time on Mercer's team in any way.

Ghost Track: Melissa

What stuck in his throat were those that impeded an investigation or held out on him. Especially on something as serious as a murder investigation.

And his old pal Leyland Francis had done just that. Mercer wanted to know why, and he wanted to fucking well know now.

He paced around the dark empty briefing room alone. Running scenarios through his mind. What to say. How to approach the situation.

He spotted Leyland walk back into the hub. Fuck it, thought Mercer. Straight into the deep end.

He dashed out of the briefing room. Leyland's smile turned to confusion when Mercer grabbed him and dragged him by the arm the six paces into an interview room. They both crashed through the door and Mercer let his grip go, slamming the door behind them. He pushed Leyland into a chair roughly.

"What the f..."

"Shut up and listen," Mercer cut him off point blank and threw the telephone record sheet onto the desk.

"You fucking explain that to me now." He emphasised the 'that' as if it were a turd on the desk.

Leyland took the sheet and scanned it hard.

Mercer was pacing the room. He turned and saw Leyland's face drop at the contents of the page.

"Well?" Mercer demanded impatiently. "I would really love some sort of an explanation as to why your mobile number appears to have called and been called by Melissa Marshalls mobile phone less than twenty four hours before her body was discovered." His breathing was heavy. Leyland's hands began to shake the sheet he was holding.

"As blindsides go this is a fucking beauty." Mercer spat in anger.

Leyland put the sheet back on the desk and swallowed hard before putting his head in his hands and elbows on the desk. He looked up, then down again. Unsure how to answer.

"Phil...I can explain...I think." Leyland's voice wavered.

"Then talk," barked Mercer loosening off his Liverpool tie and undoing his top button. The unwritten signal that he meant business.

Leyland's breathing was heavy with adrenaline. Being bundled into the room had surprised him and had his heart racing.

"I...I saw her. I saw her on the tube," he spoke slowly. Mercer ran his fingers through his hair.

"When?"

"Monday morning."

Mercer turned. He didn't give a fuck about the rules in there at that moment and pulled out a cigarette.

"Leyland. Old friend." He sparked the cigarette and pulled heavily on it.

"How could you have seen her on Monday morning when she was already dead?" There was an air of concern in Mercer's tone. Leyland let out an involuntary laugh.

"You think I haven't been asking myself the same questions since I knew who she was. And how she ended up?"

He ran through the Monday morning before he came back to work. The fall. The train stopping. The cold cold air. Melissa appearing from nowhere. The chat.

Ghost Track: Melissa

The business card. The phone call. Seeing the body. He laid it all out on the line for Mercer to pick over and digest. Leyland knew it was going to leave a bad taste in Phil's mouth.

They sat silently for a minute, the room was filled with cigarette smoke.

"Leyland. It must have been the fall or the accident. It's affected your mind," said Mercer.

"You're seeing dead people and swapping numbers? How do you expect me to react to something like that?"

"The same way I have to react to it," replied Leyland, his voice breaking with emotion. His eyes were welling up.

"By finding the truth. By finding out what happened to her and who was responsible. And nailing the fuckers."

"By getting to the bottom of what the hell happened to that girl and how she came to be where rational thinking says she couldn't possibly have been "

Mercer looked perplexed. And exhausted.

"Are you trying to tell me that you made contact with a ghost or something?" Mercer looked Leyland in the eye.

"How would you like me to deal with that? What would you do in my shoes given the fact that I'm heading up the murder investigation? By rights you should be in handcuffs as we speak being treated as a suspect. If it wasn't for the fact you saved my arse on Operation Ferry you would be."

Leyland's face dropped instantly. He knew it was a far out explanation. Completely messed up. But he had still wished that in some way, no matter how small, that his old friend could understand what he had been going through.

"If Occupational Health get wind of this you'll end up in a mental institution, you know that don't you?" Mercer questioned. "And they'll probably hang me out to dry for knowing about it as well." Mercer sucked on his cigarette.

"Everything is at serious risk. Risk of serious compromise." Mercer held his hands out.

"So tell me. What do I do now?" He asked Leyland. "Please enlighten me on how you wish to proceed as I'm stuck," Mercer explained.

"I turn you in then I lose a very good friend who is also a superb copper. For what? For experiencing some...difficulties shall we say. From your accident?"

"I don't know if that's what it was Phil. You're saying I'm mad but it was so real. I actually physically have the card. And the call that she made to me will still show on my phone." explained Leyland. "These are physical things Phil. Physical tangible things."

"Why didn't you tell me? All you had to do was come to me. We could have worked it out. Not find out like this. I could have helped you," Mercer explained looking hurt and puzzled.

"I wanted to old friend. But I was scared. I needed to get back into the job. So badly. Maybe I am crazy. Maybe I am ill. Maybe I have the ability to talk to ghosts. But one thing's for certain." Leyland paused. He was looking Mercer in the eyes and was deadly serious.

"I know what I know. I know what I saw," he said with tears in his eyes.

"So, old friend. You do what you have to do. I understand if you have to turn me over to Ferdinand. You have to do the right thing. But I will get to the bottom of all of this. I promise you that." With that Leyland stood and faced Mercer.

"I need time to think about what to do," said Mercer.

"I suggest you consider getting some extra help," he added.

This hurt Leyland to a degree. But he knew where Phil was coming from.

"Whatever happens from here on in, if you ever in any way withhold anything from me in relation to this investigation and I mean anything, then I'll call Ferdinand myself to come down and fuck you off the force. Is that crystal?"

"Of course," Leyland answered softly looking down at the table.

Mercer left the room. A tear slowly rolled down Leyland's cheek as he felt a loneliness never before experienced by him. He shouldn't have held out he thought to himself. He should have trusted.

Leyland held onto the table, shakily and unsteadily. He needed to move. To get out of there. He turned a right out of the room and headed for the nearest pub. A stiff drink was very much in order right then.

As he turned out of the room in deep thought he came face to face with Ferdinand almost knocking her off balance.

"Excuse me Ma'am," Mumbled Leyland trying to pass her with zero communication. Ferdinand was having none of it.

"Well well Detective Sergeant. Why such a rush?"

"Places to be," replied Leyland shortly, looking miserable and not sounding particularly convincing. Avoiding eye contact.

"Have you been crying?" She asked.

"No ma'am. Hay fever," replied Leyland thinking on his feet.

"I see. And how is the leg?"

"Getting a lot better ma'am. Nothing like a good session at the gym to iron out some kinks," he couldn't resist the dig at her.

"Quite," replied Ferdinand, with narrowed eyes. "But don't overdo it will you Detective Sergeant. We wouldn't want you undoing all that hard work would we?"

Leyland drew breath to answer but was stopped in his tracks when he felt a heavy hand on his shoulder.

"C'mon lad. We've got statements to take, remember?" The warm scouse tone of Phil Mercer was behind him. Still covering Leyland's arse. When he didn't have to.

Leyland would have turned around and kissed him if didn't know that would have pissed him off more than the phone records.

"Sorry to drag him away from you Petunia but the investigation must roll on," Mercer explained, ushering Leyland past her. "I'm sure you know what I mean," he added and winked at her as he walked past.

But he had a look on his face that clearly said 'Fuck you , bitch'

Leyland headed out of the building. The emotion had built up to such an extent in him that he couldn't find his voice.

He wanted to say thank you to Mercer. But the words wouldn't come out. Mercer just smiled at him and parted company with a brief "See you later soft lad."

Leyland couldn't get to the pub quick enough. If it wasn't for the limp he would be guzzling his first pint by now. He crossed Tin Street carefully and his mobile rang. He didn't recognise the number.

"D.S. Francis," he answered.

"Hey, officer Leyland!" Exclaimed the familiar voice on the other end. It was Stan.

"Hey Stan. How are you doing? I didn't think I would hear from you so soon."

"Well I thought about what you said and I decided to have a nice chat with Mrs Rosamund over a lovely cup of tea," answered Stan.

"Did anything come from the chat," Leyland asked enthusiastically.

"Absolutely." Confirmed Stan. "Can we meet up somewhere?"

"Do you know the Weasel pub at all?" Asked Leyland.

"I know it buddy. That where you hang out?"

"Not generally but I'm headed there."

"O.K. I'm on my way. You gonna need your notebook officer," said Stan.

"Meet me there can and we can chat properly Stan. It'll be good to see you."

"Sure thing buddy," said Stan and the call was ended.

Leyland walked through the doors to the Weasel. He would have to let Mercer know as he may well have wanted to sit in on the chat. Especially if it threw any useful information up.

Leyland ordered a large Vodka with ice. As he waited for his drink he punched Mercers number into his phone. Four rings passed.

"Yeah?" Mercer answered.

"I'm in the Weasel," explained Leyland.

"Bit early for you isn't it?" Mercer was shocked.

"Five O'clock somewhere isn't it?" Leyland offered.

"You've been spending far too much time with me," Mercer chuckled. Leyland's guts turned.

Did that mean he was going to cut him loose? Or throw him to the lions?

"Stan Carmouche has been in touch," Leyland explained. "He wants to meet here, he is on his way now. He has info regarding a chat he had with the landlady."

"That was quick. I'll be there in five," informed Mercer. "Get me one in," he added before ending the call.

Leyland ordered Mercer a pint, paid and started looking for a decent table in a dark corner.

Some privacy would certainly not go amiss during this meet. Scanning the pub he found a free booth at the far end. Perfect. He took up residence there and waited.

It wasn't as busy as a normal lunchtime in there which was good. He pulled his notepad and pen out in preparation for the information from Stan.

Ghost Track: Melissa

Leyland hoped and prayed it would be some big news or a decent lead. It may serve to take Mercers mind off the predicament between them.

He took a gulp of the Vodka. It was delicious and the burn hit the back of his throat and warmed his chest.

He was at conflict inside and begun to consider the effects of being thrown out of the job would have on life. No job. No pension. A fucked up leg and head case in big red letters slapped all over his record.

Not the most appealing of futures. He just didn't know what to do. Should he call his dad and go and stay with him for a bit? He would surely twig that something was wrong. His dad was always very much switched on to things like that. Leyland's train of thought was broken by the approaching figure of Mercer. Thirsty.

The two friends stared at each other. No words. Awkward silence. Mercer took a seat opposite Leyland.

"Seems that you have advanced the investigation with your little chat to Stan." Mercer opened with.

"Let's see what info he has before getting too excited," Leyland countered.

Another pause. Leyland sipped at his Vodka.

"I'm sorry I held out on you."

Mercer remained quiet and hard faced.

"Why would Petunia Ferdinand be following me?"

Mercers eyes widened a bit.

"Why wouldn't she?" He answered. "You're just the type of copper she likes to put out to pasture."

"She seems to be going to quite some lengths. Following me to the gym, things like that," Leyland revealed. Mercer nodded wisely.

"She is focussing on your weaknesses. Or possible weaknesses. She probably asked the gym staff if you've shown any signs of injuries or distress while there. That's her style. Fucking snidey. I wouldn't be surprised if she tries to take a sample of your blood when you're asleep!"

"From my neck? With her fangs?" Joked Leyland. It drew a slight smile from Mercer.

"What you wouldn't want to do," continued Mercer. "Is to let her find out in any way shape or form what you told me. That would not end at all well," Mercer warned.

"Not that I need to point that out to you. It's something you've obviously been struggling with since it happened. Am I right?" That was a touch warmer and friendlier.

"Like you wouldn't believe," Leyland confirmed to him.

"Question is," said Mercer. "What are we going to do about it?"

"Nothing right now Phil. I just need you to trust me. However hard that may be at the moment. I need you to trust I'm O.K. We will take care of this case and then I can concentrate properly on what the issues are all about. I need you to trust me my old friend." Leyland was wavering again.

Mercer knew he had the guts to see it through. After everything that Leyland had done to help him over time. He knew there was no way he could turn his back on him.

"We get through this case," said Mercer. "We get Ferdinand off your back and then we deal with you. However that needs to be done. agreed?" He asked, knowing full well what the answer would be.

"Thank you Phil," gushed Leyland.

"You keep those tears under control fella. Don't want Stan walking in thinking we're a couple of irons," jested Mercer.

"We don't mention this issue again until the Marshall case is finished. Understood?" He added.

"Crystal," replied Leyland.

"Give me the call sheet."

Mercer shoved his empty glass toward Leyland with his trademark grin fully returned to active duty.

"I think you owe me a proper drink." Mercers mobile rang at that moment.

"Hello?" He answered with a hint of snappiness.

"What? How did you get this number?" Clearly showing that the call was unwanted.

"No comment," he growled and ended the call.

"Trouble?" Asked Leyland.

"Newspapers," answered Mercer. "Sniffing around already. Fucking bone pickers." Mercer did very little to hide his discontent for tabloid journalists. They were just one more headache he didn't need at all at that time. Trouble was once they got their teeth in they very rarely let go.

And if Mercer was getting calls then it was likely a safe bet that the Chief was getting calls as well. And that meant pressure from above. It would only be a matter of time in Mercer's experience.

Leyland picked up the empty glasses and made for the bar. Mercer sat and pondered, but he wasn't pondering to such an extent that he didn't notice the leggy brunette walk up to the bar. He recognised her and couldn't believe his luck.

It was Maria Santini. Mercer had had a thing for her for a while and she had always seemed to reciprocate the interest.

"Maria! How you doing?" Mercer projected his voice.

"Phil!" Squealed the lady and rushed over to where Mercer was sitting. She grabbed him and pulled him into a hug.

"You're looking good girl. What have you been doing with yourself?" Mercer asked, beaming.

"Well since I left your team I had been moving around a bit. I kind of landed on my feet with my current post. Back at NCA HQ." She smiled.

"Although the boss is a right old bitch," she added.

"Tell me more?" demanded Mercer.

"I transferred over to Occupational Health about two months ago." Maria revealed.

"Love the post but the director is a real power tripper."

"That wouldn't be Petunia Ferdinand by any twist of fate would it?" Asked Mercer excitedly.

"That's right. How do you know her?"

"We've had our run ins over time," answered Mercer.

"And it would seem that she has it in for my oppo. Big time." Mercer thumbed in the direction of Leyland at the bar.

"Well that's no good Phil. At all. she really doesn't give up. What's he done to rattle her cage?"
"Absolutely nothing at all," Mercer replied.
"That's an issue for me you see. Leyland Francis is a very good friend of mine. And he doesn't deserve to be pursued in the way he has been. Ferdinand has a long reach, I know that. But she can't get away with trying to destroy the career of a first class officer."
"Francis? That name rings a bell. I'm sure she has him flagged," Maria revealed.
Leyland returned with the drinks. "I'm sorry, I didn't realise we had company." He looked at Maria.
"Leyland I'd like you to meet Maria Santini," introduced Mercer.
"It's a pleasure to meet you Maria," said Leyland politely and shook her hand gently.
"Lovely to meet someone that Phil speaks of so highly," said Maria. Leyland sat.
"So how do you two know each other?" Leyland asked.
"I used to be one of Phil's team," Maria confirmed. "Best guvnor I ever had." She added warmly.
Leyland spotted Stan out of the corner of his eye who had just walked into the Weasel. He rose and put his hand up signalling to him.
"I can help you," Maria whispered to Mercer. "I know stuff. I can help." She repeated.
Mercer looked at her, then at Leyland. His brain was ticking over.
"Detective Sergeant would you be able to handle Mr Carmouche on your jack jones do you think?"

Leyland looked very puzzled, but then twigged, with completely the wrong idea.

"Ah yeah. Of course I can," he answered with a smile.

Mercer was pleased. "O.K. we can catch up later buddy," Mercer confirmed as he drained his drink double quick.

Stan walked over as Maria and Mercer left the pub. Lucky bastard thought Leyland as he greeted Stan with a smile and a firm handshake. The Louisianan nearly broke bones in Leyland's hand with his massive handshake.

"Can I get you a drink?" Leyland asked.

"If you can stand me a Jack Daniels you got a friend for life," chuckled Stan, looking good in his shirt and black jeans, completed with the pork pie hat which he whipped off his head and placed upside down on the table with a smooth well practiced motion. He sat. Leyland spotted his cigarettes in the hat and smiled. Very old school.

Outside the pub Mercer and Maria had hailed a cab back to her place. Mercer was a very intrigued spectator as Maria held court as to what she had discovered about Petunia Ferdinand over the past two months and how it helped keep her off Marias back.

"I'm really not into blackmail Phil," she revealed. "But I had to use this to get some kind of space from her. I think it might help shed some light on why she is after your friend and I think I can help you beat her."

Mercer smiled.

"But only if you're nice to me Phil," Maria added in seductively, rubbing her hand gently on the top of his leg.

That was Mercers kind of blackmail. It's a dirty job, he thought to himself comically. But he would have to do what he needed to do. To help Leyland of course.

Nine.

Petunia Ferdinand sat at her desk. It was fairly dark in the office and the whir of the air conditioning was the only tangible noise in the room above the sound of a computer keyboard being tapped.
Ferdinand was scanning through some internal C.C.T.V. footage of Leyland and Mercer. She had decided to focus on the minutes leading up to her bumping into a very puffy eyed Leyland.
It made for some very interesting viewing for Ferdinand.
Why would Mercer have bundled Leyland into the room like that? What on earth went on in there? And, more importantly, how could she use it to her advantage?
She lifter her desk phone and tapped in a four digit extension number.
"Hello, S.M.I.U?" Came the answer.
"Petunia Ferdinand here, tell me are the interview rooms on level two Charlie in any way under surveillance?"
"One moment Ma'am let me just double check." Some keyboard tapping at the other end.
"No Ma'am I'm afraid not. Not with cameras anyway. But there are still voice activated recorders in the rooms. They were due to be pulled by the end of this week I think."
Ferdinand's eyes lit up.
"And if I needed one of those recordings?" She asked.
"If you email me a request I can help get that to you within the hour," came the reply.

"Superb," answered Ferdinand. "Just remind me of your email address?"

She was excited at the thought of what that recording could reveal. She couldn't resist sending off a quick text. *'Getting closer. Get ready to take your place. P'*

The reply took literally seconds to come through. *'Superb. Are we still ok for tomorrow night?'*

'Yes. Don't be late' Ferdinand replied.

She fiddled with her glasses and got down to composing the email. She could smell blood. She wanted the taste of it as well. She wanted to see fear and regret in the eyes of Leyland and Mercer before she made them clear their desks and vacate the building as mere civilians.

An involuntary smug laugh came out of her mouth.

She adjusted her glasses again and typed furiously.

Leyland Francis and Stan Carmouche were almost forehead to forehead in deep conversation in the Weasel.

"I felt it best to contact you early, given what I found out from Mrs Rosamund," said Stan.

Leyland produced his notebook and pen poised for some scribbling action.

"What did she tell you?" He asked with an excited curiosity.

Stan sipped his jack Daniels.

"It would seem that on Saturday evening she saw three people going up to Melissa's flat."

Leyland's eyes widened. "Holy shit. Any descriptions at all? Did she recognise any of them?"

"Two she had never seen before. But one she recognised. It was the guy that used to drop her home sometimes,"

Leyland busied scribbling descriptions into his notebook. This was solid gold. The kind of lead they had been seriously hoping for.

"The two guys that she didn't recognise. They caught her looking through a gap in her door. Gave her a warning that if she said anything they'd come back for her. Shook her up real bad buddy."

"How is she doing now?" Leyland expressed genuine concern for the old lady.

"She'll be ok. She's got old Stan looking out for her. She'll be cool," reassured Stan. Leyland smiled warmly. He believed the big old man.

"So," Stan continued. "These guys put her in a car and took off fast. After that, who knows. Mrs Rosamund did say that the two guys she didn't recognise had some sort of accent. She didn't know what it was though. Definitely not from these parts."

"Like a regional accent?" Asked Leyland.

"Like Phil?" questioned Stan. Leyland chuckled.

"Yeah, like Phil?"

"No no buddy. This was like another country kinda accent," Stan revealed. Leyland scribbled further.

"Ok. Well we can get onto looking for these people. You say one of them was known to Melissa?"

"Definitely. Work colleague it would seem. Boyfriend possibly. Never came in normally. But he did that night."

"Did Mrs Rosamund notice if Melissa was scared or distressed in any way?"

"She didn't say. Maybe she couldn't tell. She would have said if she knew," answered Stan.

"OK. any description of the vehicle they took her away in at all?"

"Only very vague. It was a blue car. She noticed that the number plate spelt out Silk? Is that traceable?" Asked Stan.

"Certainly is," Leyland replied. "Stan this is all brilliant stuff. I can't thank you enough for the help you have given us."

Stan looked slightly embarrassed at the praise.

"How's the leg doing now?" He asked, switching the subject and remembering their first encounter.

"Getting there for sure," Leyland answered smiling lightly, if a little bit embarrassed at recalling the incident.

"Let me buy you a drink young buddy," Stan demanded, as he rose and took the glasses with him to the bar.

"I'm gonna have a quick cigarette as well, but I'll be back."

"No worries," smiled Leyland.

He pulled his phone out of his pocket. He just had to let Mercer know the state of play regarding the developments. It rang three times and then went to voicemail.

Leyland left a quick message, as much as he hated doing so.

Phil Mercer had rejected the call.

The reason he did so was because he was, at that precise moment, enclosed in a passionate kiss with Maria Santini. And she tasted so good.

Whatever Leyland wanted it was going to wait until Phil had finished what he had started and got what he wanted. At that moment in time that was two things. The first he was getting right then.

"So. What can you help me with? Surely not just practice on my kissing technique?" He asked, gently working his lips along Maria's shoulder working his way to her neck. She shuddered, and closed her eyes with a smile.

"Ferdinand. I know things." She lost her breath momentarily and she swallowed. Mercer had made his way smoothly to the back of her neck and moving slowly across to her other shoulder.

"Like what exactly?" He whispered.

"Depends what you need," she replied gently as her breathing became more rapid. Mercer ran his hands across the front of her breasts.

"Do you want her to back of or do you want to finish her off?" A light gasp passed her lips again.

Mercer had professionally unclipped her bra and it slipped off to the floor. He spun her around and they were eye to eye.

"I want that bitch to disappear off the face of the planet darling."

Maria was undoing his shirt button by button, his Liverpool FC tie was on the floor and tangling with her bra.

They kissed heavily and longingly. Their collective breath was as heavy as lead as it left their nostrils in unison.

She ran her hands softly and slowly down his chest and her finger circled a white round patch of skin. A bullet wound.

Mercers phone rang. Again.

"For fucks sake," he cursed.

He looked at the screen briefly. it was Trudy. He just stared at the phone. A bizarre deep down feeling that all the time it was ringing she could see what he was doing. It had his stomach doing cartwheels and smashed his ardour into a million pieces.

He sat on the edge of the bed and put his head in his hands. Maria sat next to him. She softly held his hand.

"I'm so sorry darling," Mercer pleaded.

Maria wasn't pissed off. Although perhaps she had good reason, she just smiled her sweet smile.

"She always was the only one for you wasn't she Phil," she whispered to him. Holding him from behind. Feeling the intensity of his pain.

"And even now look at the effect of just seeing her name flash up."

Mercer exhaled heavily and looked at her.

"Even so. I blew with her. Feeling like this, its all part of the punishment isn't it."

Maria's smile dropped.

"No. No Phil. You deserve some peace. Some kind of release. Especially after this amount of time. You can't keep dragging a sackful of guilt around with you forever. You're fucked eventually if you do. Why didn't you follow her Phil?"

"Because, my darling Maria, I am what's commonly known as a fucking moron. That's why. And with a lot of things in my life it's too fucking late for me." His hands were shaking.

"It'll never be too late for you Phil. For her or for me. But the choice has to be yours at the end of the day. I've always been here. Always will be."

Mercer looked at her. She was beautiful and on a plate. She could do better than him. A million times better.

"Right now the choice I have is to protect a very good friend of mine from whatever your boss has in store for him," Mercer swang the subject.

Maria placed her second hand onto his. The shaking subsided.

"She will bury you if you don't get things right Phil." Her look had turned slightly concerned.

"She could try. But it ain't likely," quipped Mercer.

"She has been having a sexual relationship with a younger officer for about three months," Maria revealed.

"I found out purely by accident. Walked in on them one evening in her office when I was collecting a file."

Mercers jaw nearly smashed onto the floor. His eyes wide and a massive grin.

"You've got to be kidding me?" He shouted. "She is so by the book it's unreal!" He added.

"Madder than fucking Tranmere!" He was laughing hard. "So you landed yourself a nice safety zone then?"

"Pretty much," confirmed Maria. "The agreement was she leaves me to do my job, which I'm bloody good at incidentally. It just makes life easier without her crap."

"Well I never!" Mercer was shaking his head. "So I need to catch her in the act. Where do they meet? Any ideas?"

"I would imagine they meet at her place after that incident. I can try and find out, but no promises O.K.?"

"You're a diamond amongst pebbles," praised Mercer.

"And you'd best get your trousers on," retorted Maria with a chuckle.

Mercer shook his head. "Any chance of a brew?"

Leyland and Stan were still in the Weasel. Both a little worse for wear but both enjoying each other's company.

There was a magnetism about the Louisiana man. The conversation had flowed from Stan's information to Leyland's injury. Stan was nursing yet another Jack Daniels and had a look of surprise on his face. With a hint of horror.

"How did you survive, I mean it must have been a horrendous crash to kill the other two guys. And you walked away?"

"Not exactly walked, no," corrected Leyland. "And I have the issue every day of being the one that survived."

Stan nodded knowingly.

"And the driver was never traced?"

"The investigation found it was stolen vehicle. The driver likely to have skipped the country apparently."

Leyland gulped his Vodka. He had added Red Bull to

it in a vain attempt to slow down the getting pissed process. It wasn't proving to be as much of a success as he had hoped.

Stan moved in a bit closer and looked into Leyland's eyes.

"And what do you think buddy?" He emphasised the 'you'

Leyland paused for a moment.

"I think many things Stan. I think that there was more to the crash than a simple accident with an illegal. More than the investigation seemed to want to put into it." He looked down at the table.

"But I guess I'm just a crazy guy who thinks that there was a figure at the scene, when according to the coroner there wasn't. What do I know? We have to stand by the investigation findings, don't we?"

"Well now my friend," Stan replied warmly. "I had many years' service with the C.I.A. and it always paid not to believe things were as straightforward as they were always made out to be. It pays to follow your instinct, hell it'll even keep you alive some days," Stan revealed.

"I didn't and it ended up costing me everything I ever had," he added. "So whatever department you work in, whatever your day brings to you no matter how trivial, always take a different angle when looking at it. You'll be surprised what gets revealed."

Leyland was looking at the big guy. His smile had faded. Leyland didn't like it.

"What happened to you Stan?" He asked boldly.

Stan looked a little surprised by Leyland's directness. But it was a fair question. And was likely to be asked at some point the closer they got.

"Well now. When you run with organisations like the C.I.A. you can occasionally tangle with, shall we say 'factions' that take things very personally," Stan began to explain. His trademark jolliness was replaced with a sombre, even slightly broken look about him.

The transformation shocked Leyland and it was obviously painful for him to recollect.

"Stan. I didn't mean to pry. You don't have to explain anything to me. Just ignore me, it's the drink," Leyland waffled feeling very guilty about pushing it.

Stan lifted his hand. The gesture to suggest that it was O.K. He had started and he needed to finish.

Maybe nobody had bothered to ask him before now. Maybe he had finally found a release in the Detective Sergeant. The trust. The confidante. Even if he hadn't, it was too late now.

"My team had been tracking and trying to infiltrate the mafia for over two years in a particular area of the states. We had some success too, taking down some big hitters" Leyland was entranced by Stan's voice.

"You remember a guy named smooth Frankie Rossi?" Asked Stan.

"Jesus. Yes. I know the name for sure," Leyland confirmed.

"He was our main player, we managed to take him down after years of various agencies trying."

"That must be twelve years ago?" Leyland asked.

"Roundabout that young buddy," Stan confirmed. "We managed to get him to cough on a lot of the organisations activities. He wouldn't name the names as you'd expect but he would generally give us enough information to work out what we needed if you catch my drift."

Leyland was sitting, fixated on Stan. Hanging off his every word. This man. The underground saxophone player was instrumental in taking down one of the most notorious mafia kingpins of all time. Books and covers thought Leyland. Books and covers.

"Anyhow we got to a point in the investigation where we needed to gain further intel regarding their operations connected to the Russian mafia who had moved in on their city operations within the last year or so after the arrests." Stan was well into full flow.

"We knew that Rossi had info on these guys and their dealings. He would not say a word at all. He was scared. He would rat out his closest friends but when it came to talking about the Russians he gave us nothing."

"And when one of the biggest mafia bosses in modern times is scared of these guys, then you know you're up against some serious shit?" Added Leyland.

"Exactly that my young buddy."

"We did not heed the warnings given to us. We didn't feel like we had anything to fear. We chased the Russians down. Hard. We were the god damn CIA for crying out loud. We chase they run. Only the Russians didn't quite understand those rules."

Stan sipped his drink. He was as serious as Leyland had ever seen him.

We raided this big warehouse one morning, close to L.A.X. airport. A smuggling operation. Counterfeit money. We hit it hard. Lost three agents in the firefight that came down. Guy heading up the Russians, well he got kinda pissed that his son got killed in that fire fight. Him and eight of his people"

Stan paused again. His face, his mood had darkened.

"I mean it was a real shitstorm in that warehouse. They were laying down the kind of firepower that you'd expect from a small army. Nobody meant to hurt or kill unless there was no way out. I guess it was the same for them too. Anyways it turns out that the top four members of my team had been quickly identified by the Russians and we had prices on our heads and the heads of our families too. The head guy invested millions into getting even before they bugged out of the states."

Leyland couldn't hide the look of shock on his face. He took a large swig of his Smirnoff as Stan continued to unravel his tale.

"Two of our guys went deep underground after that. They wouldn't risk wives and children. What kind of man would?"

Stan stared down at the table. He was the kind of man that would, and the shame still seemed so fresh. So raw.

"My second in command refused to give in or run from the threats. Lasted about three days which wasn't bad by his standards. He was a fat son of a bitch!" Stan chuckled very briefly. Remembering ribbing his old colleague about the shape he was in. The chuckle died very quickly.

"They were waiting for him at home one evening." Another sip of bourbon and a shake of the head.

Leyland knew things had gone very very bad for this guy.
"Killed his wife, his son and daughter right in front of him," Stan's hands clenched into fists involuntarily.
"Then they popped him off. That little girl was only six Leyland. Six."
Leyland was sitting perplexed. Just watching the pain engraved on Stan's face. He wanted to stop him but didn't know how. Maybe he needed to get this out. It looked as though he had been hanging on to it for a bloody long time.
Stan could feel a tangible pain just talking about it.
"I thought I was untouchable Leyland. My little family was still in New Orleans. I went there as fast as my legs would carry me. I felt I could see them coming. Especially in my community. Everyone knows everyone and strangers, especially strangers that are packing a serious amount of heat, get spotted real quickly. That's what I needed to protect my family."
"And you managed to do that Stan?" Questioned Leyland desperately wanting to hear a happy outcome.
"I tried. I got to them in time and swore I would, I could, protect them. But I had to go out looking for my boy. He should have been home from college at that time and was late." Stan continued. Tears welled in the big man's eyes.
"He was found in an alley. About five minutes from college. I missed him by ten." Stan stopped. His breathing had increased greatly and he swallowed. Fighting back the emotion.

Ghost Track: Melissa

"They stabbed my poor boy around thirty times and left him in an alley like trash. There was no time to mourn properly. Have a decent funeral. We had time to grab some essentials and for me to get my family deep underground into a protection programme. You should have seen the look in Mrs Carmouche's eyes from that day onward. She had hate for Stan. For the way it all happened so quickly. To him. New home. New identities the whole nine yards."

"So how come you're here?" asked Leyland.

"Did you get assigned to London?"

"No, nothing like that buddy," Stan revealed.

"Stan here went on a different path. A path of revenge and the self-destruction that comes with it. I wanted blood. I wanted to take those bastards down for what they did to my boy. My boss passed over some information on their possible whereabouts, some cash and a passport in an envelope and cut me loose. Last I found they had come to London."

"So you came here for vengeance?" Leyland looked so confused. He could never grasp what Stan had been through. Not in a million years. Not even after his experience with the crash. This was a hundred levels above.

"But you've been here for years. Have you never found them?"

"No. Not yet anyway. My sources dried up when I got here. I was in no man's land. Nowhere to go. No family. No leads to chase. I had to put down roots and keep all channels open. Just in case that fateful opportunity came my way."

Stan paused. His mind wandering.

"It never did," he added quietly.

Leyland was astounded as to what he had just heard. He managed to pluck up some voice.

"Why not go back to your family Stan?" He asked.

"They wouldn't want old Stan back. After so long" He answered.

"They blamed me for what happened to Steven. Rightly so. My position. My job. My arrogance got him killed when it should have been me. That's all true"

"That's all unfair," jumped in Leyland.

"Nobody deserves to feel that way about what happened." Leyland defended the old man.

"You do a job, a dangerous job and there are always risks. We accept the risks and accept that things could happen to us. But not to our families. Of course we forget how things can affect them. None more so than when things go terribly wrong," Leyland explained with passion.

"That doesn't mean you should use it as a stick to thrash yourself with for the rest of your natural. I think you've done that enough by being away from your family for so long. Just on the possibility of avenging your son's death? Look at that from your wife's point of view. She lost her son. And then she lost her husband too. Because of what those terrible people did. And she couldn't bury either of you." Leyland looked into Stan's eyes.

"That's a terrible price to pay. For anyone."

Stan lowered his head. Not for the first time that evening.

"Just how close did you ever get to finding them?"

"Within minutes one day," Stan revealed.

"At their hotel room."

"The tea was still hot in the pot. I was never closer than that day. The smell of the aftershave. The television still on. How they saw me coming I will never know."

Leyland felt his pain. And it had him considering his own situation with regards to the crash. Should he pursue the possibility of it being caused deliberately? A question gnawed at Leyland.

"The saxophone on the tube?" Leyland asked.

"What's that all about?"

Stan raised a tiny smile.

"Ah well with thousands of faces passing through every day, I figured that maybe one day I would see one of those bastards pass me by. Seemed like a good place to be."

Leyland was flummoxed. But impressed in a funny sort of way. By his dedication to finding his son's killers. Assuming they were still in business. Assuming they were still alive and assuming they were still in this country too.

"One hell of a gamble Stan. They could be dead, back in Russia or even in prison somewhere," Leyland suggested.

"I may be an old man Leyland but I have retained a number of contacts from my agency days. Across the world. If their names cropped up anywhere I'd be in the loop. Trouble is after so long I've mellowed. I don't know if I could pull the trigger if the chance came tomorrow."

"That would be a hard decision for anyone to make Stan. But I'm honoured that you've shared your story with me. Thank you, Stan. And I'm desperately sorry for your loss," Leyland offered.

Stan raised his glass in Leyland's direction.

"You're a good man Leyland."

Leyland cringed, with a semi blush.

"I try," he mumbled.

"You know it's never too late to claim your life back. Never. Why don't you? Why can't you?" Leyland probed.

"It's too late for an old asshole like me to change the way things are," Stan answered as honestly as he could.

"I have to accept what is, now. The future belongs to young guns like yourself, you got the brains and the ability. When I operated it was generally one or the other."

Leyland knew that deep down it was probably out of his reach to help Stan. He had better contacts than Leyland could ever hope for. But he put something out there to him anyway.

"Stan you know if I can help in any way you must let me know. I owe you one after talking to Mrs Rosamund for us."

"That's mighty kind of you young buddy," beamed Stan.

"I may one day just call on that favour."

"Damn I need a smoke," he dropped in as he rose and headed to the beer garden.

"It's a beautiful evening. Let's take our drinks outside?" suggested Leyland grabbing the glasses and heading out into the evening August sunset. The red and orange blaze. It was beautiful. And in some strange way a fitting backdrop to the revelations of the evening.

When out in the open Stan lit his cigarette and they both sat at a picnic table style seat.

They both swigged at the same time. Stan pulled heavily on his smoke.

"You know, to reverse what you said to me, if I can ever help you young buddy then don't be afraid to ask."

"I have a lot of contacts. A lot of skills. If you ever need to call on them then just let me know?"

Leyland smiled and nodded slowly. He would have to head for home soon. But one more drink was calling to him. As it always did when it came to Vodka and Red Bull. Stan had drained his glass too.

"Another?" The old man asked.

Leyland considered for all of three seconds before confirming the same again please.

He pulled his mobile out of his pocket and tried to get Mercer again. Again no joy and he left a message for him as much as he hated doing it. But he needed to give his buddy, now his boss, the heads up on new information as quickly as he could.

Unbeknown to Leyland a familiar female popped her head slowly over the crest of the beer garden wall.

A camera appeared and softly ran through the automated process of taking multiple pictures. She checked the LCD screen and satisfied with the results; the photographer jumped into a Jaguar XJS and sped off.

As Stan wavered back with the drinks order, Leyland had switched into deep thought mode and wondered what the hell would become of them both.

If he didn't get some sort of plan of action together soon he would be fucked because mostly it felt like he was wading through mud and trying desperately to break free of all that had happened to him.

He knew how Stan did it. That motivation. Waiting for the one chance to make good on your child's death. If making good was the right expression of course.

Leyland wasn't convinced it was something that would cure Stan anymore. He had been waiting for so long that if the opportunity arose for him to carry out revenge he probably wouldn't live long enough to enjoy any sort of release it could bring him.

And having listened to the story of how Stan Carmouche came to be in good old blighty Leyland was sure that there wouldn't be any release at all for Stan. Unless he drastically changed the path he was treading. But with immense self-doubt gnawing at his beliefs Leyland couldn't see himself as the person to make Stan realise those facts.

Maybe it wasn't even Leyland's place to try and make him see. But what kind of person would it make him if he didn't at least have a go? He thought to himself. The two men clinked glasses.

"To peace," toasted Stan.

"However that may be achieved," Leyland added.

Another wouldn't hurt he justified. Besides, Mercer may come back here looking for him. That was Leyland's excuse and he was going to stick to it.

Ten.

Phil Mercer had made his way back to his place after the ill-fated liaison with the gorgeous Maria.

If some good was to come out of that situation then Mercer needed to sit and think about the information he had been given about Ferdinand. If he used it properly and at the right time, used it smartly, it would be one less thing for Leyland to worry about and, ultimately, that was Mercers aim. To protect his friend.

He had, of course, considered the nature of Leyland's confession to him regarding seeing ghosts. Mercer was a simple man and wasn't really wired to deal with those sorts of revelations in a rational way. Not at first anyway.

At that point he was at the 'let's just not mention it and carry on with the investigation' stage. But he also had to be doubly certain that Leyland wasn't going to put himself in a position where he could become a suspect. That was of massive importance to Mercer. Simply because if that sort of thing came out it would be a situation taken out of his hands.

So they definitely needed to put their heads together about that. He switched his mobile from silent, and once it got a signal almost immediately flashed up two missed calls and one voicemail message. Both calls were from Leyland.

Mercer listened to the message and checked his watch. It would be chucking out time at the Weasel. Leyland was probably tucked up in bed by then. Even so thought Mercer, he could probably get there to squeeze in a night cap.

He would have to rush. Could he be arsed? He hummed and thought for a few seconds. Then decided no. His bed was, amazingly for once, a far greater pull.

He keyed in Leyland's number. It rang five times and Leyland, much to Mercers surprise, answered.

What surprised Mercer even more was the fact that Leyland was still at the Weasel and sounded a tad pissed.

"Good news about the info buddy. Please pass on my heartfelt thanks to Mr Carmouche," Mercer asked.

"Hey come down, come down," Leyland slurred.

"It's still open, come and have a quick one mate."

"No, I decided on an early night fella. Up and at 'em early tomorrow," explained Mercer.

Leyland was, of course, shocked.

"Whaaat?" He shouted.

"I know, I know," said Phil.

"Shocking isn't it. You enjoy the rest of your evening and for Christ's sake go careful."

"Will do, will do," promised Leyland.

"See you tomorrow Phil."

Leyland was surprised. Greatly. It was unusual for his good friend to turn down the offer of an alcoholic beverage. But he was pleased that he did, and then felt bad for inadvertently trying to encourage him.

Leyland felt like he should call it a night. He was a little unsteady on his feet. The alcohol had dulled any pain in his leg. Hopefully the next physio session on it would really do the trick on it. Hopefully.

He and Stan shook hands.

"You take care buddy," said Stan. "Don't you be falling over anymore, you hear?" He jested.

As they shook Leyland cupped his other hand to Stan's.

"Stay in touch friend."

Stan nodded once his acknowledgement before turning and heading out of the pub.

Leyland wasn't far behind and absorbing the fresh night air, feeling a bit numb around his mouth and nose. He came to realise that the drink had clouded his mind and that he would likely see Stan again tomorrow when they visited Mrs Rosamund again.

The evening air was delightful and Leyland was seriously considering walking home. The realisation of how long that could take him didn't take long to sink in so he decided to hail the next cab that appeared.

He was growing too tired to walk anyway. It had been a long day and what with the alcohol. He needed his bed. Badly.

"Don't fucking move!" Boomed into Leyland's ear.

He froze and felt something jabbing into his right side.

It was a feminine voice. Fairly posh as well given how she over emphasised the h sound after the f and allowed the g to be heard at the end.

"If you struggle, run or make a commotion I will shoot you where you stand. Do you fucking understand me?"

She was closer and quieter this time.

"Yes. Yes I understand." Leyland confirmed.

"My wallet is in my inside pocket." He added. "My phone is a bit shit but that's in my right trouser pocket, if you so wish." His assumption that he was being mugged was very misplaced.

"Wallet?" Questioned the female.

"I don't want your fucking wallet you idiot. Now move toward that car."

She pushed Leyland in the direction of a beat up Nissan Micra, jabbing the weapon in his side just to make sure he remembered there was a gun in play.

She opened the passenger door. "IN!" Leyland complied and the door slammed behind him. His heart was racing. What the hell was this?

The woman dashed around to the driver's side, checked up and down the street quickly and jumped in.

Leyland got a good view of her as she checked around before gunning the car away. Navy blue Adidas hoody. Hood up. Blue jeans and trainers. Completing the ensemble was the handgun. It looked like an old Browning nine millimetre. It certainly didn't look fake.

"Face ahead." She barked. "Put your phone in the glove box and do not look at me or you're dead."

Leyland complied quickly with the order.

"Buckle up as well." Leyland clunked clicked on this trip.

"You stay silent and stay still and do as you're told and you might live." She added.

Leyland faced straight on. They seemed to be heading to the eastern outskirts of the city. There was a waft of perfume from her that Leyland quite liked.

This didn't seem like any run of the mill robbery and his mind was wandering as to what was going to happen. He toyed with some brainstorms. Taking the belt off very quickly and making a jump for it out of the door whilst still on the move. She couldn't drive and shoot. But what if he just ended up messing his leg up even more? He could even be hit by a vehicle at the rear as well. Too risky. Way too risky. Dare he chance talking? He had to.

"Where are we headed?" He asked gingerly.

"What part of sit in silence is too hard for you to fucking understand?" She bellowed.

Leyland observed her hands as she reached out for a packet of cigarettes in the cup holder by the handbrake. She shook as she lit one up and pulled heavily on it. Clearly nervous and very clearly not hiding the effects of the adrenaline on her. What the hell was this about?

She hadn't done much of this sort of thing too often, that was clear. Underworld kidnapping? Unlikely.

They would have used a pro. Everything about her body language suggested she was far from that.

The flight syndrome had Leyland wanting to run, but he knew the only choice there and then was to sit tight and be quiet.

To be perfectly honest the speed and way she was driving a local traffic unit might pull her. But then that wouldn't satisfy his very mild curiosity, not really killing the fear, as to where they were heading to. He was shitting himself. His fear was increased tenfold with an all too familiar panic feeling that swept over him ever since the accident whenever he was in a car travelling too fast. He wasn't in control. Far from it in this situation.

When Mercer was driving, it wasn't so bad. Leyland had confidence in his abilities behind the wheel. But this crazy bitch he did not know from Adam and for all Leyland knew they could get wiped out in a split second. He couldn't hold it in any longer.

"I'm sorry but if you're trying to alert every uniformed unit in the area to yourself, the way you're driving should really do the trick."

"Shut...up!" She shrieked at him. Leyland was a little too far into panic mode to give up there.

"I just assumed you wouldn't want to get caught having kidnapped someone at gunpoint." He added still looking straight ahead.

"If I get caught then I'll plug you first you gobshite. Now SHUT THE FUCK UP!"

Leyland left the conversation there. He clutched his fingers together. A cold sweat had enveloped him. It wasn't the end to the day he had quite anticipated, that was for sure.

Two minutes passed and the car was bought to a screeching halt that filled the evening air with the scent of burning rubber.

They were at the rear entrance of a cheap and grubby hotel. Probably in favour with the local prossies and dealers.

She killed the engine. Her hood was still pulled up over her head covering around eighty percent of her facial identity.

"Here's what's going to happen." She began to inform.

"You'll walk through the entrance there." She pointed. "And I will be right behind you. With the gun pointed at you." She picked up the weapon from inside the door.

"If you so much as look at anyone else, I will shoot you where you stand. Are we clear on that?"

"Oh crystal." Leyland answered.

"Were going to room fifty two. Do not stop until we get to the door."

Leyland nodded his acknowledgement. The adrenaline had a severe grip on him. He was playing scenarios in his mind. Ways out. Options. There weren't many. He wondered what awaited him up there.

She got out of the car and walked cooly around to the passenger side and let Leyland out.

He walked ahead as instructed to the entrance, trying to look down and not make any obvious eye contact with anyone. Not that it was very busy. He could hear the footsteps behind him and knew that his kidnapper was indeed, as promised, a couple of paces behind him.

He couldn't help but let his mind wander to past cases. Would any that he'd been involved in warrant this kind of thing? He certainly couldn't pinpoint any at that time. What if the accident, as he had thought, wasn't an accident and he was going to get finished off in jolly old room number fifty two? It had sobered him up pretty damn quickly that was for sure.

Having a gun jabbed in your ribcage did that. And he realised that he had left his crutch in the Weasel. His leg was starting to become painful and he didn't want that slowing him down.

He limped through it as best he could.

They took the stairs to the fifth floor. Avoiding the lift. It was a struggle.

Thankfully room fifty two was only a couple of doors along the corridor and as Leyland reached it he couldn't help but put his hand on the wall to take his weight and raise his leg slightly to relieve it.

He saw her hand pass his side with a key card in it and disengage the door lock. Before he could place the full weight back on his legs equally Leyland felt the whoosh of being bundled through the door and pushed to the floor of the hotel room. The door slammed behind them.

"Please!" Leyland cried out in pain.

"Get up." She demanded. Leyland complied as the gun was extended at him once again.

"Sit on the end of the bed"

Leyland lowered himself steadily onto the bed and was then very much looking down the barrel of a gun. Literally.

She moved the weapon into the grip of her right hand and with her left whipped back her hood revealing just exactly who it was Leyland was dealing with. He recognised her instantly.

"Felicity Marshall?!" He announced with shock.

"So you know my name," she sneered. "I guess you know the name of my sister as well?"

Leyland nodded.

Then maybe you could tell me why her murderers are still walking the bloody streets then?" Felicity cocked the weapon. Leyland swallowed hard.

"I'm on the investigating team," he revealed, dry mouthed and wishing he was in a million other places than there.

"I know. Do you think I grabbed you because of your looks? You're all corrupt and looking the other way and I want to know why. Now!" She looked ferocious. Even with the obvious family trait of gorgeous eyes.

Leyland didn't know exactly what she was talking about, and he didn't know how much time he had left to find out. He had to be direct.

"I'm not corrupt Felicity. I don't know why you would think that. I'm certainly not looking the other way with regards to your sister's murder investigation." He was as calm as possible under the circumstances.

"Bullshit," she spat. "I passed information to you lot days ago. And nothing happened. Why?" Tears of anger and frustration were welling in her eyes.

"They'll come for me next you know that don't you?" Her first indication of any vulnerability or softness.

"Who will?" Leyland probed.

"Don't take me for an idiot. I sent emails. Lots of them. Full of evidence or full of information as to where to find evidence to nail those bastards and you lot did nothing about it," She snapped again at him.

Leyland's breathing had become heavier as dawning of what was being suggested here hit him. A snake in the ranks. A mole. A leak.

"I know nothing about that," Leyland answered. "But if what you say is true then we can get to the bottom of it. Together." He was trying to calm her. Reassure her. She was getting out of control.

"Who is it that you think killed Melissa?" He slowly rose from his sitting position. She stared him out. Hard. Leyland didn't, no, couldn't flicker.

"Why should I trust you? You haven't a clue what's going on. You're either very clever or completely inept not to know," Sneered Felicity.

"Why should I trust you?" She stepped up to him and shoved the gun in his face.

Leyland had to go for it. The risk was heavy. But he had to prove to her he was trustworthy. He reached slowly round to his back pocket with his other hand held out in a 'wait' pose.

Felicity backed off a pace. Leyland pulled the business card from his pocket and held it up in front of him.

"Because she trusted me." Leyland threw the card on the bed. He emphasised the 'she' so that Felicity was in no doubt. He hoped to god that in some way pacified her.

Silence. Her eyes were wide and Leyland noticed a shake in her hands.

"I can protect you. But I need to know everything about what she was involved in."

Felicity lowered the gun. She moved slowly over to the bed and picked up the card and stood, fixed on it.

"You can believe what you like," Said Leyland in a softer tone.

"But she came to me," he said.

Tears streamed down Felicity's soft cheeks and she lowered the gun to her side. Leyland moved in gently and pulled her into his arms. He couldn't help but shed a tear at the same time as he took the gun from her grasp and threw it onto the bed. He held Felicity Marshal close and tight. She had lost her sister in a brutal way. And she felt betrayed. Leyland needed to know everything. They sat and he pulled out his notebook.

"Now," he announced. "Tell me everything that you know."

Eleven.

Phil Mercer was having trouble sleeping. His mind was running at a million miles per hour. Trudy. Maria. Leyland. Melissa Marshall. They were all serving to put the mockers on the benefit he would have gained from his early night.

Too many situations. Too many feelings. What to do. What to do and how to do it.

Maria had provided him with a solid gold angle in which he could get Ferdinand to back right off. He just had to get his timing right to gather the evidence he needed. He'd take great pleasure in rubbing her nose in it. Telling her to piss off. He looked forward to that in a very big way.

His mind drifted to Trudy. His anger had subsided to a degree about the situation with her. It was a bit hypocritical for him to start throwing his toys out of the pram because she had finally found someone else. God knew she had held on for long enough. Waiting for him.

She had held the door open for him in Liverpool for a long time and he had never even come close to walking through it for her. It still hurt though. The thought of some other bloke playing daddy to his boys stabbed him in the stomach. It sickened him. But what sickened him more was the fact that it wouldn't have taken too much effort to do a better job than he ever had. And how could he ever make that up? Would they grow up hating him? Or, even worse perhaps, end up pitying him? Would they still want to know him? No, of course they would. Trudy would never let them forget who their dad was. She wasn't the kind of woman to let that happen. She always was a good one. And at that moment he felt the realisation of his situation.

Feeling pretty alone. He couldn't jump Maria's bones because Trudy was in his mind. And that was because he had not drunk enough to forget. Which, again, was unusual. Maybe he was finally growing up. But what a shame that is was probably far too late.

He had an urge to call Leyland but then realised that he would likely be fast asleep with the amount of alcohol he sounded like he had consumed earlier. The ghost spotter thought Mercer. Jesus. He didn't know who was the craziest right then.

Leyland was still at the hotel with Felicity. He was in automatic mode arranging through his own team some protection for the sister of Melissa Marshall.

She had spilled her guts to him about what she knew. She had passed this information before and it wasn't acknowledged. Let alone acted upon. Leyland had to presume that there was a traitor in the midst of the investigation. He didn't like feeling like he had to look over his shoulder and in protecting Felicity his witness protection team were the only people he would turn to, or trust, to protect such an important person under those circumstances.

He needed it cleared and arranged yesterday.

"John, Leyland. Sorry to disturb. I need a two person detail for a witness. Twenty four hour in situ cover. Can I request Rix and Connor if you don't mind?" Leyland was frank, to the point and business-like on the telephone to John McTavish. Leyland's understudy and current temporary team leader of Leyland's team. Leyland was, to a degree, embarrassed that John would have to move aside when Leyland returned to full duties.

"Superb. Again sorry to disturb buddy." Leyland was obviously pleased with the response from his protégé.

He walked into the bedroom area where Felicity was sitting clutching a cup of tea.

"O.K." Leyland began. "I have two officers coming here and they will provide you with an armed guard at your door until we can move you to a safer location."

"We can trust nobody." Felicity said to him, concerned.

"How do you know these guys aren't on the payroll or involved in the cover up?" She asked.

"These officers are fully trustworthy." Leyland was trying to be reassuring and, understandably, Felicity was highly paranoid at that time.

"I requested them personally from my team. I trained them. I worked with them and I know them both extremely well," he continued.

"I will not involve anyone other than those I can trust and rely on one hundred percent in this process. I can assure you of that," he added.

Felicity seemed only very slightly reassured by Leyland. She had been stuck in this room for five days solid and was jumpy as hell.

Leyland couldn't help thinking that the quicker Rix and Connor got there the better. Not to just keep the bad guys out. Whoever they may be but, just as importantly right at that time, to keep her in.

Running around town with that gun was a no no. She wouldn't hand it over either. Leyland could understand the sense of protection it afforded her. He was still slightly uncomfortable in leaving it with her but he had bigger fish to fry.

"I need to get in touch with my Detective Chief Inspector, Phil Mercer", announced Leyland.

"If I'm not available then he is the only person to trust with any information. Do you understand?"

Felicity nodded in the positive.

"And you definitely trust him do you?" she questioned before draining her tea.

"With my life Felicity," Leyland countered without hesitation and with a look in his eye that said it all to her.

"Try and get some sleep if you can," he added.

"I'll let you know when the guys get here. As soon as they are settled in I will need to head off and check through some of the intel you've given me, O.K.?"

"You will come back though?" Felicity asked with concern.

Leyland pulled a reassuring smile. "Of course. As long as you promise not to come and find me again!"

Felicity allowed herself a little smile at the thought of their car journey and laid out on the bed.

"D.S. Francis?" She asked.

"Please, call me Leyland," he answered.

"When did you meet my sister?" A perfectly legitimate question by anyone's standard. Leyland couldn't answer truthfully though.

Out of respect and not wishing to open a can of worms on that night he just answered quite simply.

"She found me on a train. Please just get some rest."
He was feeling pretty knackered himself and decided that five minutes in the chair wouldn't hurt too much.

He lowered into it. It was so good to take the weight off his leg for a moment or two.

He leant his head right back into the fabric and closed his eyes.

The adrenaline had subsided pretty much and the effect of his pickled evening had returned to haunt him. He breathed deeply. He could hear the sound of Felicity fidgeting as she tried to settle in the hotel bed. She probably hadn't slept properly all week. Poor girl.

Leyland's mind continued travelling.

To Stan. His awful predicament that brought him to this country. His futile search for revenge. Leyland was drifting into a light sleep and he found himself above the crash site and looking down on it. Months ago. Back in time. He could see very clearly the overturned car with its radiator bellowing out angry hot steam.

McGuinness was positioned about ten feet away from the vehicle having been thrown so violently from it during the impact.

He was quite obviously very horrendously injured. But Leyland was dreaming? This couldn't be real? Did this happen? Was he seeing it as it was? Or was his imagination playing tricks on him? Should he trust this as some sort of vision similar to Melissa's?

A figure approached the car.

He didn't seem intent on helping. The figure bent down and peered into the passenger area at the rear.

Ghost Track: Melissa

He reached in. Leyland couldn't see why, but he reached in and pulled his hand out. And walked away. Where was he going? He just walked away, speaking. Leyland strained. He could only hear the voice very faintly. But he couldn't make out the words. Was the voice accented?

His breathing quickened in his dreamlike state. Sweat began to form. What was this? What was going on? Why was he seeing it?

He strained. What accent was that? What was he saying? Why wasn't he helping?

Leyland awoke with a jump and a cry. His eyes were now wide open and beads of perspiration trickled down the side of his face. Or was it a tear? Felicity Marshall was standing next to him with her hand on his shoulder.

"You seemed to be having some sort of nightmare," she said.

"Are you O.K?

"Oh...oh yes. I'm fine. Just been a long day," he faked a smile but jumped a mile high again when there was a heavy knock on the door.

He got up and stood to one side of the opening.

"Who is it?"

"Its Connor and Rix sarge," came the familiar voice. Relief was hard to hide for Leyland as he swung the door open and beamed at the two guys.

He made introductions to Felicity and Leyland got down to the briefing. It was a simple one.

"Nobody comes into this room unless it's me or D.I. Mercer, O.K?"

"No exceptions whatsoever. At all."

"Got it boss," confirmed Rix.

"I'm available on my mobile at all times."

"Boss, it's covered. Why don't you go and get some sleep?" Suggested Connor.

"Too much to do buddy. Too much to do."

"But it's really good to see you chaps again," he added with a grin.

"Been shit without you sarge," Rix added.

"McTavish has turned into a right wanker as acting D.S." he informed.

"Get your arse back soon will you?" Connor backed Rix up. As they always did with each other.

"All in good time fellas. Just you make sure you keep her safe. And Felicity, try and get some sleep. You have the very best at your door tonight," he said with affection. Felicity smiled lightly.

"See you soon," he parted with and headed out of the room and toward the lift.

As he descended the realisation of the task ahead of him kicked in. He hadn't slept at all, had been out on the piss with Stan and now was heading back to NCA headquarters to dive into Melissa Marshall's email accounts to try and find why she was killed and, hopefully, to reveal who Felicity passed the information to.

Leyland stepped out into the night air and hailed the first cab he saw.

When he was ensconced in the back his thought process turned to the approach he would need to gain some form of tangible evidence by morning to justify the resources he pulled in to protect Felicity.

Not only that, he felt compelled to prove himself to Mercer. To prove to him that attaching him to his team was a good move and that Leyland had what it took to stay on the force.

He knew that a decision like that was out of Mercer's hands but he needed to show it anyway. If anything by way of repayment for his faith in Leyland.

The trip back to HQ was considerably smoother than the trip to the hotel and as he paid the driver and turned to the main entrance he checked his watch. Half past one. Sleep was off the menu probably for hours but the thought of this didn't bother Leyland in the slightest given that he was a step closer to nailing Melissa's killers.

He was very keen to get a result and to do justice for the girls.

He swiped in and acknowledged the night staff in reception as he quickened his pace to the investigation hub. Not a soul around and the only noise in contrast to the bustle and banter of the daytime hours was the white noise whirring of the air conditioning units which Leyland found both unusual and comforting.

He sat at a computer desk and pulled out his notebook. He had a hell of a lot of information to process and follow up. What was worse is that he had to cover it himself to keep his promise to Felicity about taking her claims seriously regarding someone working for the bad guys. That would be the tricky bit. He had to tell Mercer. But then what? They were in the middle of a murder investigation. Certain people needed to be involved with the information.

Leyland considered that someone on the team wanted information of this detail to disappear. That couldn't happen again. He wouldn't let it happen again.

A few minutes of tapping away at the keyboard and Leyland was immersed in his own world.

"Working rather late aren't we"?

Leyland jumped out of his skin.

"Or working early. Whichever it may be?" It was Ferdinand.

Leyland winced after the Goosebumps had disappeared. He didn't have time to get into conversation. Especially with her.

"Well sometimes there is an urgency to some tasks. Not that you'd understand that in your department." It had left his lips slightly before he realised how spikey it sounded.

"Rather late for you as well isn't it?" He added, in a softer tone. The look on Ferdinand's face told him it was a bit late.

"Well in the course of my duties, which as you know I take very seriously, I like to make sure any issues with our officers are addressed. Like alcohol dependency. Things like that Detective Sergeant," she retorted.

"And dealt with appropriately," she added.

"Oh I'm sure," mumbled Leyland as he turned back to the computer screen.

Petunia paused. How dare he turn his back on her. Disrespectful little shit, she thought.

"How was your little session earlier?" She asked him. "Have the effects worn off already? I would hate to think that you were drunk on duty."

"Well Petunia, I'm not drunk. I'm perfectly sober and capable," Leyland defended, choosing his words carefully that time.

"But I really appreciate you stalking me just to make sure I'm ok. Beyond the call of duty. It really is," Leyland didn't want to tangle but she was out of order. He felt the frustration of their office meeting rise up in him.

"What would your department advise for such obsessive behaviour Petunia?" He asked sarcastically knowing full well that calling her by her first name would grind her.

Ferdinand's face turned into a full on snarl and Leyland had superb indication that his words had hit a nerve. Adrenaline shot through him again.

"You'll be the only one needing my department sooner rather than later you jumped up little shit. You and that prick Mercer." She spat. The mention of Phil got his interest. Ferdinand was in flow through.

"Getting pissed on the job? Following in his footsteps aren't you. What a role model. No wonder his wife got as far away as she could," she added.

"He's fifty times the copper you are. In every way ma'am," bit back Leyland.

"And John McTavish is fifty times the copper you'll ever be," she slipped. There was silence.

"You and Mercer will cross the line and you'll both be scrubbing my toilet by the time I've finished with the pair of you."

"Good luck with that Petunia," retorted Leyland who turned his back on her completely signalling that the conversation was finished. He started tapping out on the keyboard again. "Goodnight," he chirped.

He heard her leave the room and a rush of breathe left his lungs in relief.

He felt sick. Should he have bitten like that? Too late. She shouldn't have mentioned Trudy like that. And the shit about McTavish. What the hell? Did they have a thing going on? Leyland would have to speak to him about it.

He couldn't have that sort of compromising situation going on. No way. Leyland hated the feeling he was experiencing. Not being able to trust colleagues. He needed Mercers help and experience and would have to wait till morning to fill him in on events.

At least had had found success in accessing Melissa's email account with the password that Felicity had given him. His eyes were tired and the hundreds, if not thousands, of communications in front of him were going to take a hell of a long time to process.

He rubbed his eyes, took a deep breath and dived in down to business as the early hours ticked away from him.

Twelve.

Phil Mercer was up and about before his alarm. As much as he would have celebrated that one small victory he was more focussed on not spilling tea on his beloved Liverpool tie.

He sparked up a cigarette in the kitchen and whilst using the sink as a makeshift ashtray he checked his mobile phone for messages.

No missed calls since last night but one text message. From Leyland.

'Major breakthrough. Felicity M found me. Lots of new info but we may have a mole. Hub at 10:00 for updates. L'

Mercer felt a surge of excitement. What has his ghost spotting compadre been up to now?

It was a little after seven. Mercer decided to head to the hub early for once. There was no point in him staying home and tapping his feet. He was up. He was fresh and he wanted information. He grabbed the keys to his Audi and headed out of the door.

Leyland was still sat at the same desk in the investigation hub. He was tired, irritable and stinking. The long forgotten quantities of Vodka that he had consumed last night had started to make their presence felt at the front of his head.

Uncharacteristically unshaven he had managed to close his eyes for half an hour in between chasing email trails of information. Frustratingly he had barely made a dent in the backlog.

He had checked in a number of times through the night with Connor and Rix at the hotel. It had remained quiet all night.

Leyland would need to make a decision soon as to whether to keep her there or make a move into protective custody. To add a further daytime detail at the hotel would mean liaising with McTavish again. After last night's tete a tete with Ferdinand he was very apprehensive to discuss anything operational with him until he could satisfy himself that all was above board. And he had a horrible feeling that it really wasn't.

He liked McTavish and always thought he was a good cookie, but with Felicity appearing on the scene shouting about Police corruption and cover up he was going to have to play his cards very close to his chest. For a little while at least.

His phone vibrated. A text message from Mercer.

He was already in the building and demanding Leyland put the kettle on. He nearly fell off his chair. He had set the briefing with him at ten because he didn't think he would haul his arse out of bed before then.

Leyland stretched and then winced. His leg was aching and his muscles were stiff, and his crutch was at the Weasel. He would have to grin and bear without it for a while. But not for too long. He had to keep his sensible head on and that would mean getting serious with the painkillers and utilising his support systems or he would be facing another embarrassing fall such as his on the underground.

That was not top of his bucket list at that time.

He made an attempt to get out of the chair he had been stuck in for the best part of six hours when the familiar grin of Phil Mercer entered the room.
"Well this is madder than Tranmere," he boomed in his broad scouse accent.
"You here all night investigating and me having a sober early night and no hangover," he continued.
"What the hell has gone wrong with the world?"
Leyland smiled and prised himself out of the chair and onto his feet.
"O.K." he began. "Shitloads of emails on Melissa Marshall's primary account, but I've managed to find the ones that may relate to the case," he announced, grabbing his notebook off the desk.
"It seemed that Melissa was concerned about large overpayments on legal bills through the firm she worked for," he paused for effect. "Legal bills paid, or overpaid, in cash sums and being recredited in bank transfers or bankers drafts. As clean as you like."
"So a kind of money laundering scheme?" Mercer questioned.
"It would seem to be, yes," Leyland confirmed.
"Any indication as to who or why?" Mercer asked again.
"Nothing to indicate within the emails, but I reckon fraud squad should get down there and start pulling their accounts apart," Leyland suggested.
"Melissa had gathered a lot of information from what I could gather, but unfortunately for us that information is somewhere on a memory stick. Location unknown," he scanned Mercers face.

"If the people involved in the scheme knew that Melissa had the drop on them we have our motive," announced Mercer.

"Possibly. Most likely," answered Leyland.

"But we don't have a weapon. Or a suspect. We sure as hell need that memory stick."

Mercer couldn't help but almost burst with pride at his temporary protégé He had struck bloody gold with his work. And secured the sister. His mind ticked.

"So you had a memory stick with explosive evidence on it and you felt unsafe with it. But you needed to keep it secure. Where would you put it?" Mercer challenged the room.

Leyland jumped in with a concerned look on his face. "Give it to someone you know and trust very very well," he said out loud. His eyes met Mercers.

"Felicity," they said in union.

"My assumption would be that she has the stick or knows where it is. I think she is waiting to see who she can trust," Leyland suggested.

"Why wouldn't she trust us with it?"

"Because she claims to have contacted a police officer on our team previously and then found herself being hunted down by some bad fuckers. What she suggested would put a mole in the midst of us. In the midst of the investigation. One of the girls Phil"

Mercers face turned to thunder at the mere whiff of such a thing

"She'd better be fucking wrong," he spat. "Where is she?"

"Premier Lodge in Stockwell. I have Connor and Rix with her." Mercer nodded approvingly at the names. Good lads.

"She knows to talk to me or you Phil and no other person. Not until we can pinpoint who might be on the payroll elsewhere. All we know is that the person is female," Leyland emphasised the 'might' part of the conversation. Nothing was for certain.

"She needs to be able to trust us one hundred percent if we are ever going to be able to unravel this," added Leyland. Mercer was nodding slowly but approvingly.

"Bloody good work lad."

They were interrupted by a rap at the door. Their faces dropped when Ferdinand was standing there.

"Ah good morning," she announced. A little too friendly.

"I'm glad to see you both here." She had an evil, almost manic, smile plastered over her face and it was then that the two officers noticed she was flanked by two very burly guys in ill-fitting suits.

Leyland piped up, "Ma'am this is bordering on a joke."

"Oh it's no joke Detective sergeant. No joke at all," she held out some paperwork for Leyland.

"I'm afraid you're being sectioned under the mental health act," she informed.

"What the..." a confused Leyland couldn't quite process the situation. Mercer was looking through slitted eyes at Ferdinand.

"What the fuck do you think you're playing at?" he hissed at her.

"Playing? It's no game Detective Chief Inspector. These gentlemen will escort you to hospital. Please don't put up a struggle," she added.

The two enforcers moved forward and each took a side of Leyland and led him away.

He looked back with fear etched on his face.

"Phil?" He bellowed. "Do something!"

Mercer was at that time powerless. And Ferdinand knew it. She stepped in front of him.

"Don't even bother. If you make waves I'll take you down too. Drinking again? Withholding important information in a murder investigation? Letting a bloody lunatic loose on your evidence? How about we say forty eight hours for you to jump before you get pushed?" She snarled. Pitbull style.

Mercer was professionally powerless to do anything.

She had somehow got some very tight information about Leyland. He had to take a seat. His world spinning.

"How did you know? About the ghost stuff. How?"

Ferdinand stepped slowly toward him and narrowed her eyes into his. She shoved a disc into his hand.

"Recording from the interview room. Your little chat with Francis in all its glory," She revealed.

"Happy listening." She waltzed away. The stench of her strong perfume choking the already thick atmosphere.

Mercer held his forehead in his hand. The world, the investigation had literally been getting somewhere. Somewhere positive in amongst ten tons of shit. And suddenly those ten tons had hit the fan. The hub was silent. There hadn't been too many people about but those that had arrived early for their day were in a stunned silence. And they were looking to Mercer for some kind of subliminal guidance.

He was trying to think. And think fast. He was the kind of copper that always thrived on the sort of pressure that needed quick, smart and decisive thinking. He needed a very good plan. What, and who, did that plan need to involve and solve?

Getting Leyland out. Taking down Ferdinand. Solving the Marshall murder. There. A nice three point plan. Forty eight hours. Forty eight hours to do all that. There was only one way to see if it could be achieved, he thought. He rose from the chair and looked at the almost infant like eyes on him.

"You lot know what to do. Keep digging," he ordered.

His first stop. Felicity Marshall.

Leyland was struggling to keep up with his goon escort. They were holding an arm each and guiding him toward the rear entrance of the HQ. They wouldn't take a madman through the front.

"Would you mind slowing down a bit please? I do have an injured leg," he asked.

No response from his personality free tour guides.

They even had matching suits. Ferdinand's clones.

He was feeling incredibly apprehensive and scared as to what delights the bitch would have in store for him. Electric shock therapy? Perhaps she would watch. If she wasn't controlling the voltage. How to get out of this little jam, he thought. What would Mercer be doing?

If he was being sectioned there wasn't much his friend could do. His mind wandered on to Felicity

Marshall. What would she do if she felt she couldn't trust anyone else? Raw frustration started to tense his body. They had just broken through in the case. Got close to answers. Why that girl was killed. Shot dead in cold blood. And because of that bitch Ferdinand he was being prevented from seeing that through.

Fuck it. Fuck it he thought angrily. The grip on his arms became tighter as his escort manhandled him through the corridors.

They must have felt his body tense involuntarily with his temper edging away from him. He did consider the possibility of breaking free and making a run for it. Then he put sensible thought into gear and realised he wouldn't stand a chance with his leg. And that would present them with the excuse they needed to handcuff him, or worse still drag him out of HQ in a straight jacket.

Stay cool Leyland, his minds voice kicked in. Play ball. See what happens. Where he was going. Deny everything or explain it away as reasonably as possible somehow.

They couldn't keep him if he could show he wasn't crazy. All was not lost yet. And he knew at the back of his mind that Phil would be trying his damndest to help him as well. And that was a reassuring thought. He was a powerhouse when he got the bit between his teeth.

At the back door a car was waiting and Leyland found himself being unceremoniously bundled into the back of it. It was a plain car with blacked out windows. His chaperone party sat in the back with him. One either side. Blank expressions. Looking straight ahead with no emotion. Leyland envied their coolness. To be able to do your job without feeling any kind of guilt or sense of injustice. How nice that must be he considered quietly.

At the wheel was what Leyland assumed would be a firm driver. The front passenger door swung open and the party was complete when Petunia Ferdinand jumped into the car.

She looked over her shoulder at Leyland briefly and sneered. She gave the order for the driver to go.

Phil Mercer had dashed down to his Audi. He got in and gunned it away at speed toward the Premier Lodge. He needed to speak to Felicity as soon as possible and arrange a permanent residence of protection for her. The priority for this was high, but had just been escalated to stratospheric importance given that Mercers gut was telling him that a stitch up job was going on. If what had happened to Leyland was anything to go by then he had to work fast before she came for him. In forty seven and three quarters of an hours' time.

Felicity also held the key to the murder case. And he wanted that key very badly right then. And quickly.

He sucked heavily on a ciggie as he navigated the streets of London at high speed. Frustration was burning his chest with every red light and pointless piece of congestion he encountered slowing him to his destination.

He was very much the type of person who was grateful for small victories and mercies. And when he had noticed that Leyland had left his precious notebook on the computer desk he had been slaving away at all night, Mercer managed to conceal it from Ferdinand. When she left he pocketed it quickly and hadn't had a chance to look at it but he was pretty confident that given the amount of scribbling that went into the book it was likely going to be a very useful aid over the next day or so.

He had it and Ferdinand didn't. That was a small victory in his eyes, in amongst all the shit going on.

And he knew that he had to keep scoring little victories until he could lay his hands on the bloody FA cup final of victories over that bitch. He needed to be able to remove her or discredit her. He didn't care which. But he needed Leyland back. And soon. He just hoped and prayed that the lad would play it smart. The last thing he needed to be doing was to be spouting off about how he could talk to ghosts on the London underground. He would never get him out if he went down that road.

Mercer had to tell himself to stop. Calm down. His mind had raced and that was no good. Leyland wouldn't be that stupid. He thought back to how difficult it was for Leyland to even reveal it to him. And given all the hard work he had put into the case overnight Mercer could see that sensibly speaking Leyland would keep his mouth shut and his brain engaged.

He lit another cigarette and tapped the steering wheel with his clammy thumbs. The next problem, he thought. Getting the memory stick from Felicity Marshall.

Mercer sensed that he was going to have to play this one very very friendly. With luck and the grace of god Leyland would have laid down a lot of the trust groundwork. He just had to go in there and be Mr Nice and Mr Trust me all rolled into one to keep the momentum going.

Finally, he needed a very solid plan in which he could manipulate Petunia Ferdinand.

No mean feat that was for sure. And possibly the hardest part of the jigsaw to get to fit. He needed an ally. A strong one. Someone on the inside. Someone who knew the score.

He fiddled with the hands free in his Audi. There were four rings.

"Hello you!" came the answer.

"Maria. About last night. What happens to you and your career if Ferdinand is gone?"

There was an awkward pause.

"Well, in all fairness I guess everyone moves up a notch on the pay scale. Why do you ask?"

"Because I need the bitch gone. And I need your help to do it. And quickly," he said, to the point and pulling hard on his smoke.

"Phil. Did we not talk about this? Its more than my career could be worth to get found out trying to shaft her," Maria answered. Phil could see her point.

"I understand darling," he countered.

"But understand that a good friend and a good copper is in deep shit because of her."

There was another pause. Phil jumped into the silence.

"All I need is the right call at the right time. I take the risk. I do the legwork. All I need is a call."

"Jesus Phil. This will not end well. I'll see what I can come up with. And only because it's you Phil," she added sweetly.

"But for Christ's sake be careful," she warned. He didn't need the warning. He had seen first-hand her handiwork.

"I need something soon," he pushed.

"The sooner the better."

Maria exhaled deeply down the line.

"Leave it with me," She answered simply. And ended the call.

Mercer was only two minutes away from Stockwell.

Leyland Francis and his delightful clone escorts had arrived at St Thomas' hospital acute assessment wing. That was where they treated and processed a lot of people with mental health issues. Leyland had heard things about the place. Not all good.

It was seen as a kind of stopping off point before being transferred either back into community assistance or Broadmoor.

Given the state of affairs as they were for Leyland he certainly wasn't going to rule out a trip to Oxfordshire being on the cards.

Ferdinand sure had gone to a lot of trouble to try and fuck up his career. And as much as he didn't want to in his mind he was trying to prepare for being held for a while.

His brain had turned to potential escape plans. How long could he last out on the street, in the open? Where would he go? Who would he trust? His mind would tick away.

He knew that the best time to attempt an escape was before you got too far into the system, too far into the infrastructure. The further you went the more secure and better organised it would be.

"Handcuff him," Ferdinand ordered.

He was helped from the car and escorted into the wing.

"Ah good morning doctor," exclaimed Ferdinand, in a way that was much too cheerful for Leyland's liking, given the circumstances.

He shuddered as they were greeted by a very official looking man. He was flanked by two men dressed identically. Leyland was going to joke about that but noticed the latex gloves they were wearing and kept his mouth shut. It looked like he could be in for an uncomfortable induction onto the wing.

Ferdinand's henchman undid his cuffs and the two latex orderlies took over. He was marched to an eight foot by eight foot clinical box marked 'search room'

Ferdinand had signed some paperwork and chatted briefly with the duty consultant.

"See you soon Detective Sergeant," was her parting shot as Leyland was taken into the room.

He looked around and saw the demonic smile of the woman who thought that she had got the better of him. And Mercer.

Thirteen.

The doctor pressed the 'stop' button on the CD player on the desk and looked up with a smile. Clicked his pen into action and poised for reaction.
Leyland was sitting opposite the doctor and had just been played a recording of the conversation with Phil Mercer in the interview room back at NCA HQ.
The table and chairs were bolted to the floor, which was an annoyance to Leyland who felt a natural urge to pull his chair in toward the desk a bit more.
He had been stripped of his clothes and was at that time sporting a delightfully snazzy pair of blue hospital scrubs. They were so not his style.
"So Leyland," began the good doctor.
"Do you believe in ghosts?"
"Certainly not doctor." Leyland answered confidently.
"This recording would suggest otherwise though wouldn't it?"
"It's been misinterpreted doctor."
The doctor feigned surprise and forced a laugh.
"Oh really? How so?" Semi sarcastically as he scribbled.
"Well doctor. Shortly before the incident I was describing to Detective Chief Inspector Mercer I took a bit of a tumble and banged my head." He was playing this as straight as it got, looking the doctor straight in the eyes.
"I believe that bang on the head affected me a bit more than I wanted to admit at the time. I must have

been concussed or still unconscious when those things appeared to have happened."

"I may even have dreamt it. Have you ever had a dream that seemed real, until you woke up but it stayed with you for the rest of the day?"

The doctor remained non-committal. His pen was working like a dog.

"You see doctor it's very easy to explain. I shouldn't be here. We both know that. It was a strange experience and not one I would want to repeat. But it certainly doesn't mean I'm a mad man. Nor does it render me incapable of carrying out the duties assigned to me, which I would like to emphasis, were duties connected with a very important case." Soapbox time.

"Tell me about the business card Leyland," the doctor asked softly.

"Again something I dreamt or imagined. You've searched me thoroughly. Went through my stuff with a fine tooth comb. Did you find the business card at all?" Leyland knew that they hadn't. It was with Felicity.

"No. I have to say we didn't. But that doesn't mean it could be somewhere else does it?"

"Doctor," Leyland chuckled. "Are you trying to tell me a business card given to me by a dead person's ghost is in existence somewhere?"

"Maybe we should swap places?"

The doctor suddenly stopped his furious note taking and put his pen down. He looked at Leyland and realised he had been boxed clever.

"O.K. Leyland, perhaps we shall leave it there for now." He pushed a button under the table and two orderlies entered the room and took an arm each. It wasn't so bad but Leyland did wish that they would actually lift him and perhaps he could rest his leg a bit more. Even so, he complied. Playing the game. Biding his time.

Phil Mercer was at the door of room fifty two of the Stockwell Premier Lodge. Or prossies dealer central as the locals called it.

He had flashed his credentials to Rix and Connor who wouldn't have asked for them as they recognised him almost instantly.

Felicity Marshall was standing by the large main window looking out and over the city.

She jumped when Mercer strode into the room. A look of concern hit her face.

"Where is DS Francis? Who are you?" She questioned.

"I'm Detective Chief Inspector Phil Mercer," he introduced and offered his warrant card to her.

She grabbed it from him and scrutinised it in the manner of an East German border guard.

"Where is Leyland? He said he would be back. What's going on?"

Mercer raised his hands. Palms out and signalled for her to calm down.

"D.S. Francis had been processing the information that you passed to him last night," Mercer lied, knowing full well that the truth would send her running for the hills. Again.

"D.S. Francis mentioned me and my role in the investigation I take it?" He queried.

"He said to only speak to him or speak to you. The only two people to trust on the investigation he said."

"There you go then. What I would like to know if I may Felicity is who you first passed the information over to?"

Felicity just stared at him.

"You see if someone on my squad is batting for the bad guys I sure as hell want to know who before we go any further." He was very serious. And cold. His eyes were steely.

Felicity looked down at her feet for a second or two.

"I don't know who it was. All I know is that it was a woman. A female. I don't know her name. Not long after I reported it two guys showed up at my home and tried to attack me. I managed to escape through the back door and decided to stay well under the radar. Until I made contact with Leyland."

Her revelation almost made Mercers legs give way. One of his girls. On his team. Rotten. He breathed heavily and was desperate for a smoke. He tried his hardest to keep a cool facade. He couldn't risk spooking her at all. Not at the crucial stage of things. The truth was Mercer only had two females on his team involved in the investigation. It had already been well narrowed down for him.

"And what of the memory stick?" He asked. "Where would that be found?"

"It's safe," she answered simply.

"It will stay safe as long as I do. And as long as I trust in you and Leyland," she added sternly.

"You might like to know that as an investigative journalist the information you want, and any information regarding any possible cover up or simple funny business with my sister's murder investigation could be revealed through any number of outlets. Fuck with me and I will fuck with you. Understand that?" She wasn't messing around and Mercer could tell that. A rookie could have picked up that she wasn't.

"Have you eaten?" was Mercers response. It caught her on the back foot after her posturing.

"What? Err no I haven't properly for days I guess," She tried to remember her last proper meal.

"Right. Let's go get lunch," he announced. "Get your things together."

"Won't take long," she back chatted. "I travelled light." She shoved a small hand held video recorder and her gun into a cloth drawstring bag and threw it over her shoulder. Mercer stared.

"Ready," she announced.

"Maybe you should leave that with me," Mercer pointed to the bulge in the bag.

"I don't think so. Solve my sister's murder and it's yours. Until then go fuck yourself," she smiled sweetly at him.

Saved by the bell, Mercers mobile blared out.

"Shit, I have to take this,"

"DCI Rawlins," he answered. Then cringed.

"I want you to drop what you are doing and get your arse in here for a chat," he was pissed off and very direct.

"A chat sir?" Mercer half-heartedly tried a blag.

"About your friend Mr Francis," he added.

Mercer took a deep breath.

"On my way sir." There was a time to stall and bullshit. And there was a time not too. This was the latter and Phil knew he had better get back sharpish. He turned to Felicity.

"Sorry. Lunch is postponed. Let's go."

"What's happened? What's going on?"

"My boss needs an urgent word with me. And we need to get you somewhere safer than here," he explained.

After handshakes with Connor and Rix, Mercer and Felicity were down the stairs and into his Audi in double time.

Mercer was ticking over in his brain where to take her. The hub? The risk with that would be dropping her into the lap of the mole. Not the best idea in the world.

As nutty as he considered Leyland was, he couldn't half have done with leaning on him at that time.

He may well have talked to ghosts. But he was wholly trustworthy. And you couldn't buy that kind of quality and it was smacking Mercer in the face. If he hadn't had the chat with him in the interview room, he would still be a free man and sewing the case up single handed most probably.

He had to prepare himself for Rawlins as well. Word had obviously spread from Ferdinand.

An arse chewing was on the cards at the very least.

He could even leave that office career less. Minus one pension. He had to assume that the worst of the news had risen up top and that the worst possible picture had been painted of the whole damn situation.

He pulled a cigarette from the box in his cup holder, lit and pulled hard on it exhaling the smoke through his nose.

"Do you mind awfully if I pinch one of those?" Felicity asked.

"Oh...sorry ...of course help yourself love."

"Terrible habit I know. Melissa was always trying to get me to give up." Mercer smiled at her comment. Sounded just like Trudy.

"Without much success I'm afraid," she added.

"What was she like?" Mercer asked.

"Melissa? Well...she was a major pain in the arse when I moved to London. Ringing me every five minutes to check up on me."

"Big sister. Of course she would look out for you," chipped in Mercer flicking ash out of the window.

"She became very protective when mum and dad died. When she got the transfer to Philips and she was over the moon. It meant she could move to London and be closer to me."

"Just so happens around the same sort of time I got the opportunity to further my career and ended up dashing around Libya during Gaddafi's takedown. We caught up when we could, things were fine. But the night she came to me about what she knew she was scared. I mean really scared about what was going on. I promised her that if she passed information to me I could follow it up. She was reluctant to involve me. But I gave her little choice in that."

"And did she pass much to you?" Asked Mercer.

"She passed me very little at first. But she seemed to suddenly give me everything she had collected. Almost in a panic. I think she knew that she had been found out. It wouldn't surprise me if she involved the Police the way I did and chose the wrong ones to trust. I think that led to her death. I won't be making the same mistakes." Her voice started to shake.

"She's dead. I'm alone and in the midst of some corrupt bastards. If I live through this it will be a miracle." Tears ran down her cheek and she turned and stared out of the passenger side window in a useless attempt to shield her emotion from Mercer.

"Let me tell you something for free. Leyland and I will get to the bottom of this mess. We will bring your sister's killers to justice and we will hang, draw and quarter whoever is working for the bad boys," Mercer insisted. Felicity wiped away tears.

"I know that trusting is a hard thing to do when everyone seems like they could be a bad egg. But I give you a cast iron guarantee that when you made contact with Leyland you went to the best possible person in the world. You came into contact with me because of him. You have two people in you corner who you can depend on completely."

Mercer noticed that under the emotion on her face a slight smile had appeared.

"Came into contact with you in a slightly different way to Leyland."

Mercer looked puzzled.

"I kind of kidnapped him," she revealed. Mercer drew on the last of his fag and looked even more confused.

"When he came out of the pub I kidnapped him at gunpoint and drove him to the hotel," she added.

"Ahh...I see! I bet he enjoyed that! Was it a speedy drive?"

"Just slightly," Felicity confirmed.

"Oh my goodness," Mercer laughed. "Was he a bit pale at the end?"

"He didn't look all that clever. I put it down to the drink, why?"

"He has a bit of an issue with fast car journeys ever since his accident," Mercer revealed.

"Oh yes, he was limping a bit going up the stairs. When will we see him?"

Mercer had to think quickly with that question.

"Soon hopefully. If I know Leyland then he will be throwing himself into the information you gave him," said Mercer tactically.

"We need to sort you out with a safe place to stay," He added changing the subject.

"I can only think of one place but it might not be up to the standard of that hotel."

He didn't know why he hadn't thought of it before. He had been juggling too many balls in the air that's why.

He flicked the indicator and changed direction. Taking her to the HQ wasn't the best solution in the world and if he wanted to keep her under the radar of any potential rats on the investigation then he needed to be the only person to know where she was.

"I think rather than trying to arrange a safe house at the moment it might be better if you stay at my flat," He announced to Felicity.

"Your flat? Is that wise? Is that safe?" She questioned.

"It's the safest place I can think of and the last place anyone would expect you to be," Mercer countered.

He didn't know why he didn't think of it before and gave him one less thing to worry about for a bit while he was dealing with Rawlins and praying that things weren't spiralling out of his control. Well, anymore out of his control than they were at that point.

Leyland was lying down and thinking. He did a lot of that in between the bouts of intensive interviews. Shrouded with the term 'assessments'.

His main train of thought always stuck around one particular subject. How could he escape?

He had given his room the full Monty in terms of searching for any gaps or weak points. He had found none.

He smiled to himself as he ruled out digging a tunnel. Even if he could and did manage to get out, where could he go?

Ferdinand would make sure that he manhunt was huge and ratchet up how 'dangerous' an individual he was and not to be approached by the general public.

She would probably go as far as trying to implicate him in the murder of Melissa Marshall somehow. But despite all of these things he couldn't just lie in this place and rot or let them take what was left of his marbles.

He knew he wasn't crazy and by god he had certainly questioned his sanity recently. More than these shrinks ever could. The difficult thing to accept was that he knew that what he had experienced were real events. Not imagination and not because he fell over and bumped his head.

Leyland stretched out on the bed and let out the heaviest of sighs. His mind wandered to Mercer and what he would be doing. He didn't think that his old friend would have cut him loose and hoped to god that he had some sort of plan he was putting into action to get him out of that place. It would take time and he knew that his predicament wasn't the number one priority for Phil given that he had to look after Felicity. It would take time to get round to Leyland. But he had time. For a while.

He couldn't help but feel the faint light of hope knowing that all the time Phil was on the street doing his thing; he would come for his friend at some point. The downside was it was nearly dinner time. And in that place it was clearly a part of the punishment.

Phil Mercer had left Felicity in the safety of his flat and after apologising for the state it was in, he demanded that she not touch his scotch collection. Oh, and to not answer the door to anyone.

He was back on the road and heading for his showdown with Rawlins back at HQ. It was going to be uncomfortable which is why he needed the buzz of yet another ciggie.

He sparked up and loosened off his Liverpool tie as he tried to play out in his mind how he was going to handle this 'chat'

He knew damn well it all depended on what kind of mood Rawlins was in and who was leaning on him. He couldn't, and wouldn't, throw Leyland to the wolves but he knew equally as well that he had to retain his own status and freedom to be able to take care of Leyland's incarceration and the murder case.

Getting his arse kicked out of the force would, of course, mean that none of those situations got dealt with. Not properly anyway.

He could even find himself fighting prison on a conspiracy charge. No doubt Ferdinand could get that shit to stick if she put the effort in. And for Mercer she would certainly put the effort in.

He had to get Rawlins on side so using his intelligence skills he knew that Rawlins was very partial to a drop of Glenfiddich. Stopping by way of an off licence to purchase a bottle was, by his own admission, a bit of a master stroke.

He parked up his Audi at HQ and made his way through the rear entrance to and in the lift up to Rawlins office.

"Hello Janet love, how are you?" he greeted Rawlins PA positioned outside his office.

"Oh hello Phil," she returned with a light smile.

"What sort of mood is he in?"

"A bit dark to be honest honey, you in for a bollocking again?"

"Am I normally up here for anything else?" Mercer quipped.

Janet chuckled and shook her head whilst she pressed a button on her telephone console.

"D.I. Mercer for you sir," she announced.

"Send him straight through," Rawlins barked.

Mercer made to walk to Rawlins door. He turned back and pointed to Janet's reading material.

"Can I borrow that magazine?"

Janet looked confused.

"So I can shove it down the back of my trousers. Might soften the canning a bit," he winked.

"Get yourself in there before he goes off on one!" she ordered.

Mercer pulled the door open.

"Ahh Phil. Come in. Take a seat." Rawlins was standing with his back to the door looking out of his window over the cityscape.

Mercer walked over to the hulking desk and popped the Glenfiddich down. He sat.

Rawlins didn't move.

"Detective Sergeant Francis," he said simply.

"Why was he not arrested in connection with Melissa Marshalls murder Phil? Why is that?" Silence. Rawlins continued.

"Is it not true that DS Francis was probably the last person to see her alive? And that he phoned her mobile number shortly before her body was discovered?"

"Not strictly true Charles," answered Mercer.

Rawlins spun around. He looked Mercer in the eye and then spotted the bottle on the desk.

"You always did go for the good stuff Phil," he complimented with an approving nod. His train of thought ever so slightly interrupted, he pulled his chair out and sat down.

"I'm sure you can appreciate Phil that when I'm presented with a recording of you and an officer under your command," he pulled two glasses from his desk drawer.

"Talking about how that officer has perhaps had an encounter with the deceased and has contacted the deceased," Rawlins was on a roll. Mercer knew not to interrupt.

"Questions get asked Phil. Even of me as to why that officer seems to have been protected rather than being questioned as part of that investigation," he poured two large measures from the bottle.

"Not for me sir," Mercer raised his hand to protest.

"It's O.K. Phil. You're with a friend. One won't get you sacked. Or reported to occupational health. And I think we both need a good shot of this stuff."

Mercer leaned over and gripped the glass. He watched Rawlins sip and did the same.

It tasted bloody good.

Rawlins held his hands out, palms up as if to say 'well?'

"DS Francis, I believe, didn't have that contact Charles. He may have believed that he did possibly, but we agreed after that conversation that what he described was as a result of him banging his head in a fall on the underground." Mercer had to at last try the bullshit card. He sipped his whiskey again. It made him desperate for yet another cigarette.

"And the phone call?" questioned Rawlins holding his glass up to the light.

"Part of the investigation procedure." Rawlins raised his eyebrows at this.

"You see DS Francis was aware of the victim's phone being missing. He called it when we visited the scene to see if it could be located in the vicinity," Mercer was in full flow now. Detective Chief Inspector Billy Bullshit.

"I see," said Rawlins, hard staring Mercer.

"Well that certainly sounds reasonable. And I assume that the timing of that call would coincide with the time that you were both at the scene?" Mercer could see that he needed to sway this.

"Leyland Francis is an extraordinary copper," he offered.

"He was close to answers and he is locked up on some mental wing because of an unparalleled vendetta against him brought about by a power mad senior occupational health officer."

"We're talking about Petunia Ferdinand I take it?" Rawlins already knew of course, and sipped his gold watch.

"She is out of control, and nobody seems to have the bottle to cool her heels Charles," Mercer knew it would provoke a reaction. A challenge to his authority always did.

Rawlins slammed his glass down.

"It's not about bottle Phil, it's about who keeps their jobs. You know how well connected she is," he rose from his seat and faced the window again.

"Phil you have twenty four hours to get a result. After that it's out of yours, and my, hands. The press are screaming for information. The brass upstairs are screaming for blood. I don't fancy offering up a vein. Not yet. Not for the hell of it.

You know I will always take hits for you because you have always done the business and given me bragging rights. In the end that's the only reason you're still holding rank and position after the episodes you've had. OK?"

"Then I need Francis. He was close to answers. Solid answers."

"Then find a way to get him out Phil. I'll back you but you'll need something very solid with Ferdinand," warned Rawlins.

"Nice drop this," he added draining his glass. "You always did know your scotch."

He turned and stared at Mercer again.

"I know you won't let me down Phil."

"No pressure then," Mercer cheeked, sinking his glass, sensing the meeting was over. The men shook hands and Mercer left the office.

His mind was racing. His plans were fragmented and he needed desperately to glue them together if he was going to make any sort of progress.

The scotch had him needing another drink and he decided to head in the direction of the Weasel.

His time was limited. He needed to get back to the flat and check on Felicity before long. He didn't want her taking off at a crucial time as that was.

As he stepped out of the front entrance flashes went off in his face as a group of about thirty reporters bore down on him.

A thousand and one questions were being thrown at him. Was he any closer to catching the murderer of Melissa Marshall? Was it true that one of the investigating officers was a suspect? Had Felicity Marshall suffered the same fate? Was there a serial killer on the loose?

How the hell did they get hold of this stuff, thought Mercer.

Was the mole leaking information? Was it Ferdinand? It could be anyone connected with the case and Mercer knew it. It sickened him. His pushed his way through the crowd as Dictaphones were shoved in his face. He stayed cool, sidestepping, firmly and simply saying "No comment. No comment at this time."

He knew the drill well. There was a time when giving the press certain information could help the case. But this was certainly not one of those times. Not yet.

Mercer knew they would follow him if he went on foot so he raised his arm and hailed down a cab for the short journey.

The cab spilled him out a few minutes later and Mercer gave no tip much to the dissatisfaction of the driver for such a short journey.

Mercer burst through the Weasel's doors and made straight for the bar, and the top shelf.

"Large scotch please Harry," he ordered to the landlord on serving duties. Harry raised an eyebrow at Mercer. The look on Mercers face told the story and sent the message 'Don't even go there' as Harry shrugged and turned to the optics.

Mercer paid and took a big slug of the booze. He breathed deeply as the burn hit the back of his throat. It felt good.

He scanned his surroundings and double took.

Sitting alone in one of the snugs was a recently familiar face. Mercer strolled over with his glass.

"Can I get you a drink Mr Carmouche?"

Stan jumped out of his daydream and looked briefly puzzled. His familiar big smile spread across his face as he recognised the person standing over him.

"Officer Mercer! Take a seat my friend," he gestured at the space in front of him.

Stan's smile faded slightly.

"You don't look so happy officer Mercer. Is there anything I can do to help?"

"Please, call me Phil." Mercer corrected the big man.

"Call me Stan."

Phil smiled very lightly.

"Well, Stan, I don't think anyone can help with my problems," Mercer revealed. Stan looked puzzled.

"Well why don't you reveal all to Stan and see if we can't help find some kind of solution." Stan was serious and looked confident.

"Is it woman trouble?" he asked.

"Of a kind," replied Mercer.

"Is my young buddy Leyland OK?"

"He's not really OK Stan. Not at all. And I'm not sure how to help him."

Stan took off his pork pie hat and laid it on the table.

"I think we might need a couple more of these," he revealed holding his glass up to Harry, who nodded an acknowledgement.

"And then you can lay it all out for Stan to chew over."

Mercer nodded an agreement. And, reluctantly, started to spill the beans.

Fourteen.

The frosted glass on the door window separated into strips allowing the night shift nurse to peer in.

Leyland Francis was lying on his bed in the eight foot by eight foot room. He was being checked every hour and if he did manage to drop off to sleep, the sound of keys hitting the door was enough to pull him out of his slumber.

He was stretched out on the bed in the blue scrubs he had been given on his admission and he lay with his hands behind his head. Thinking. He had a lot of time for that. Thinking hard. Worrying.

He was worried about Felicity and wondered where she had ended up. It wouldn't have taken long for word to get out that she was being guarded at the hotel. He hoped and prayed that Mercer had been able to get to her and find someone safer.

He worried about Mercer as well. Worried as to whether or not his friend was watching his own back enough, given the revelations about someone on the team. He knew Felicity was a tough cookie and capable of protecting herself to a degree, given the way that she introduced herself to Leyland. But she needed him. And he needed her. He needed to prove to her that her sister's murder wouldn't be buried or covered up. He had promised to prove that to her and it pissed him the hell off to be stuck in this hole not being able to make good on it.

He stretched his bad leg out. It was still painful. He was trying hard to ignore it and had refused the offer of a brace. He didn't want the limp to personify him anymore. As much as it hurt on occasions. He was going to get out of that place and get answers. He was going to solve the mystery of the crash ultimately. And he was going to do it without those bloody crutches.

That was his determination. He felt under the side of the plastic mattress. He had managed to acquire a plastic knife when the evening toast was put out. He knew full well that they counted the metal cutlery used at dinner so ruled that out as a target. The plastic knife would still be taken seriously if threatened in the right way. He felt sick at running through his plan but he wasn't lying there for another night. He had considered the consequences. And he was still going to go for it. All he had to do was take a hostage and get them to open the doors. Then he would make his way quickly as he could and get some sort of jumper or hoodie or coat. He wouldn't look as conspicuous in the scrubs that way. He would look like an off duty hospital worker. There were plenty of them floating around London at any given time.

He then planned to head straight to Mercer's flat. Hide out for a bit and see what stage the investigation was at. Once they had solved it he was going to the top to push for another opening of the investigation into the crash. His gut was telling him that he had to go for that. Something was not right with what happened. The way it happened and after so long he was going to follow his gut instinct. Finally.

He closed his eyes again. Things were going to get busy tomorrow. He just hoped that his nerve would hold and that if he did go through with it that he could evade being caught. At least until he could straighten things up.

Phil Mercer was in full flow after a couple of whiskeys. He had reeled off the whole situation to a wide eyed Stan. The whole stinking mess that they were in.

Stan was non-judgemental of course. He liked Leyland and he enjoyed Phil's company too. He found his lack of bullshit refreshing.

Mercer found some kind of warmth and comfort in the old man too. He wasn't entirely sure that levelling with him on everything that had happened was very ethical, but he needed some kind of second pair of eyes on it all. And Stan was that pair of eyes right at that time.

"Of course I was there when he took his tumble," Stan revealed.

"Helped him onto the train and stuff but that stubborn son of a bitch wouldn't stop for an ambulance or any kind of medical assistance," he added to Mercer's surprise.

"You were there? It was on that journey he had his incident, shall we call it? You could provide some vital information to back up the fact that it was because of the fall?"

"I could. I would. But if what you have told me is true then we're gonna need something more hard-core for leverage." Stan sipped his drink. "I don't know if Leyland ever got the chance to mention it but I have acquired certain... skills shall we say, in my time."

Mercer looked very curiously at Stan.

"I'd be happy to look into hacking those email accounts if it helps. Unofficially of course," Stan offered almost as matter of fact as offering a cigarette. "It's usually something I've kept close to my chest but I think now is not the time for modesty if we're gonna get the kid out of his predicament."

"You could do that? Under the radar?" Mercer questioned, unsure.

The big man beamed. "If I can't, which is unlikely, then I know someone who can. Don't worry. One hundred percent under the radar," Stan reassured a Mercer with mixed feelings.

"That leaves you free to get to work on springing our little buddy from his hole."

Mercer nodded. Slowly but positively. What Stan had suggested made sense. And frankly under the radar seemed to be the only way to get anything done on this investigation. It would cut out the potential of the mole finding any new info.

He would have to make sure Stan's involvement was as far away from HQ as possible. It left him with one nagging issue though. Felicity Marshall.

Did he continue to bullshit her about Leyland or was it in his, and her, best interest to just come clean about what was going on. And risk her bolting for the hills. Stan stood up and offered his hand.

Mercer shook and pressed a small piece of paper into his palm.

"Thank you Stan. Thank you," Mercer blurted. This guy was a godsend and Mercer was putting almost all of his faith, and his future, in his hands. And

Leyland's for that matter. Stan tipped his pork pie hat in acknowledgement.

"I won't let you guys down," Stan said with a serious and determined look in his eye that Mercer didn't think possible from such a jolly man.

He drained his glass. He needed a smoke very desperately so he ordered another shot, one for the road, and headed out to the beer garden and sparked up.

His mobile vibrated and his 'You'll never walk alone' ringtone drew some funny looks from the cockney boys giving it large in the outside summer air.

It was Maria.

"Hey you. Just can't keep away can you?"

"You wish," she chuckled. "Just a quick one may or may not be of interest to you, but Ferdinand has a liaison with her toy boy this evening I do believe."

"Bloody hell, are you sure?" Mercer needed this.

"As sure as I can be Phil. I checked her diary when she was out of the office for a bit. It was in code but I kinda worked it out."

"And this fella is job?"

"She is going to a lot of trouble to keep it quiet. It has to be someone on the force. I'm sure of that," Maria revealed.

"Just be careful Phil. She will do just about anything to protect her position and reputation."

"Don't I know it. Just look at Leyland."

"So he's not a head case then?" Maria asked.

"Not in the sense of mentally unstable, but he does hang around with me an awful lot."

"Take care darling," Maria ended the call.

Ghost Track: Melissa

Mercer drew hard on his ciggie and exhaled through his nose. This was likely to be the one and only chance he would get to nail Ferdinand.

If it was definitely happening then he needed to be on it. His mind whirled. Could he do it on his own? He was almost certain he would need some kind of back up. How was he going to approach it? He knew where Ferdinand lived. Did he just go steaming in?

At that very moment a stunning plan hit Phil Mercer right between the eyes. How to kill two birds with one stone. Ensnare Ferdinand and keep Felicity safe and in the loop. What better way to capture quality video evidence than by utilising the skills of one investigative journalist, with her own camera no less. The hard part was going to be explaining everything to her and hope that she would want to help, and not shoot him. It would not be easy. But he had to convince her. Failure would mean serious problems. And by serious he meant the nuthouse for Leyland and prison for him. With Petunia Ferdinand holding the keys. Mercer shuddered in the summer sun at the thought of that. He pulled on and stubbed the last of his smoke and headed for his flat.

Leyland was pulled out of his slumber by the door to his room flying open and hitting the wall behind it with a heavy, ominous bang.

Sweat was dripping off him in the terribly ventilated space and he was out of breath with the shock, almost physically panting. Six orderlies piled into his room.

"We need to search the room Leyland. Don't make a fuss," said the lead guy.

Leyland was disorientated and got up off the bed. He was immediately boxed into a corner of the room and handcuffed.

"Is there anything in particular you're looking for?" He asked.

"Calm down!" Shouted the orderly holding his arm.

Leyland looked puzzled. It was a perfectly reasonable, and calm, question given the way they came into his space. He certainly hadn't shown any aggression to warrant cuffing.

"I am calm? What the hell are you lot on?" He joked.

"I said calm down!" Came an even more aggressive reply.

Leyland's mattress was thrown up in the air and off the bed frame.

"What's this then?"

"It's a plastic knife."

"Clever prick. Why is it hidden in your room?" snarled the searcher.

A great sense of unease hit Leyland's stomach with the intensity of these guys' actions.

"Maybe the person before me hid it there?"

"RIGHT... Paul, sedate him."

"What?!" Leyland was sure they couldn't do that for no reason, or for a bit of backchat.

"You just tried to attack three of us with this," explained the orderly, waving the plastic implement in front of Leyland's face. "What do you expect?" He was grinning. Ferdinand's reach was extensive and she had obviously given orders for his stay to be a very uncomfortable one. He had to hand it to her. Anything to make him look dangerous.

The orderly holding Leyland's arm spun him quickly and forced him face first into the corner. It took Leyland by surprise and he instinctively threw his good leg up. He caught the orderly clean in the testicles and he collapsed in a retching heap on the clinical floor. Split seconds told Leyland it was a stupid move and the rest of the gang jumped on him and forced him face down. He felt blows and kicks rain down on him. His head, kidneys and back. One particular shot caught him in the leg and he howled in pain and begged them to stop, it was impossible to protect himself with his hands in the cuffs. On the verge of passing out, he felt a sharp scratch in his arm followed by a cold sensation.

As he tried to continue his protests, the beating stopped. Time began to slow down. Voices in the room lowered in pitch and Leyland felt as if he was going to float from the ground, half convinced he was dying from the vicious assault he had just been subjected to.

"Relax. You're going to be here for a long time," the voice was almost comically deep and slow. Leyland wanted to laugh but all that came out was a throaty rasp. The taste of blood trickled into his mouth.

He floated onto his bed. The room started to spin. Spinning and fading very slowly.

He heard the screech of tyres. Where did that come from? The crash of vehicle bodies colliding. He was drifting into a nightmare and couldn't do a thing to stop it. A foreign accent? A different language? He heard deep slow words.

"Umeret sviney."

And again. Swirling words.
"Umeret Sviney."
Everything was fading fast. The spinning got faster. He felt sick. Fading. Black.
"Umeret' Sviney Ublyudkov."
Black. Echoes. A scream. Nothingness.

Fifteen.

The modern apartment at Java Wharf was host to the owner and one other that night.
On the fifth floor it gave a view of Canary Wharf that was usually only within reach of bankers or stock market high rollers.
The interior was immaculate and gave the air of someone who was extremely particular about how things should be.
Petunia Ferdinand had bought the place after her promotion to Occupational health director. Promotion was the term used to cover what was, in effect, a bloody coup to get rid of her superior at the time. Get rid of him she did though in her own unique way. Underhand tactics ruled in Ferdinand's world.
And after beating off the challenge of Tony Martinez for the job she was set.
Tonight she was entertaining. Two tumblers of Brandy sat neatly side by side on her coffee table which was centred to the millimetre in the living area.
Ferdinand was on the sofa and the younger man next to her was getting hot under the collar. He kissed her neck gently and slowly from her collarbone slowly up to her ear. He reached up and released her hair from its tight beehive and it cascaded down to her shoulders.
"I think we need a little something before we get going," said Ferdinand.
The younger man stopped and clutched at the two glasses.

"I meant something a little stronger," she demanded, with a tight smile.
"Did you bring it?"
The man stared at her for a moment and then dived into his trouser pocket and fished out a small clear bag containing white powder.
"That's more like it. You'll go far. I'll see to that. Like I said before if we look out for each other there is no limit, no boundaries to what we can do."
"No boundaries?" Questioned the man. With that he drained his glass and in an ultra-quick movement he ripped open Ferdinand's blouse and moved to take her glasses off as buttons bounced around.
"No! They stay on," she ordered.
She snatched the bag from him leant forward and emptied half the contents on to the coffee table and neatly arranged four identical lines ready for snorting. The young man smiled and picked up a small plastic tube ready to get his fill of narcotics. He leant down toward the lines.
"That's not for you," Ferdinand informed sternly. A look of confusion and mild disappointment took over the man's face.
"This is for you." She leant back and sprinkled the remaining drug over her breasts. The man's eyes widened with delight and as Ferdinand leant back into the cosiness of the sofa she held her arms out.
"Come to mummy," she threw at him. The young man dived into the arms and cocaine covered bosoms of Ferdinand, savouring the illegal delights of the Charlie on her skin.
CRASH!

Ghost Track: Melissa

They both jumped up with a shock.

The front door had been kicked in and before they could regain coordination and disrupt and destroy the neat lines of drugs on the table, Phil Mercer and Felicity Marshall were standing over them. Mercer was grinning as Felicity was stone faced holding her video camera. Filming the sticky scene for posterity.

Mercers grin dropped when he identified the male with Ferdinand who was sitting with white powder on his nose, the posture of a naughty schoolboy.

The figure of John McTavish was sheepish.

"Fuck me at Anfield," he exclaimed. "You? You?"

McTavish looked down at the floor.

"Of course. Of course. You and her." The penny had dropped.

"You want to know why Leyland is where he is?" Mercer turned and asked Felicity.

"Get a good close up of what's on the table there." She zoomed in over the Charlie.

"Meet Leyland's rival for his job," Mercer announced.

"John McTavish. Current head of the witness protection team in Leyland's absence. And the longer he is absent, the longer he keeps the job. Convenient eh?"

"And if Leyland is stuck in a nuthouse?" Asked Felicity for effect rather than information. She knew where this was going.

"Mr McTavish gets the promotion on a more permanent basis," explained Mercer. His face twisted.

"You fucking backstabbing piece of shit. Do you know what's been done to your colleague? Your friend? Do you?"

McTavish shook his head. "It's not like that," he tried to explain pathetically, rising to his feet.

"Leyland is unwell and is in the best place to get the help he needs."

"Is that right? Is that the opinion of the wonderful occupational health director is it?"

Ferdinand slowly fastened what buttons were left on her blouse.

"I don't know what your game is but get the hell out of here. Now," she was calm under the circumstances.

"You wish," chipped in Felicity. "You stitched up the guy who could have solved my sister's murder. Time for some role reversal, wouldn't you agree Chief Inspector?" She looked to Mercer.

"I think we've got enough footage," he confirmed and looked at his watch.

"You've got six hours to get Leyland released and the recording of us destroyed. And I mean all of the recordings," he demanded.

"And you," he pointed at McTavish and narrowed his eyes. "You might want to seriously consider your future in another line of work. Within the same time frame."

"And if I decide not to do as you ask?" Ferdinand trod the thin line.

Mercer smiled very lightly at her.

"Then I guess me and Commander Rawlins will be having a little private viewing of that footage," he pointed at Felicity's camera.

"And just in case there will be copies dotted around various places. Should anything happen to me or Leyland in the meantime." They hard stared each other. Mercer knew he had won this round. And seriously needed it was.

"Let's roll," he told Felicity.

"Wait, Phil!" McTavish shouted, and chased after him, placing a hand firmly on Mercer's shoulder.

With barely a seconds hesitation Mercer spun on the spot and planted a peachy right hander square on McTavish' chin that made a very satisfying 'Schlaap' sound as it made decent contact.

McTavish' legs went from under him and he crumbled to the floor. It was a good shot from the short scouser. He knew just how to play rough when needed.

"Don't ever touch me again. And it's Detective Chief Inspector to you, shit head. I earned my rank pretty honourably compared to your way," Mercer growled. They left the apartment.

As Phil and Felicity entered the left and pressed for the ground floor Mercer turned to her.

"Thanks for that," he said simply.

"Thanks for what? Just a bit of filming. Done it a million times," Felicity replied.

"There aren't many people that would have stuck around after hearing what I told you. Let alone help me."

Felicity considered this briefly.

"Maybe not. But Leyland assured me that he would protect me before he disappeared. And he did just that by sending me you. He kept his promise," she explained.

"And you've both been working your socks off to find Melissa's killers. Seems to me you've both been screwed over so I'm happy to help turn the tables on that."

They looked at each other as the lift plunged.

"Can we please find the fuckers that killed my sister now?"

"Took the words right out of my mouth," said Mercer, who faced ahead of him again.

The lift doors pinged open and as they headed back out into the docklands air Mercer offered her a cigarette. She accepted glad fully and pulled a face when Mercers phone blared out.

"I've cracked the accounts," announced Stan.

"I'm in the process of collating any relevant information and I will bring hard copies to our meet. Where and when officer Mercer?"

"Let's say the Weasel in an hour? Is that doable?"

"Sounds good to me. First ones on you," Stan chuckled and ended the call.

These lucky breaks can keep coming, thought Mercer. First Maria's tip off and then his very own CIA trained case assistant. Brilliant.

"News on the case?" asked Felicity.

"Sure is. And big news as well. Leyland had made the breakthrough originally but we lost his work and notes when he got sectioned. When you can't trust your own people sometimes you have to run with unorthodox methods," Mercer enlightened, breathing smoke out through his nose.

"That's where Stan comes in," he added.

Mercer flicked his keys and the Audi unlocked. They both got in and Mercer threw the engine into action in a heartbeat.

"When do you think we will hear about Leyland getting out?" Felicity asked.

"Most probably tomorrow morning. It would be good if we could be there to pick him up."

Felicity nodded positively and flicked her ciggie butt out of the car window.

"What can you do about the mole?" she asked.

"Find out who it is, and then nail her to a cross."

"How?"

"Smoke her out somehow. That's a plan to think on while we are slamming the cell door on your sister's killers," Mercer added.

"Once we have the copies of the emails I'm going to need the memory stick," he added.

"Sure. Shouldn't be too much hassle." She smiled.

"Pleased to hear it," reacted Mercer. "Something to do with this crap pile needs to be straightforward."

The Audi slipped into the car park of the Weasel and they both made their way quickly to the bar. Stan was already ensconced in one of the booths the pub had to offer, his pork pie hat on the table and glass in hand. He raised it as soon as he spotted Mercer.

"Orange juice please, what you having?" he turned to Felicity.

"Vodka and coke. With ice please." She needed something stronger than orange juice and with their drinks they went and sat with Stan.

He had a half inch thick pile of papers on the table.

"I know you don't I?" Stan asked Felicity, squinting at her.

"You lived downstairs from my sister," Felicity replied to him.

"Oh my, yes of course. Where are my manners," said Stan looking slightly embarrassed with his memory. He rose from his seat and his massive frame towered over Felicity as he planted a soft kiss on both cheeks.

"I'm so terribly sorry for your loss", he added.

"Your sister lived above me for a year and was a delightful young lady to know."

"Thank you so much," Felicity acknowledged. She had reddened with a mixture of pride, grief and vodka hitting her system.

"I remember seeing you a few times when I first came to London and visited her. She always mentioned how lovely you were to her," Felicity blurted.

"That's too kind." Stan shuffled in his seat with an uncomfortable slight embarrassment. He didn't take compliments easily.

"I was hoping that these would go some way to helping solve what happened. But I'm afraid to say probably not." He pushed the papers to Mercer who looked confused. Disappointed.

"Seems that a large number of messages were deleted at some point. Don't know how or who by I'm afraid to say. Not even I could retrieve them."

"Shit." Mercer's response couldn't hide how he was desperately hoping for some kind of clue in the emails.

That was a massive let down.

"Hey, thanks for trying Stan," Mercer thanked the big guy and sipped at his orange juice.

"There may be little bits of info in those," Stan pointed to the pile and then changed the subject.

"What's happening about our little buddy?"

"He should be a free man by the morning," Mercer confirmed. It bought a big beam to Stan's face again. It didn't stay away from his face for too long if he could help it.

"Sure do hope so. That guy's been through enough that's for sure."

"Well we can keep a very close eye on him once he is out. It will do him the world of good to be around people he can trust after everything," Stan added.

"Certainly not much to trust about his understudy," Felicity revealed to Stan. "Made me sick."

Stan look puzzled.

"The guy that had stepped into Leyland's position temporarily had designs on making it a more permanent arrangement. In cahoots with a senior officer as well," Mercer explained.

"But with Felicity's help it has been dealt with quite well."

Stan sipped his drink and nodded in positivity.

"He's gonna be OK. He'll be over the moon to see you again," Mercer put to Stan.

"He's a good kid. Gotta lot of sense and an old timer like me can appreciate that," Stan chuckled.

"I'll let you know as soon as he is back with us," said Mercer.

"I sure would like that officer Mercer."

Phil drained his glass of the OJ and fiddled with the knot on his Liverpool tie.

"Right. Time to head for home and start sifting through that lot." Mercer picked up the wad of papers and stood. Felicity gulped at her drink and kept an ever present clench on her cloth bag with the camera in it. She offered her other hand to Stan.

"Really nice to meet you Stan." Stan stood and gently kissed her hand.

"Keep strong young lady. Justice will be done for your sister." Felicity smiled lightly. Mercer and Stan shared a crunching handshake.

"Can I help you go through those emails?" Asked Felicity as they left the pub.

Mercer cackled.

"You don't think I'm going through them all on my own do you?!" They both got into the car.

"Didn't think you were going straight to bed when we got in did you?" he smiled.

Felicity looked dog tired. She took Mercer seriously.

"Not that you're getting the bed anyway," Mercer added cheekily.

"The sofa is very comfy!" He winked.

"Thanks!" retorted Felicity. "What a gent!"

"Oh. And I'll need that memory stick as well. Where is it?" he questioned.

Sixteen.

There were distant voices and echoes that slowly bought Leyland out of his sleep. His vision was seriously blurred and his head was pounding. The after effects of the sedative forced on him last night.
He could also feel swelling and the ache of bruising on his face and deep in his ribs.
They really did give him a good kicking. For no reason at all other than he was at the mercy of fucking Ferdinand. And Ferdinand's puppets getting their kicks. Literally.
Leyland sat up and the room span lightly. He checked the clock on the wall. It was hard to gauge time in that place. No windows meant he really didn't know if it was day or night.
The voices were being drowned out by each other. The mixture of that, the room spinning and the remnants of the sedative hangover was making Leyland nauseous and he moved as quickly as he could to the toilet and puked.
He sat on the bare floor and wiped his mouth. A cold sweat had formed on his brow. As a, generally, peaceful guy Leyland Francis was certainly entertaining some very dark thoughts about how he was going to get out of that place. Ferdinand's Muppets had obviously been given the green light to have their fun with him and he was certain that it wouldn't be too long before they got bored and decided to pay him another visit.
He had heard stories and wondered how far their levels of depravity would sink. He feared what was to

come that night. If the day shift didn't fancy a crack at him, of course.

The fear for Leyland was that, as proved last night, if he did fight back or defend himself, however unintentionally, or if he showed any degree of aggressiveness, no matter how badly provoked, they would use that as an excuse to move him further along into the system.

He had zero qualms that Ferdinand would in some way love to ship him off to ultra-high security custody. And Broadmoor scared the shit out of him.

Hour by hour had turned into minute by minute that he prayed for some kind of news from the outside. From Mercer. Time was running out. Very quickly.

A set of footsteps echoed in the corridor.

Leyland listened intently as they came closer. And closer. And louder. His guts tightened and adrenaline spiked into his system making his legs shake slightly.

From what he could make out it wasn't a mass of people coming his way. Not like last night. Two maybe three at most. It could still be a very unwelcome visit even with those shorter odds.

Shoes skidded to a halt outside of his door with a slight squeak.

The small window on the door was still in privacy position. He awaited the familiar heavy clunk of keys hitting the door. In a split second he decided to make himself look as passive as possible and dropped into the furthest corner of the room with his hands visible. The door swung open and Leyland braced himself. Scared.

There in the doorway stood Dr. Martinez. To his left the doctor who had carried the constant questioning of Leyland. He was holding a bag with Leyland's possessions in it.

Martinez looked stunned at the sight of Leyland. Leyland looked awfully confused.

"What the hell happened to your face?" Martinez questioned as he strode toward Leyland.

Leyland's confusion manifested in his inability to speak properly.

"What? What are you doing here? Why are you...?"

He slowly got to his feet from the corner of the room and the pain in his ribs expressed on his face as he did so. Martinez rushed to help him and stood face to face checking the bruising on his face.

"Mitchell, how did this happen?" he asked the assessor, angrily.

"Night shift reported that he became aggressive and attacked them during a routine room check. They claim self-defence and had to forcibly sedate him." His initial eye contact had dropped to the floor.

Leyland mock laughed. As much as he could to the point where it didn't hurt his midriff.

"Yeah of course," he croaked. "I really went for it on your guys. Fucking idiot."

"Did they hurt your leg at all?" Martinez asked looking down at Leyland.

"About the only bit of me they generally left alone. Took a kick I think but nothing bad."

"Get dressed and we can discuss this more when we have got you home," Martinez revealed, to Leyland's shock.

"I'm leaving?" he was flabbergasted.
"How so?"
"I received a call very early this morning from Petunia Ferdinand asking for me to take care of your release. All a terrible misunderstanding apparently."
"Well well," chuckled Leyland. He didn't know the details but he was pretty sure Mercer must have struck solid gold for this to happen.
"A misunderstanding?" he pointed at Mitchell.
"You tell the boys that did this to me last night that there won't be any misunderstanding when it comes to me fucking their careers. Make sure you pass that on won't you?"
Mitchell was pale and shifted nervously on his feet.
"I'm terribly sorry Detective Sergeant."
"Save the bullshit and let me get dressed in peace," Leyland cut him off and nodded toward the door. He grabbed his bag of belongings from Mitchell and he and Martinez vacated the room.
He pulled his phone out of the bag. It still had some charge in it and he tapped out a swift text to Mercer.
'Leaving soon. Don't know how you did it but thank you my friend.'
He sent it and pulled his clothes out. They were creased to buggery and Leyland, for a second, considered leaving in the scrubs.
He couldn't wait to get out into the fresh summer air. His mobile buzzed on the bed.
'You owe me a pint! Who would you trust in your team?' Need Felicity guarded. McTavish is a no no'
Leyland read and re read the message. John McTavish was his deputy. Why would he be a no no?

What the fuck was going on? He tapped out his reply, remembering his conversation with Ferdinand and her comment about John.

'Connor and Rix all the way. Why? Where shall we meet?'

He buttoned his shirt as he anxiously awaited a reply. What he wouldn't give for an ironing board at that moment. Another buzz.

'The cafe opposite the unit. Contact no one. Tell no one'

He pulled on his suit jacket. He had a good idea it would be too warm outside for it, but it covered most of his shirt thankfully.

He sat on the bed and pulled his shoes on. It took some effort and Leyland grimaced through the pain of his ribs. As he stood up gingerly and made to leave the room he took a glance in the plastic mirror set into the wall.

He looked at his face. Swollen and purple on the left side. If he came across those fuckers he was going to force feed them their own testicles.

He hadn't been in for long but as he made to leave the room he looked back. That room personified everything that he needed to know to keep quiet from there on about what happened on the tube that morning.

He walked along the corridor with Martinez. He counted seven other rooms along that long walk and wondered what treatment the other poor bastards in there would get during their stay.

At the reception desk Mitchell was standing and waiting to discharge Leyland. Sat at a computer was a familiar face. An instant spike of rage coursed through Leyland and he couldn't control his reaction.

"Hey tough guy," he bellowed.

"Fancy trying your hard man shit on me without your wanker mates to back you up?" The guy looked up and horror spread across his face. Leyland was desperately trying to control what he wanted to do to the man. Martinez stepped in quickly.

"Leyland this isn't the time for that. Let's just get you out of here."

Leyland's stare was fixed. Narrow eyed and full of hate.

"How do you feel, prick? Feel big do you? Well come on. Let's have round two." His eyes were bulging. Various members of staff wandering through the area had stopped and were watching the stand-off in silence. Martinez held Leyland's arm. Mitchell turned to the guy.

"Go and get yourself a coffee or something." He seemed rooted to the chair with fear, but swallowed and backed out.

"Fuck the coffee," bellowed Leyland.

"I want to hear what he has to say for himself. Pussy." Martinez walked around and into Leyland's line of sight. He had to get him out of there or there was a genuine chance he could book himself a longer stay.

"I'm sorry. Things got out of hand," offered the orderly pathetically.

"We were just following orders."

"Fuck your orders!" Spat Leyland. "And fuck you and your buddies. Keep looking over your shoulders."

Martinez manoeuvred him with some friendly force toward the main doors. Once outside and immersed in air of the fresher type he cooled slightly and Martinez loosened his grip on his shoulders.

"Jesus Leyland. I know what they did to you was despicable but you're better than that. You can't go shouting threats with so many potential witnesses around."

"Doctor. I don't give a flying fuck, with all due respect."

"Well you should. Just because Ferdinand has had to let you go, doesn't mean she won't try and stick it to you some other way"

The sunlight was hard on Leyland's eyes as he scanned for the cafe.

"Thanks for getting me out of there."

"No problem. I came as quickly as possible. Just as well really as I wouldn't want to be the one scraping him of the carpet. And besides, I owed you one."

"Do you have time for a coffee?" Leyland asked pointing to the cafe.

"I have time for a quick one, certainly."

Leyland pushed his hair back with his hand. He was surprised by how quickly he had dropped his temper.

It had been a tricky couple of days with not much sleep and a good kicking added into the bargain.

He was bound to be a bit snappy. That was his justification anyway.

"You'll have to buy doctor," Leyland laughed.

"Those bastards emptied my wallet."

Martinez shook his head in disbelief at the revelation as they crossed the road to the Bay City cafe.

Seventeen.

Detective Chief Inspector Phil Mercer stood in his flat.

Felicity was still asleep on the sofa. He would have to wake her soon as her guard detail would be arriving to look after her whilst Mercer went to link up with a freshly released Leyland and go and retrieve the famous memory stick.

He didn't realise it but Leyland's aggressive feelings may just prove useful for the mission and where it would take them.

During the evening before and whilst they were sifting through the email mountain Felicity revealed to Mercer that she had hidden the memory stick inside a biscuit tin. No big deal.

But the biscuit tin was located in the upstairs living area of a pub that her ex-boyfriend worked at.

Again not too much of a major drama to deal with.

But when she revealed it was the upstairs living area of the Dockers Broom in Millwall then things once again started getting bloody complicated for Mercer.

It was one of the most notorious pubs in East London. And not in a good way.

Mercer knew the place well by reputation and as an experienced copper he knew he couldn't go in single handed. Not if he wanted to walk out in one piece.

He considered the problem of going mob handed. Who to trust. They would have to keep their wits about them and hope that none of the locals fancied taking on the law that night. The chances of that weren't even fifty fifty.

Ghost Track: Melissa

He considered who to take with him. No females. That was the first rule. Not because he was sexist and didn't want any of his female officers in danger, but because the only lead he had on the mole was that she was female. Scott and Blondie were off the operation. They just didn't know it yet.

He had his gut feeling as to who that may be, but he wasn't risking anything on a trip like the one to the Broom.

McCall was quite tasty when the going got a bit rough. Lewis could handle himself. Smith and Dalton. They'd be up for it. So that gave him six.

He hoped that would be enough. Uniformed were always a backup plan. As a very last resort. If he wanted to keep that part of the assignment well under the radar then the last thing he needed was a whole load of uniformed crawling around needing paperwork signed.

Mercer pulled the curtain to one side of the window upon hearing a car pull up. They were early.

Mercer opened the front door to give Connor and Rix access. He strode over to the sofa and couldn't help but notice just how peaceful Felicity looked as she slept. Almost angelic. He tried to stay detached as far as possible with murder investigations over the years. That wasn't to say he was cold toward families affected by the sudden loss of a loved one, usually in pretty grizzly circumstances. There was a fine line between being sympathetic and supportive and getting way too close. The facts were though that he didn't really have much choice as far as circumstance had allowed with Felicity.

They had been thrown together by Leyland's incarceration and not being able to trust too many people. He knew this was far from standard procedure. But she was scared, alone and dangerous. But she trusted two people to do the right thing And Mercer was one of those people.

He didn't want to wake her, but she needed to know that Connor and Rix were taking her to a nearby hotel for a little while. He gently kissed her forehead. No stirring. He gently shook her shoulder "Felicity," he whispered softly.

Her eyes opened slowly and she gave a little smile then stretched. The brief smile disappeared when she fully awoke and the reality of life was remembered again. Sleep must have been such sweet escape for her.

"You need to get ready. We're moving on for a short while," he explained.

Felicity looked confused.

"Why can't I stay here?"

"It's just for maximum safety," Mercer reassured.

"Connor and Rix you know. They will take you to the Marrion hotel. You'll be on the top floor. Multiple escape routes. Just precautionary while I pick up the stick."

"You're familiar with these two guys from before. They'll look after you and I will come and get you as soon as I'm finished at the Dockers"

Felicity was pulling her hair into a pony tail and aimed a smile and nod in the direction of Connor and Rix whom she recognised from her first meeting with Leyland.

Ghost Track: Melissa

"Phil please take care in that pub. I've tried to get a message through to my friend Don who works there but I've had no response. He could help keep things calm in there. They don't like Police in that place."

"I know the pub, and we'll take it as softly as we can," answered Mercer, trying to alleviate her anxiety.

"But the bottom line is we need that stick. End of." He added. Connor spoke up.

"We can always be available if needs be sir?"

"Much appreciated lads, but your one and only concern is to keep this young lady safe. But thank you."

"Right, I'm ready," announced Felicity.

"OK. I will call you when en route to the hotel as soon as I can. In the meantime just sit tight and relax, OK?"

"Fair enough," conceded Felicity.

"Maybe finish going through the email pile, only if you get bored." Mercer grinned.

"Speak soon lads," Mercer shook the hands of Connor and Rix firmly as they headed to the door of the flat.

Getting into his Audi, he first watched Connor speed off to the hotel before he switched the ignition and screeched away for his cafe rendezvous with Leyland.

"So how is it that I'm so suddenly out of that place?" Leyland asked the obvious number one question. In the absence of Mercer, Dr Martinez was in the line of questioning.

Leyland was sitting opposite the doctor, a steaming latte in front of him. His anger has settled somewhat since leaving the secure unit and he was now looking for valid answers as to what had been going on.

He tore open some packets of white sugar and poured them into the drink. The coarse granules settled the frothy head for a few seconds before disappearing into the milky depths.

"All I can tell you is that I received a call from Petunia Ferdinand this morning to arrange your immediate release. Why I don't know. Why me I also do not know, but of course I was happy to come and get you out Leyland. I did, after all, owe you one."

Leyland smile lightly recalling their conversation in Martinez office.

"I heard some whispers of how you came to be in that place and I was very surprised. I didn't pick up on any ghost talk in our session."

"That's because its bullshit," snapped Leyland, lying defensively. "I want to know why she had me put in there. Why she was on my case so much".

"That I can't answer. But what I can tell you, in my opinion for what it's worth, is that she is on the back foot. That's good for you. And good for me too. I suggest we look to topple her sooner rather than later. I do hope Detective Chief Inspector Mercer can help us in that respect. It would pay you to put your trust in someone like me Leyland. I think we both know you need support."

Leyland looked puzzled, and embarrassed. What was he referring too?

"With your flashbacks," Martinez added almost telepathically reading Leyland.

Leyland looked down at the table and took a swig of coffee.

"Maybe," he said non-committal.

"There are bigger priorities to worry about. The murder case has to be taken care of. I will do nothing until that is sorted out. That's nonnegotiable."

Martinez nodded positively.

"Well that's not a no Leyland. I'll take that. Promise me that you will find me when it's done. Come and see me. I can help. I promise you that."

"If that's what you want. If you think you can help me, then fine. I give you my word. As long as you promise I won't have to see the inside of that place again." He thumbed in the direction of the unit.

"That's one promise I'm happy to make," assured the doctor.

"But seriously drop the thoughts of revenge Leyland? They will serve you no good at all."

Martinez drained his cup and stood.

"I need to head back," he offered his hand.

Leyland stood and looked Martinez in the eye as he shook firmly with the man who had released him from hell. He couldn't help but question why he wanted to help him so much.

"Speak to you very soon Leyland." They would be seeing a lot more of each other soon enough.

"Thanks for the coffee," Leyland blurted as Martinez left, he raised a hand in acknowledgement.

As Leyland sat and swigged more of his delicious beverage he couldn't help feel a tense knot in his stomach at Mercers lateness.

He was agitated and needed a decent shower, shave and change of clothes. He had been pushed way out of his comfort zone for way too long.

He stared out of the massive frontage window onto the street scene. He couldn't help but hear a favourite quote of his run through his mind. It certainly represented what was happening recently.

'Sometimes when things are falling apart, they may actually be falling into place'

Well things had certainly been falling apart. And he wouldn't know what was falling into place until Mercer got his arse into gear and turned up.

One thing he had rediscovered, he thought, was a steely determination. It had been smothered by the confidence destroying accident and subsequent injuries. He didn't feel vulnerable anymore.

He knew full well that he would be jettisoned if Occupational Health suspected deterioration in his mental well-being, regardless of who was pulling the strings. He felt the fight within him returning and he wasn't about to let himself get kicked out. Not after the crap that had happened. No way.

He secretly hoped that Mercer would still want to keep him close. He had come round to the idea of working with his old friend. Despite his love of the team he had. They would survive, maybe thrive without him. It still gave him pangs of guilt to think about leaving them behind though. That was to be expected after so long with them.

His train of thought was interrupted by the familiar Audi mounting the pavement right outside the cafe and the unmistakable short stocky build of Mercer getting out.

He spotted Leyland through the window and flashed his trademark grin. His Liverpool tie was flapping in the breeze. A sense of ease overcame Leyland. A sense that things were ok.

Mercer strolled into the cafe and ordered a strong tea.

"You want a fresh one, soft lad?" he shouted over. Leyland gave the thumbs up, covering his bruised face with his other hand. In some way embarrassed about the injuries even thought they were way beyond his control.

Mercer waited for the drinks and paid the ropey old assistant with a cheeky wink.

He took the drinks over to the table, taking care not to spill a drop, placed them carefully down and sat opposite Leyland.

He saw his face and the grin disappeared.

"What the fuck happened to you?" He barked.

"Night shift decided to have a workout," Leyland replied, half smiling.

Mercers face had darkened.

"No doubt at the request of Ferdinand. So tell me, how did you get me out?"

"There's a lot to explain my friend. Not least as to why she had it in for you. That's no longer a problem. Me and Felicity sorted it."

"Felicity. How is she? Is she safe?" Leyland questioned naively. He should have known that Mercer would have her covered. His head had been fuzzed by the drugs and the kicking. He engaged his rational thinking.

"She's with Connor and Rix?" Smarter thinking.

"Yes. She's at the Marrion with them. Safe and sound," confirmed Mercer.

"What's going on with John McTavish?" Leyland asked as he slipped more sugar into his fresh Latte.
Mercer looked down and pursed his lips.
"McTavish wasn't happy being your deputy."
Leyland looked baffled. McTavish always seemed to look up to Leyland in a funny sort of way. That's how he came across.
"He was shagging Ferdinand. With a view to taking over form you permanently. With her help of course. That's why she was so intent on trying to tuck you up."
If Leyland jaw didn't drop physically, it certainly did mentally as he took in the revelation.
If he hadn't been through what he had been through he may have even found it somewhat amusing. McTavish and Ferdinand. And a shit load of hassle for him. That was just the cherry on top of the cake for Leyland.
"I did give my word that if she got the release sorted out and destroyed the recordings from the interview room then I'd leave her be. But looking at the state of you I do think we need to burn the bitch." Mercer offered, looking for Leyland's reaction.
The anger in Leyland was rising again. His thoughts, his ideas seemed to be taking on a dark angle. He was hurting physically and emotionally. Mercer could see it in his friend.
"Save it lad. Save it for later when we retrieve the memory stick. You might well need it then. It's going to be tricky."
"I don't give a shit," answered Leyland.

"Let's nail this case and then get rid of the trash back at HQ." Leyland drained his cup.

"First port of call is a bath and a shave. Let's go." Leyland got up and Mercer duly followed him.

"Cheers love," Mercer chirped to the old girl serving as he placed the empty cups on the counter. She smiled so hard it was likely the highlight of her week so far and her false teeth nearly fell out.

Mercer shadowed Leyland to the Audi. To home comforts.

"Your leg seems to have improved," Mercer noted.

"Just as well," replied Leyland, "Going to need it with the amount of scores to settle."

"Ever heard of the Dockers Broom pub?" Mercer asked.

"Jesus, yes. That place has a black flag on it. Uniformed always have to go mob handed there. Isn't that where Harry Davison settled after his release? I remember the stir it caused, why?"

"That is indeed the very same pub." Acknowledged Mercer.

"He got a twenty five stretch for murder. Gangland related. One of the first investigations I headed up," he added.

"I don't think old Harry will be too pleased to see us stroll into his boozer later on!"

Leyland looked very puzzled.

"Why the hell would we want to be going to his pub? You developed a death wish suddenly?"

"That's where the memory stick is hidden," Mercer revealed. A look of utter disbelief, followed by horror hit Leyland's face.

"Phil. We can't go in there. Not after you nicking him all those years ago. You've got to be kidding?"

"Don't worry lad, I'm not that bloody daft. We'll be going in mob handed. Hopefully I can get my hands on it without too much trouble. Good job you'll be there with me. You can unleash some of that pent up aggression if the shit hits the fan!" Mercer chuckled.

"Fucking hell Phil." Leyland felt sick, and he looked out of the window. This was going to be yet another very long, very messed up day.

"There is something I want you to consider for me as well," Mercer dropped into the conversation.

"Jesus, what else have you cooked up for us tonight?!" Leyland joked, dreading to consider.

"All this business of seeing ghosts. Do you believe it was real?"

Leyland was quite taken aback by Mercer's sudden matter of factness of the subject.

He took a deep breath. He was past trying to hide his thinking to Mercer. It was take it or leave it time.

"It was as real as you sitting next to me. Don't ask me how. Don't ask me why because I do not know. But she spoke to me. She called me. She gave me a business card. When she was already dead. I know no more than that Phil."

"Fair point lad. I ask because...well you hear of people who claim to have gifts like that don't you. The Met have used mediums and psychics for years on cases. Unofficially of course."

"What's your point Phil? Should I purchase a big pair of hooped earrings and a crystal ball? Get people to

Ghost Track: Melissa

cross my palm with silver in the canteen?" The sarcasm wasn't lost on Phil.

"I wasn't taking the piss. All I'm suggesting is maybe join me on a permanent basis. I could cover your arse; maybe you could help us if you ever got any more 'insights' Just a thought."

Leyland had to keep looking out of the window so Mercer couldn't see the tears welling up in him.

"You make a massive assumption that it could happen again. That I would want it to happen again. Whatever 'it' was."

"I'm not assuming anything. I just reckon you'd be an asset. Ghost chatting or no ghost chatting. At least I could keep an eye on you."

"Yeah, and more importantly I could keep an eye on you too!" Leyland chipped in. Mercer smirked.

"We could get pissed every night with Ferdinand out of the picture," He belly laughed.

Leyland swallowed back his emotion, and looked at his friend with a shaking head. Incorrigible. But such a solid friend.

"Just step on it will you. If I don't get out of these bloody clothes soon I'm going to kick off."

"Roger that, David Banner. Did you hear about the two gay ghosts?" Mercer queried.

Leyland sighed. He knew a crap joke was about to be unleashed.

"No. No I didn't hear."

"Oh? Well they both kept trying to put the willies up each other!"

Leyland rolled his eyes. "Might be best if you don't talk to me for the rest of the day," he demanded.

"Madder than Tranmere!" roared Mercer.

Eighteen.

The view from the thirtieth floor offices was nothing short of magnificent. The square mile glistened like a diamond in the summer sun.
The traffic below was heavy, but muted from up this high. It couldn't be heard. Couldn't be smelt.
You paid your money you took your choice as to how high in the atmosphere you wanted to sit.
The uber rich could sit so high above the working class below that the smell of shit was a long forgotten memory.
If you were fortunate or indeed ruthless enough, to be as rich as Viktor Petrov and the memory of that smell ever made an unwelcome return then you could pay someone ten times over to remove that smell.
The plush offices that Petrov relaxed in was as a result of treating business rivals, enemies and obstacles very much like the smell of shit. And he had never been renowned for his hesitation when it came to removing them in the same way.
Petrov's number one enforcer stood before him.
A towering six foot three hulk, weighing in at sixteen stone, he may have had the look of a meathead about him but this guy was a million miles away from thick.
Anatoly Vasilievich had worked for Petrov for many many years and had proven himself to be loyal, merciless and unhesitant when it came down to 'eliminating' problems.
His abilities were in no small way attributed to his training received as part of Spetznaz for seven years.

That was where he caught, the then, General Petrov's eye and where the early bonds were formed.

Fast forward to the office in the Gherkin and the two had no less than fifteen years of history together.

Elevated from simple and cheap contract killings on the streets of St. Petersburg all the way up to a slick Ecstasy manufacturing and distribution operation, political blackmail, money laundering, high level bribery and corruption and whenever still required, good old fashioned understood in any language bullet to the head. Or heart, if you happened to be the unfortunate Melissa Marshall.

"I'm worried about Montague," said Vas. (Vas to his friends, of which they were not many)

Petrov reclined in his massive leather chair.

"Why? Why worry Vas?" He asked.

"The guy is a fucking weasel. Look at how he was when we took the girl. He nearly pissed his pants. What if he talks?"

"Talks to who? He knows if he steps out of line then he'll get buried. Pricks like that don't risk their own necks. He may talk within the firm, but that's good. That'll reinforce the message to the rest of those stiff arseholes and maybe they'll keep their shit in line."

"I don't fucking like him or his sort," reinforced Vas.

Petrov raised his hand.

"We've been through this. We can't waste time or worry on him. He'll comply. What's starting to piss me off is the cop. She is saying that the sister is well protected, but she doesn't know where. She doesn't know where the stick is. We are paying her a lot dollar for fuck all."

Vas nodded an agreement and pulled a cigarette packet out of his trouser pocket.

"How many times? Not in here Vas, for Christ's sake."

Vas huffed and pocketed the pack again. His mood was darker still.

"Boss let me lean on the cop a bit. She knows what she is being paid for. She knows what to expect if she doesn't deliver."

Petrov considered, and then nodded.

"We need the stick more than anything. The police are probably close to it. If they get their hands on it we will have to skip town again, and Vas, I like this office. And I like English pussy. I don't want to move on yet." Petrov got out of his chair. He was a lot shorter than his deputy but nonetheless was in a similar athletic condition. He stared out of the window down onto London.

"We own this city Vas. There are no limits to our powers, but only if we stay tight. Sloppiness will fuck everything. Just like in America. That can't ever happen again," Petrov explained, shaking his head slowly and stared at the photo of his boy, beautifully framed on his desk.

Vas nodded in agreement.

"America was extremely lucrative. Fucking shame what happened."

At that moment the telephone on Petrov's polished walnut desk rang out. Vas answered. The least likely secretarial wannabe.

"Yes?" He answered sulkily. "OK and where are they now?" he began scribbling on a memo pad on the desk.

"Are you sure? Make sure you follow him. If he's going for the stick we want to know about it yesterday."

Petrov's ears pricked up and he spun the chair to face Vas as he put the phone down.

"The cop just came through." said Vas, he turned the pad and pushed it into the view of his boss.

"They have the sister at that hotel."

Petrov looked at the pad and rubbed his chin. He was in deep thought.

"What of this Mercer? Who is he?"

"He's the investigating officer. She seems to think he knows the whereabouts of the stick and she will watch for any activity."

"Do we need to pay him a visit?" asked Petrov.

"Maybe wait and see what she can find out. I don't think we should leave it too long though."

Petrov tapped his fingers on the desk, thinking.

"I have a better idea. Vas, go get the sister. Bring her here. Do what you have to do my friend."

Vas, although slightly surprised by his boss' decision, knew immediately that doing what he 'had to do' would be by means of violence and killing.

He nodded to Petrov and left his office. He knew to never question or ask twice.

He would need others with him and punched into his mobile phone.

"Get your fat arse ready for a job," he ordered into the mouthpiece.

"And wake Vitali as well. I'll be there in twenty. We need the tools as well. And Yuri..."

"Yes boss?" queried the voice on the other end.

"Make sure you shower this time. I don't want you stinking the car out again, or I'll pop you off myself."

Vas ended the call. Good help was hard to come by since the warehouse in America.

He needed to plan this out as clearly as possible in his head. Killing cops bought a lot of heat and had, again as America had shown, cost a lot of dollars to put the heat out. Both needed to be avoided, but the sister was coming with him. One way or the other. That he was certain of.

Leyland Francis was underwater. Echoes of music were penetrating the hot layers. He was feeling an intense sense of relief and relaxation, despite the recent events and those that were forthcoming.

The stress was melting into the steam. Leyland rose out of the water and wiped the stream of water from his hair away from his eyes. The bath felt magnificent and he lay back, clutching at the beer bottle from the corner of the tub and he swigged deeply from it.

He was feeling relatively relaxed despite the consideration that in about an hours time or so they would be wandering into one of London's most anti police pubs in the hope that they might just get their hands on Felicity Marshall's memory stick without a tear up.

The odds were, quite frankly, against them. But they had to try. It was likely the only way of nailing Melissa's murderers. So get the stick they must, by any means required.

"Your milk's off. How am I supposed to make a brew?" came a shout from the kitchen.

"And you've got bugger all in to eat."

Leyland swigged and smiled.

"What do you expect when I get chucked in the nut house without as much as a detour to Tesco's?!"

"Bloody hell." Replied Mercer. Leyland heard the top of a beer bottle being popped of.

"Easy on the booze you." He shouted out to Phil.

"Just the one lad. And move your arse will you? You've been in there nearly an hour. I'm not taking some wrinkled up scrote into the Dockers with me for back up!"

Leyland laughed loudly. "Then piss off there on your own!" he jested and pulled the plug out.

He emerged from the bathroom in a towel, drying his hair with the towel around his neck.

"What suit would you recommend?" he asked Mercer, half seriously.

"Mmm...well a good one might end up with claret on it," Mercer answered, giving his fashion critique.

"A shit one might get you pulled for vagrancy," he added.

"Middle of the range then," concluded Leyland and he shuffled into the bedroom. Opening his massive wardrobe revealed an impressive range of suits, shirts, ties and shoe sets. It paid ultimate testament to how much effort Leyland liked to put into his image.

He pulled his trousers on and noted that when he did the belt up he needed to go up a notch. The recent goings on had clearly taken a toll on his diet and his weight. He exhaled in slight frustration and pulled on a nice crisp well ironed shirt.

The adrenaline tinge was just beginning to make its presence felt in his guts. He knew full well he would need it to keep him sharp and alert tonight.

"Who else is coming?" he shouted to Phil from the bedroom.

"Lewis and McCall will be here in ten," shouted Mercer in reply.

"Couple of others are going in as normal punters to check out the lay of the land and show themselves if need be when we get there. Six in total. He hoped that would be enough, but he had a nagging doubt that it wouldn't be.

He prayed that Felicities message had got through or they wouldn't be getting out without some physical.

He picked up his Asp. He hadn't carried it very much whilst with the witness protection team, but tonight he covered all the angles and flicked it out to make sure it still worked properly.

He heard the familiar tone of Mercer's phone going off.

A muffled commotion of expletives came from Mercer's mouth and Leyland quickly kicked the door open whilst buttoning up his shirt.

A look of concern was painted on Mercer's face.

"Where are you now?" he barked into the phone. "Fuck. We're on our way."

Mercer turned to Leyland.

"Get your arse into gear. Connor is dead and Rix is badly injured. Felicity has been taken from the hotel," he revealed.

Leyland stood perplexed for a couple of seconds. Connor dead? A split second thought hit him that this could be a wind up, but this wasn't Mercers style of humour. He shook himself and sprinted back into the bedroom, pulled on his socks and shoes and grabbed the first tie his hand touched in the wardrobe.

"Let's go. You drive" and they bundled out of the apartment toward the lift.

"Who called it in?" Leyland questioned.

"Rix did. He sounded fucked up, couldn't breathe properly it sounded like. Might have just been adrenaline though," Mercer was quick to slightly correct his synopsis of Rix in Leyland's presence, in light of what happened to McGuinness.

"Bollocks." Leyland's anger rose again at the thought of what had occurred at that hotel to two of his closest and most trusted colleagues.

That was the only reason they were there. Because he trusted them so tightly.

"Who the hell would have known she was being kept there?" Leyland asked through gritted teeth.

"Easy fella," Mercer placed his hand on Leyland's shoulder.

"Let's find out what we can when we get there." Mercer had a sick feeling in his stomach. Ever since the revelation of a female mole in his team he had been very careful to fence what information went to the girls involved in the investigation.

As the lift descended he knew full well that it was one of two people, and the possibility of having blood on his hands if one of them had led the bad guys to the hotel.

"The chances are whoever took Felicity are just as desperate to get that memory stick as we are, so it's likely she is alive until she talks." Mercer offered.

"She's a tough one. I don't think for one minute she would give it up easily." Replied Leyland, and as the words rolled from his tongue he began to have flashes in his mind as to what they might do to her to make her talk. Melissa's face flashed through. Two sisters. Dead. He couldn't let it happen.

He closed his eyes and took the deepest of breaths as Mercer began getting agitated at how long the lift was taking to reach the ground floor.

"How's the leg?" Mercer asked, randomly.

"It's holding up. Don't worry about it. I'm strong enough to take down the motherfuckers who did this." He didn't hide his anger, close to boiling over.

Mercer considered silently. He would need to keep close to Leyland and help him keep a lid on it. Until the time came.

Leyland looked to the floor.

"Connor. He had kids." He shook his head. His jaw ached with keeping his emotions under control.

"Just like McGuinness. More fatherless children. For what?" Someone was going to pay. That's all that he could think.

"Inside information Phil. Has to be."

Mercer remained quiet. The lift doors pinged and opened and as the two dashed through concierge to the Audi, they prepared for the scene that awaited them at the Marrion hotel.

Nineteen.

Felicity Marshall was scared. Her hands had been cuffed by Vas and his crew using Connors handcuffs.

If that wasn't an insult to the guy then she didn't know what was.

His blood had spattered her face and neck as he had tried to protect her and usher her out of the room. He took a round from Vitali's Glock straight to the forehead and killed him instantly.

What saved Rix' life? The fact that he was on the toilet when the Russians crashed the party.

He had got off three shots in the confusion. One hit Vas in the arm and the other two ended up in Yuri's chest and stomach before Vitali's Glock punched two bullets into his shoulder and arm.

The two surviving Russians pissed off out of there thinking that he was dead as well as Yuri. Wrong on both counts.

Rix had an opportunity, if he could keep Yuri alive, to interrogate him for information, but needing urgent medical attention himself he knew he would have to leave it.

He had called through the hotels internal system and requested urgently the duty first aiders.

They would probably shit themselves at the sight of gunshot wounds but he had to move fast.

His call to Mercer was made just before local uniformed turned up and despite Rix's protests they took Yuri to Hammersmith Infirmary under armed guard.

He wanted to keep him there, for Leyland and Mercer to deal with but as his strength depleted, so did his ability to control any of the situation there.

The boot of the car was pretty clean, but the fumes were nauseating as Felicity considered if she was the first to be transported this way in this car. She was scared but trying to get into the survival mind-set. She had been given a degree of training and advice before she was assigned to report in Libya.

If kidnapped and locked in the boot of a vehicle, try and kick or punch a tail light out and wave furiously through it.

Her hands were cuffed but she wriggled to try and get into a position where she could try and kick one out and try and stick her foot out. There was little room to manoeuvre in the cramped and pitch black boot, and the position she was in placed tension on her midriff and back but she kept wriggling. It also didn't help at all that the driver was throwing the car around corners very aggressively.

Bang. Bang. She kicked. Mustering as much muscle power as the position would allow.

She couldn't actually see so was praying that it was generally the right area for the light.

Nothing gave.

Two more kicks. Nothing.

One massive lunge with all her strength, born of fear and frustration. Felicity howled in pain as the force of the kick made something in her ankle pop. But the foot had broken through something. A small sliver of light pierced the tiny gap.

The traffic noise had increased and Felicity wanted to kick again, but the ankle pain was holding her back as she fought back the urge to vomit. Tears streamed her face. In her mind she pictured her beautiful sister. Her sister who had been put through a lot worse by these fuckers. The chances were that a couple of bullets would be for her judging by the way they took out the guard detail at the hotel.

If that was anything to go by these people obviously didn't give much of a shit about who you were generally. Melissa flashed into her mind again.

Emotion and anger flew through her body and in a final desperate lunge a massive kick back took out the rest of the light. Her ankle was well and truly screwed. She was fighting to stay conscious with the pain.

Her body was going into shock and was close to shutting down. An unconscious Felicity couldn't signal to any traffic behind. She had to stay with it. Trying to control her breathing. The pain was horrendous and of a nature that she hadn't felt before. Like electricity flying up and down her leg. Manoeuvring was out of the question and she was thinking hard as to how she could signal.

She curled into as much of a ball as possible. Using her left foot was a no go. She shuffled.

Trying to get into a position facing the front of the car she could hook her good foot through the gap. It slipped through, just, and scratched her skin as she eased it to the knee joint.

She moved the foot as much as possible to the outside world.

She didn't know if anyone would see it. And even if they did would they bother to report it? It was out of her hands. All she could do was try, and hope that Leyland or Mercer were in some way aware of what had happened and come to the rescue. But given what happened to her sister, knights in shining armour were hard to come by, obviously.

They had been travelling for what seemed like the longest five minutes in history.

The car had stopped and started a few times which Felicity put down to traffic lights. She thrashed her leg furiously at any opportunity like that. The traffic sound had changed, almost disappeared. Felicity became aware that the sound was like being in an underground car park. The tyres squealed with every corner.

The car came to a halt one more time, but this time the engine was killed. Final destination.

Felicity gritted her teeth through the tears as the pain seared through her again as she pulled her leg back through the hole. She prayed hard that they wouldn't notice the hole.

The boot popped open automatically and she heard both driver and passenger doors slam shut.

"You bring the girl in," a voice barked from outside and Vitali lifted the boot door open all the way.

He was an outstanding pistol marksman, but really wasn't the sharpest knife in the cutlery drawer.

To Felicities relief he was far too involved in getting her out to notice any damage.

He lifted her and as they cleared the boot, he allowed her to put her feet on the ground with Vitali supporting her upper body.

She screamed as the pain hit again as soon as her left ankle made contact with terra firma and crumpled weakly from under her.

God knows what she had done to it, but it hurt like hellfire.

"I can't walk," she rasped through tears looking up. Vas was holding his shoulder, supporting it inside his suit jacket. A dark wet patch was clearly visible on the jacket. He'd been hit and Felicity hoped it hurt as much as her ankle. Even worse than that she wished on him.

"You'll have to carry her." He ordered to Vitali. This didn't seem to impress the overweight hit man but he got on with the job of scooping Felicity into his arms and carrying her toward the lift.

Vas was looking around to make sure they hadn't been seen. With Vitali carrying the girl and his wound the last thing they needed was a call to the cops from some curious passer-by.

They squeezed into the lift and Vas punched button thirty.

A thin layer of sweat had formed over his closely shaven head and he was pale. Even paler than a typical Russian in the English climate. He didn't look at all good and it was obvious that Rix's bullet had caused some serious damage.

Vitali was perspiring too, with the struggle on his unfit body of carrying Felicity. The lift doors closed and the upward motion swirled Felicity's stomach and her breathing became heavier at the thought of what awaited her at the thirtieth floor.

Mercer and Leyland had pulled up outside the hotel.

It was crawling with uniformed officers and multiple armed response units. Leyland was scanning the scene, looking for an indication of where Rix may be. Mercer pulled the handbrake and they both jumped out.

Leyland started with the nearest ambulance and hurried to the open back doors. It was empty but the stretcher was missing giving him the assumption that the paramedics had gone into the hotel to treat Rix. He approached a second ambulance that had an armed officer at the rear, only one of the doors were open and Leyland could see paramedics attending to someone in the back. He turned to see Mercer busying himself getting the lowdown with the scene commander. As he turned back the armed officer had the drop on Leyland.

"Stop right there," he ordered. Leyland wasn't the least bit taken aback and flashed his warrant card.

"Detective Sergeant Francis," Leyland confirmed clearly. The AR officer stepped up and checked the credentials then lowered his weapon. They were obviously tetchy about one of their own being taken out.

"Where is Rix?" Leyland asked.

"In this one," the officer thumbed to the back of the ambulance.

Leyland climbed onto the back and caught eye contact with Rix who was struggling to breathe. The paramedics were tending to a gunshot wound to his chest.

"Rixxy, what the hell happened?" he asked loudly, over the shoulder of one of the medics.

Rix lifted his hand and waved Leyland toward him, despite the protests of the medical team there. Leyland moved beside him and put his ear close, Rix took his oxygen mask off.

"Check the room, check it properly. They left something behind," he gasped.

"Its ok my friend, its ok. We'll look over it thoroughly. Just stay cool and breath." Leyland placed the mask back on Rix' face and squeezed his hand for a second or two.

"We need to move now," the paramedic informed Leyland, he acknowledged and stepped out of the ambulance, he turned to catch Rix' eye again and gave him a thumbs up.

"Bloody well take care of him," he bellowed just as the doors closed.

Leyland turned to walk toward the hotel entrance and Mercer had now caught up with him.

"How's your boy doing?"

"Not good. Not at all good." Leyland was ashen faced. Mercer patted his shoulder.

"Come on; let's get a look at this room."

Inside the foyer another armed response officer was guarding the lift entrance. The doors had been locked open and Leyland and mercer peered inside at the blood smeared walls.

"At least one of those bastards that made it down took a hit," murmured Mercer.

They paced over to the working lift on the further side of the foyer and travelled up to the room.

"I cannot wait to see what the C.C.T.V. throws up on this," Leyland commented.

Mercer nodded his agreement.

"We need to be swift up here lad. The quicker we can get that memory stick the better. You can bet that's why these bastards have taken her."

"Quick in and out then. No fucking around at the Broom either. We need as many bods as we can muster." Leyland announced.

"Shouldn't be too hard to rouse the troops with a dead officer on their minds," chipped in Mercer.

"Well, we're not leaving without the stick. It could save her life. And even if it doesn't it means we can nail the bastards responsible. I'd rather she didn't end up like her sister though."

"Understood," Mercer answered with a seriousness that was unusual for him.

The truth of the matter was that they had both grown fond of Felicity and felt the deep sense of responsibility of finding answers regarding her sister's murder.

Having Felicity end up the same way did not sit well and, as far as they were concerned at least, it wasn't going to happen on their watch.

The lift juddered to a halt at floor thirty four and as the doors opened the two officers hastened their pace to the room.

Two armed guards were at the door already and as Mercer and Leyland entered it was pretty clear one hell of a fire fight had gone off.

Leyland's guts turned as he noticed the almost black blood stained wall were Connors brains had ended up. They trod very carefully around the room. It was an active crime scene after all and they took care not to disturb various bullet casings scattered on the carpet.

Leyland bore in mind what Rix had told him. He scanned carefully. An unusual black metallic object caught his eye. It was peeping out from under the bed. He crouched down to look it over. He was pretty sure it wasn't an unwanted dildo left behind by the previous occupiers.

"Phil," he called out and pointed to the object.

"Ooh," Mercer replied.

He joined Leyland crouching and studying the weapon.

"One of your lots?" Mercer asked.

Leyland shook his head.

"No. Not one of ours. I'm pretty sure it's not the one Felicity pulled on me either."

"Russian then?" Asked Mercer.

"Could well be. We need this tested yesterday. Ballistics could match this to the bullets taken from Melissa's body."

Mercer pulled an evidence bag from his inside jacket pocket and gently wrapped the gun within it.

"O.K. Let's go check the C.C.T.V. and then we'd better hotfoot it over to the Broom," Mercer ordered.

"Cheers guys, stay safe," Leyland offered to the guards as they left.

Twenty.

Felicity Marshall was blindfolded.
She had been tied to a heavy office type chair but her legs were free on account of the fact that even if she could get up and run she was pretty certain by that time that she had broken her ankle in some way and couldn't run for shit.
The officer she was in was warm and smelt of new carpet. She could hear the muffled sound of an argument. It was close, possibly in the room next to hers. She could make out a female voice and a male. The female was clearly pissed off about something and Felicity tried hard to tune in.
"You stupid idiot. You killed a Police officer in cold blood. One of you gets shot. It's only a matter of time before the pieces get put together. And when that happens not even I can stop the shit from hitting the fan. I covered your goons as best I could at that hotel. I cleared the C.C.T.V. and got rid of the other car but those incompetent pricks made it impossible to clean the scene."
Petrov raised his hand, in a gesture of 'Enough'
"Don't think I don't appreciate what you've done. But just remember who you are calling an idiot." His eyes were cold and stony and pierced into hers. She looked at her feet as he continued.
"The life of a police officer is worth very little within this organisation. You'd do well to remember that," he warned.

"Now maybe go next door and get the girl to tell you where the memory stick is before we pop her off like her sister."

She did not like the road that this situation had found itself going down. But it was way too late for her to get out. Petrov called the shots and she was way too deep into the Russian payroll to start arguing and growing a moral compass. She inhaled deeply as she opened the door to the room where Felicity was tied up. The murder squad team mole was about to introduce herself.

Felicity looked up. Upon hearing the door open she moved her head around trying to pick up any noise. Any clues as to who it was, and what they might do. She was shaking. Scared.

"Hello Felicity."

"Wh...who are you?" She asked.

"I'm the person who can get you out of here alive or send you the same way as your sister. Which one we go for is entirely dependent on you." The mole spoke softly.

A chill ran up Felicity's spine at the mention of Melissa.

"You know what happened to my sister? Who was responsible?"

"I'll ask the questions," retorted the mole, pulling a chair with her as she walked toward the shaking captive. She sat close and opposite to her.

"Where is the memory stick Felicity?" She questioned.

I don't own a memory stick. I don't know what you mean."

Ghost Track: Melissa

"Really?" Reacted the mole.

"Do you know who I am Felicity? Do you know how I know about the stick?"

"I can't see you and I don't recognise your voice," Felicity answered honestly.

The mole stood up and whipped the hood from Felicity's head. It wouldn't matter if she knew what was going on and who she was. She would be dead as soon as she gave up the information. So getting identified really had little consequence at this stage for the mole.

Felicity squinted as the orange light from the sunset hit her eyes.

The mole held out her Metropolitan Police warrant card and thrust it in Felicity's face.

"I'm Detective Constable Roxanne Lilywhite. If you want to live then you had better tell me where to find that stick." She smiled sweetly with a fake sickly tinge to it. Playing the good bad girl.

Felicity felt the full horrifying notion of what had been going on and it was written all over her face.

"You're...you're working for them? You're bent?"

"Oh please," retorted Lilywhite.

"Spare me the holier than thou bullshit. This is about survival. Now where is the stick?"

"I don't know about any stick."

Thwack. Lilywhite planted a firm backhand slap across Felicity's face. It made the prisoner gasp.

"I have heard all about it. Seen evidence regarding it. Tell me where it is. Now."

Felicity shook her head and a tear rolled down her reddened cheek.

"You were at the hotel weren't you? I saw you. Why were you there?"

Lilywhite exhaled loudly. Looked to the floor nodding.

"Oh I was there." She stepped forward and grabbed Felicity's face in her hand.

"But like I said. I'm asking the questions. Where is that fucking stick?" She squeezed her face and the words came through gritted teeth.

Felicity tried to pull out of her grip but couldn't break free. In a moment of panic she sunk her teeth into Lilywhite's hand who recoiled in shock and pain and broke her grip.

"You fucking bitch!" Lilywhite howled and looked at her wound. Anger buzzed through her and she landed a hard punch square in Felicity's face. It sent her tumbling backwards, the chair tipping over. As she looked up blood trickled from her nose and she was struggling to catch her breath with the shock of the blow. Lilywhite regained a small amount of composure and wrapped her hand in a white lacy handkerchief. Felicity spotted red on the cotton and had a feeling of small satisfaction.

Lilywhite moved forward and towered over her.

"I guess we'll do it the hard way then." She pulled Felicity from the floor and sat her back in position, placing the hood back on her head. There was something in her eyes though. Felicity caught a flicker of it before the darkness of the hood enveloped her senses again.

"You're scared aren't you? If your Police colleagues find out about you. Or if the Russians find they have

Ghost Track: Melissa

no use for you anymore. Or worse still they think you're playing them. Either way you really are fucked aren't you Roxanne?"

Lilywhite dabbed at her hand and split a small grin before delivering a punch to the side of Felicity's head. She managed to stay on balance in the chair but the shock of the blow made her yell out. She heard footsteps pad out of the room and a door slam.

"What do you mean it's gone? Gone where?" Mercer's voice grew in volume.

"The policewoman dealt with it. I have to say she was here very quickly after it happened," revealed the receptionist.

"Other woman? What other woman?"

"She was a police officer, for sure. Showed me her identification and everything. She said she needed to access the CCTV urgently. I put it down to needing information on the incident quickly. She was only here for a few minut..."

Mercer raised his hand.

"Whoah, hang on. What was the name of this officer?"

The receptionist of the Marrion hotel raised her eyes up trying to tap into her memory.

"Erm..it was..oh god, a flower sort of name."

"This is extremely important ma'am," Leyland added, remarkably calmly.

"Lily... lily something."

"Lilywhite?" Asked Mercer.

"Lilywhite! That's it!" She exclaimed.

Mercer and Leyland locked eyes.

"So the camera footage of the time period just before, during and just after the incident has gone?" Leyland wanted to confirm.

"Yes, she must have wiped it."

"And you didn't think that unusual at all ma'am?" Asked Mercer.

"Well she was Police. You guys know what you're doing, so who am I to question?"

"Thank you Tracy," Leyland flashed her a smile and they both headed out of the hotel.

Mercer had a face like thunder.

"Looks like we have our insider," Leyland stated the obvious.

"It was her or Scott. I would never have believed it was either of them until now. Fuck!"

"Don't beat yourself up Phil."

"You don't understand lad, Connor and Rix, it's because of me. I let on to Roxanne as to where Felicity was being kept. I gambled. I thought it would flush her out. I told Scottie a different hotel. I thought it would be her. Never in a million years did I think it would be blondie."

Sickness rose within Leyland.

"You did what? Knowing that there was a possibility that they could have all been killed? What the fuck where you thinking? You saw for yourself the state of that room? Jesus Phil."

"I thought we would have her out of there quickly. If it was Lilywhite I didn't think she would move so quickly on it." Mercer lit a cigarette. He couldn't look at Leyland.

He pulled his mobile out and dialled in.

Ghost Track: Melissa

"This is D.I. Mercer. If Lilywhite returns to the hub I want her apprehended and in a cell, got it? No information is to be passed to her regarding any of the ops on the go. Me and Leyland need a chat with her but don't go pursuing her to that effect, ok?" He got the answer he wanted and the call was ended.

"I'm sorry lad. I did what I thought was best. I never wanted anyone to get hurt."

Leyland was looking at his feet. Breathing heavily. He had trusted in Mercers judgement every step of the way. He got that one completely wrong. Leyland knew that he wouldn't put lives at risk unduly. He believed that Phil genuinely wanted to move Felicity quickly. Events just got in the way. Like getting him out of the nuthouse. He felt that he needed to take his share of the blame in that respect.

"Let's go and get this fucking memory stick." Leyland put to Phil as they weaved through the throng of uniformed and paramedics. A crowd of journalists and TV cameras had arrived at the perimeter as well.

Leyland patted Mercer's back as a gesture of reassurance and as they once more climbed into the Audi, they screamed off in the direction of the Dockers Broom public house.

Twenty One.

Vasilevitch was looking, and feeling, like crap. His visit to 'the doctor' was a painful and unpleasant one, as he knew it would be.

He couldn't exactly pitch up at A and E with a bullet wound as that would lead to all sorts of awkward questions. Nevertheless Rix's bullet still had to be removed and the services of Petrov's ex military surgeon, now practicing quite legally in London, were called upon.

Vas was swigging Smirnoff to try and numb the pain. His arm supported by a sling under his suit jacket taking the pressure of his heavily dressed shoulder.

He relaxed as best he could in a plush comfortable chair in Petrov's office and had expressed his desire to have some 'one to one' time with Felicity. She had remained tight lipped.

"Two minutes. She'll talk," he expressed.

"Vas. Vas, please. We must try and appear to be more caring of her life. We don't want to look entirely bad if we have any chance of her spilling. That won't happen if you bounce her off the walls. Besides you need to rest." Petrov reasoned.

Vas gulped more Vodka. He looked even more pissed off.

Petrov straightened his tie and stepped out from behind his sprawling desk and took a pistol out of his top drawer. He strolled into the office next to his, where Felicity was still bound and hooded. Petrov shook his head. He didn't like to treat the girl this way. But what else could they do to get the information? He gently pulled the hood from her head and she squinted again as the office lights burned her eyes.

Sitting in the chair opposite her, Petrov smiled warmly. He had concealed the pistol inside his suit jacket.

"Miss Marshall. I must apologise for the treatment you have received. I'm to blame for that. But you must understand that you have an item that I need. My freedom and liberty depends upon it you see. So I have to do things, very horrible things I grant you, to protect that freedom."

Petrov was calm, warm and clear.

Felicity was scared but surprised by the demeanour of the very well-dressed man in front of her.

"You killed my sister." She spoke quietly. Petrov paused and considered before speaking again.

"I didn't. But one of my colleagues did. It was not meant to happen. I had every intention of letting your sister live her life. She was going to give us the stick. But she decided to struggle. She was never meant to get hurt. It wasn't necessary. And I'm sorry for your loss."

Emotion hit Felicity like a freight train and she couldn't control the tears that flowed from her, as much as she wanted to appear tough.

"Would you like vengeance Felicity? For your sister? Would it help you?"

She looked puzzled at the question. Exhausted. In pain. Almost beaten.

Petrov walked to a desk in the corner of the room and picked up the telephone.

"Send Vitali in here," he ordered and removed the gun from his jacket. He held his hand out as a gesture for Felicity not to worry about removing the magazine with a click and a slide. He removed the first bullet from it and loaded into the chamber of the weapon and cocked it. Safety on.

Felicity's head was spinning and she felt close to the edge of fainting. What was this?

Fat Vitali slinked into the office.

"What's up boss? You want me to smack her up a bit?"

Petrov mock smiled at him. Vitali was a fucking pig but so very good at his job. A good man to lose.

"Vitali. You shot the sister didn't you?" Petrov asked for Felicity's benefit, for the added drama. He knew the answer.

"That's right boss." He looked confused.

"Your knife Vitali. Please," Petrov held out his hand as Vitali reached to his back and pulled out a concealed butterfly knife. He handed it over.

Petrov, in a smooth quick motion, flicked it open and faced Felicity.

He cut her shaking hands free. Was this it for her? Was this where it ended? On the thirtieth floor of a luxury office suite in Canary Wharf?

It's certainly not where she thought she would cash in her chips. Baghdad maybe. Helmand Province. Could have been. But not here. Not like this.

"Don't be scared," Petrov tried to reassure.

He held the gun out and explained.

"One bullet Felicity. One bullet. Use it as you wish. Shoot Vitali if you want revenge. Shoot me if you blame me. If there is no way out of this in your own mind then maybe use it on yourself." His steely eyes bore into Felicity. She was shaking. Confused. Unsure.

Petrov held the gun out to her. Vitali shifted uncomfortably.

"Boss?"

Petrov remained still and silent. Felicity was glued to the chair. He stepped closer and held the gun out for her to take. Her hand slowly moved to it. Shaking. Her puffy red eyes didn't move from Petrov's.

She touched the cool metal.

"One bullet," Petrov whispered to her.

She had the gun in her hand. She studied it for a second or two then flicked the safety off.

She looked to her right at Vitali. Beads of sweat were forming on his forehead. His eyes darting between Petrov and the gun.

"Boss. What is this?" He was rattled. Petrov raised a dismissive hand.

Felicity stared ahead of her. At Petrov. One bullet. Could she? Which one? The one left would surely kill her? Her breathing became more and more rapid with the dilemma. If she turned it on herself then it was all over. No more pain. Mercer and Leyland would probably solve the case anyway. She could take the knowledge of the stick with her. But what if they didn't see the Russians coming? They would surely know that's who took her though? Maybe they had already got the stick?

Petrov rested his chin on his hands. Waiting. Her hands began to shake even more. The tears flowed again. She aimed at Vitali. Then at Petrov. If she shot now the chances were that she would miss anyway as she couldn't control the shaking. She placed the barrel under her chin. No. She couldn't do it. She couldn't do it. She dropped the gun and it made a heavy clunk on the carpet as she sobbed heavily with her head in her hands.

Petrov picked up the weapon as Vitali exhaled his relief. Touching her shoulder Petrov spoke.

"It would be very sad if any more lives were lost because of this situation," he whispered to her.

He turned and took aim at Vitali and fired with a clean head shot. Felicity screamed with the bang and Vitali's blood and brains sprayed onto the tinted windows.

"It's at a pub. The Dockers Broom," she wailed.

Petrov slapped the magazine back into the gun and concealed it back into his suit jacket.

"Thank you," he responded calmly.

"We should get ready."

Mercer and Leyland were sat outside the Broom in the Audi. There was silence. Five further cars were parked in various places adjacent to the pub and all five carried officers from Mercers team. Tooled up to the nines. A few of Leyland's colleague's had joined with them as well after a quick call around Leyland found extra help easy to come by after the demise of Connor. For many this was personal. And that included Leyland. He held a tight grip on his gun, a spare magazine on his belt. His thoughts drifted to Felicity and his guts twisted at the thought of what they may have done to her.

Mercer clicked the button on his radio unit.
"Everybody stand by. We're going in."
He looked at Leyland.
"Ready then soft lad?"
"Let's do it," confirmed Francis.
They decamped the Audi simultaneously and breathed in the night air. The buzz of noise emanated from the open windows of the broom and the two friends strolled to the doors. Paused before they went any further, and then went in together.
Silence hit the entire place as the locals realised that these weren't just two strangers at the door. But filth as well.
"Well well well," came a voice from behind the crowded bar, its identity obscured. Mercer knew that voice though.
"You've got some bollocks showing your face in here scouser."
Ordering drinks was on the backburner for the punters at that bar as they parted, Mercer and Leyland walking slowly forward, revealing the landlord of the Broom, Frankie Davison.
"Evening Frankie. Lovely to see you again too." Mercer leant on the bar.
Davison scowled, tea towel in hand, wishing it was a shotgun probably.
"What the fuck do you want in here then?" He spat.
"Couple of pints would be nice for starters," replied Mercer. Semi-serious.
Leyland scanned the surroundings. There was a universal look of hate of hate on the faces around

him. He felt that the shit was going to hit the fan in any second.

His look caught the eye of a younger man behind the bar, listening intently to the conversation.

Leyland tipped him a slight nod.

"You want to do you and your mate here a favour and fuck off out of my pub while you've still got your kneecaps," Davison growled.

"Come on now Frankie, a couple of pints and a chat for old times' sake. Might be to your benefit."

The younger man strolled over to Frankie and moved close to his ear.

"Dad, maybe you should take this out back."

Leyland's ears picked up on the 'dad'

"You Don Davison?" He asked.

"Who wants to know?" Replied Don, looking Leyland up and down.

"Oh I think we have a mutual friend. Felicity? Ring any bells?"

Leyland saw the penny drop in Dan Davison's face almost straight away.

"Dad!" He urged.

"I don't want fucking filth in my boozer," he snapped.

"Well they're here and the punters don't like it. So maybe get them out of the way then argue the toss?"

"Got a smart lad there Frankie," Interjected Mercer.

Frankie lifted the bar hatch. "Out back," he grunted and they made their way through the bar to a modest dining room housing a table and a fridge. Frankie pulled up a chair.

"Well sit then," he ordered.

Ghost Track: Melissa

Dan walked through with a bottle of scotch and four glasses and sat down with the three.

His dad stared at him and wondered what he was playing at.

"It's alright dad, Julies got it under control out there."

He poured the spirit and passed out the glasses.

"Well, what do you want then?" Frankie questioned.

"Is this about Felicity?" Don interrupted, looking at Leyland, who paused and looked him in the eye before answering.

"I think you know it is Don. And you know why?"

He nodded negatively.

"She's in trouble and there is an item of hers that she stored here. We need it to help her."

Frankie chipped in. "Is that the bird you were seeing a while ago? The journalist?"

"Yes Dad, be we were just friends. I know how you feel about journos Dad."

Frankie turned his attention to Leyland.

"What makes you think it's here then? And what gives you the right to stroll into my boozer just because you think something of hers is here, eh?"

"Because," Mercer took over the chat, "If we don't get that item you'll have about twenty tooled up Russians tearing your pub apart for it as well."

"They could fucking try," Spat Frankie.

Mercer mock laughed. "They kill coppers for the fuck of it Frankie, much like your lot used to. They're not going to worry about an old has been like you. Or your family." Mercer nodded in the direction of Don.

"Do you know where the memory stick is lad?"

Don froze for a second and looked at is father. Frankie wanted to know just as keenly as Mercer and Leyland did.

"Yeah I know where it is. But why should I let you have it? Can you promise it will make her safe? Why shouldn't I just hand it over to the ruskies for a price?"

Frankie smiled at his boy. He'd taught him well.

"Because," informed Leyland, "The minute you do that she is dead. Just like her sister. And you think they'll pay for it? Like Phil said, they'll prise it from your dead hand rather than do a deal. If you having any feelings for her at all then you'll help us to keep her alive."

Mercer swigged his scotch, draining the glass in one, and stood.

"It's really up to you lad. I've got officers outside who can protect you all if the Russians come here."

Frankie belly laughed. "Don't worry yourself about that. If they come here they'll wish they hadn't. You forget who you're talking to Mercer."

Mercer shot him a cold stare.

"No Frankie. I'll never forget you. Or why our paths crossed all those years ago. So maybe count yourself lucky I'm looking out for you, and your boys, safety because it would be quite easy for me to let those fuckers come in here and put holes in you. Just like you did to Peter Quinn, eh?"

Leyland and Dan looked at each other; the level of needle was surprising to both of them. The name that Mercer mentioned rang some bells with Leyland but he had neither the time nor the desire to search his memory so deeply at that time.

"Don, the stick please?" Leyland asked.

He looked at his dad for some sort of guidance.

"You can help her? For definite? Man to man, not copper to Davison."

"Yes. We can help her," Leyland confirmed.

Don nodded. "OK I'll get it." He disappeared up the stairs. Mercer took his seat again and poured himself another drink.

"Why don't you invite them here to collect it?" asked Frankie. "Tell them to bring the girl then pop them all off. End of problem."

Mercer chuckled. But it was as fake as a porn stars tits.

"Is that how you'd do it is it Frankie? Trouble is when you were running round in what you call your prime; you still wouldn't have come close to these people. You certainly wouldn't want to be inviting them in for Vodka. Lovely offer though, thanks." He shook his head in disbelief as Dan reappeared with a small plastic bag. It was wrapped tightly around the visible purple stick as he held it out to Leyland. Dan held is grip on it.

"Bring her back in one piece," he said with a glare of meaning business.

"If they come here don't mess about. Call us in," Leyland said softly to Don.

"You've got what you came for," Interrupted Frankie. "Now fuck off."

"Charming you southerners aren't you!" chirped Mercer in Leyland's direction. They headed out of the pub the way they came in, albeit somewhat quicker, to a chorus of abuse. As they took deep breaths of fresh air Leyland rasped a "Fuck me" as some colour started to return to his pale face.

"Did you have to rattle him like that?"

"Dunno what you mean lad. Just a bit of banter. We go way back. If he lives tonight it will be a miracle. Still, live by the sword and all that."

"Peter Quinn?" questioned Leyland.

"Another time lad," Mercer dismissed. They had business to attend to and that wasn't the time for a history lesson.

"Got a plan?" asked Leyland.

"Will do shortly," he confirmed, lighting a cigarette. He held the radio up to his mouth.

"Stand down everyone. We have the item."

A voice crackled over the airwaves in reply.

"Boss, we've just had some intel come in on the Russian in hospital." It was McCall.

Mercer and Leyland headed to her car and got in the back. McCall and Scott were sat in the front.

"What do we have?" Mercer questioned.

"Been identified as Yuri Gladvid. Prints flagged up on the Interpol database as an associate of Viktor Petrov."

"And he is...?"

"He has been linked to several Russian mafia fronted businesses in three different countries. The gun that you and Leyland found..."

"The gun that I found, blind bollocks here didn't see it," cut in Leyland, mock smiling at Mercer.

"The gun that you found Leyland has been ballistically matched as the weapon that killed Melissa Marshall." Revealed McCall.

"So we've got them then? Let's go and bring them in." Leyland announced with some excitement.

"Hold back fella. We've got nothing on anyone other than a half dead Russian. This is what implicates Petrov, and anyone else," Mercer held up the memory stick.

"And as things stand we barely have time to check what's on it."

"So what's our next move then?" Questioned Leyland.

"Scott, what are the chances of finding an address or number for this Petrov character?" Mercer asked, Scott was one of the more resourceful of his officers, and given the intel on Lilywhite, she was back on the op.

"I thought you might ask." Scott passed a folded piece of a4 to her rear.

"Current business address and a mobile number. Everything we could possibly check shows him to be legit. I'm guessing whatever is on the stick will tear that down." Scott informed.

"Interestingly though, there was a link to that address from a number of reports from members of the public of a leg hanging out of the boot of a car. Now who would we know that might have been in the boot of a car and would possibly try and signal that way?" Scott asked.

"Registration plate was a fake. But last known report was of the vehicle heading into the underground car park at that address. Strange coincidence, eh?"

"Bloody good work," Mercer praised.

"Maybe you can give us some info guv?" Scott asked.

Mercer looked slightly confused. "About what darling?"

"Lilywhite. With what happened to Leyland's guys. Was she involved? We all need to know. She's been off the radar since the shootings."

Mercer shifted uncomfortably in his back seat. He had been duped by her and he wasn't at all comfortable with admitting it. But the team needed to know.

"She's bent. She was helping the guys who took Felicity. She wiped the C.C.T.V. at the hotel. I assume that she has been protecting them and feeding them information all along. Fact is she got ID'd at the hotel. So yes, she is working for them."

"Bitch," spat Scott.

"Save it," Mercer replied. "If she doesn't already know that we know then she will do very shortly. Her hand will be forced one way or another."

The atmosphere was tense in the car.

"We need to regroup and get out of this shit hole," Mercer announced.

"No!" Exclaimed Leyland.

"This is perfect. They'll come here, soon. And we'll be waiting for them. Take them all at once."

Mercer stared out of the window.

"The last thing we need is a fire fight on the streets. We have lost enough good officers for one day. And

Ghost Track: Melissa

do you really think Felicity would have given up where the stick was hidden?"

"I don't think she would have had a choice in the end. You know what these sort of people are capable of. At least if we wait its better than going to them and them seeing us coming. We need, and have, the element of surprise." Leyland explained energetically.

Mercer rubbed his chin, and then got onto the comms network.

"Is everyone carrying?" The air crackled and one by one the names called back in. All in the positive.

"And you two?" He asked Scott and McCall.

McCall held up his Glock seventeen for Mercers approval. Scott moved her blazer aside to reveal hers in a side holster. Mercer nodded and looked at Leyland who he knew was packing. He nodded slowly. Leyland had a very good point.

"Then we wait," he announce, cracking open the window to light another cigarette.

Fifteen highly trained and well-armed police officers ready to spring into action.

Mercer checked his cigarette packet. Much to his annoyance he had three left and begrudged having to consider rationing them.

A shot of adrenaline would kick in every time a car slowed near the pub, only to speed off again or reveal the markings of the local taxi firm and spill its contents of revellers onto the pavement nearby.

Seconds seemed like minutes. Minutes disguised themselves as hours. They waited.

Forty five minutes had passed, but seemed like twelve hours, since they had left the Broom a convoy of three identical black Range Rovers pulled up. Blacked out windows meant that the occupants couldn't be seen but within seconds they had all decamped. Mercer counted twelve. They had a numerical advantage.

"Stand by, stand by," crackled Mercer over the network.

"Any I.D. on Petrov in this lot?" he asked Scott who was flicking through her file on the Russians.

"Can't see him guv. Or Vasilievitch."

"Oh fuck!" Exclaimed Leyland, "It's Lilywhite!"

A single female stuck out like a turd on a snooker table amongst Petrov's enforcer group.

"We need to get her," said Mercer.

"How the hell are we going to do that with those meatheads covering her?" questioned McCall.

Mercer wracked his brains as the group of Russians made for the doors to the Broom.

They had to separate her somehow. Even just for a moment. Mercer dialled into his mobile just as the first pair walked through the doors. Lilywhite was right at the back of the group.

Mercers call was ringing at the other end. He spied Lilywhite dive into her pocket and check her call.

"Hello guv?" she answered.

"Roxanne. We have some information and are heading to the Dockers Broom in Millwall. It's where the memory stick is. Can you meet us there?" Mercer questioned, his quick thinking would hopefully give them some time.

As the watched they noticed her holding back from the group going into the pub.

They had to time this just right to not be spotted. He signalled to Scott and McCall to go. Two Russians left on the street just about to enter. Lilywhite was holding back and waved for them to go in.

"I can meet you there, I'm not far from that area," she answered.

Time to strike and he gave Scott thumbs up.

"See you soon." He ended the call and got straight on the comms network.

"All stand by to back up Scott and McCall's extraction." He ordered.

The position of their vehicle had allowed some cover and their approach was almost to the rear of Lilywhite as she pocketed her phone and made to enter the pub.

She had about ten paces to the door and she could hear swearing and arguing coming from the Broom and knew that her visitors were not being welcomed with open arms.

McCall broke into a sprint. Five paces from the door Lilywhite heard heavy footsteps behind her and she turned.

In a split second and a blur a hand had grabbed her and covered her mouth.

He manoeuvred her forcefully away from the pub doors and Scott ran in to assist by planting a heavy punch to her solar plexus that forced Lilywhites breath out and through the gaps in Scott's fingers. Hers legs crumpled and McCall grabbed both of her ankles and manoeuvred back to the car as she gasped to regain her breath after the windings of all windings.

There wasn't much fight left in her after that.

"Good call," complimented McCall.

Once back at the car Mercer jumped out and helped bundle her into the back and she was positioned between him and Leyland.

Mercer immediately got back onto the comms.

"R.V. at St James car park. Let's get the hell out of here."

Lilywhite looked awful. Her mascara had run and she had dribbled down her chin due to McCall's contact. She was retching and gasping still.

"Sorry love, we arrived earlier than anticipated." Mercer aimed to Lilywhite.

"We saw you had company though," said Leyland, whose eyes had narrowed into slits.

"Why did you let that happen to Connor and Rix? And then scrub the C.C.T.V? Why?

Lilywhite gasped a laugh. Dangerous, but she couldn't suppress it.

"You know full well why," she rasped.

"Were you really in that deep love?" asked Mercer, surprisingly calm considering that Lilywhite had been one of his most promising officers.

"That there was nowhere else for you to turn? That you had to allow colleagues to get killed? People with families?"

"We've all got families Phil," she countered.

Just as the convoy drove away from the pub, a chair crashed out of one of the windows. Leyland looked back. Mercer called into control.

"Control this is D.C.I. Mercer, Trojan units to the Dockers Broom Public house Walthamstow. Urgent.

Major incident in progress. Multiple firearms involved."

"Roger that, Trojan units dispatched." Crackled the reply.

He and Davison may have clashed years ago. He might have been a cop killing piece of shit but he considered that his boy was in there as well and they kind of owed him one by handing over the stick.

"They won't give up until they get what they want. And if you have it they'll take you too," advised Lilywhite chillingly.

"What, this you mean?" Mercer waved the memory stick in front of her face.

"I'd hazard a guess that most of Petrov's top lads were in that pub. Consider them out of the game. Who'd be left Scott?"

"Petrov himself wasn't I.D.d at the pub." confirmed Scott.

"Wouldn't dirty his own hands would he?!" cut in Mercer.

"And Vasilievitch, his number two, wasn't spotted either."

"Considered to have been injured in the shootout with Connor and Rix." Leyland informed.

"Remember Connor?" he aimed at Lilywhite. "A fellow officer. With a family?"

"I couldn't stop it. I couldn't do anything. I was in too deep." She protested.

"And now you're fucked because we know. And shortly your Russian boss will know you've been pinched. Maybe he'll consider that you're telling his secrets. He'll want to shut you up won't he?" Leyland antagonised her. Angry. All he could visualise was Connor.

"Stop!" she gasped. "There is no need for that. You've found me out. So use me. I can help you. Protect me and I can help you."

A collective laugh rang out.

"Protect you like you protected my guys?" asked Leyland, shaking his head in disgust.

"I couldn't give a fuck what happens to you. Is the girl still alive? Felicity?" He asked.

Lilywhite looked down to her lap.

"She is still alive."

"Where is she?" asked Leyland. His voice softened slightly at the pathetic sight of what Lilywhite had become. He looked her in the eyes briefly before she turned away to her lap again.

She looked shamed. Grey and shamed. Leyland concentrated his stare on her. Willing the effects of his aura on her.

"She's at Petrov's office. He is with her waiting for word on the stick."

The convoy pulled into St James car park. Mercer had to consider his plan very quickly. He called everyone out of their vehicles and set about an impromptu open air briefing.

He needed everyone to be sharp and on top of their game. If they weren't then the chances were that someone would catch a bullet. Mercer did not want any further dead officers because of that Russian prick. It was time for he and Leyland, with the teams back up, to end this. Tonight.

Twenty Two.

Viktor Petrov was generally a very cool customer, but on this evening he was uncharacteristically unsettled and nervous.

Felicity Marshall was sitting opposite him across his large walnut desk. She had been afforded a meal ordered in but the pizza sat on the desk in front of her. Untouched. Although she hadn't eaten for many hours her appetite had left her in the presence of that man.

Vasilievitch sat seven feet to her left. His arm was still being held up in a sling to take the weight of his shoulder wound and he seemed to have a bit more colour about him but he was still popping pain killers like smarties.

Petrov had a shot glass and a bottle of Smirnoff Red in front of him and he span the top off, pouring a generous measure and knocked it back in one. He let out a slight 'gahh' as the alcohol hit the back of his throat.

They were waiting. Waiting for word from his guys that they had retrieved the memory stick but so far it had been quiet. Far too quiet. He didn't like that and Mr Cool was perspiring more than he would ever let anyone see. He would excuse it to the summer evening heat but Vas knew.

And so did Felicity. He didn't care about her knowledge though. As soon as he had the stick she would be going for a one way skinny dip in the Thames.

His mobile phone danced into vibratory life across the desk.

"I have the stick." It was Lilywhite. "I'm bringing it in."

"What took so bloody long" Petrov demanded.

"It went smoothly until the Police turned up. Mercer's lot. All hell broke loose. I managed to get out. But only me."

"Fuck," Petrov muttered. "Just get back here quickly with it. I've had enough of fucking around."

"I'm five minutes away," she updated and killed the call.

"Good stuff," approved Mercer standing next to her. They were downstairs to the offices. Ready to crash Petrov's party.

The rest of the squad had been ordered to position around the complex ready to thwart any kind of escape attempt. Or get into the building quickly if things went bad up there. They were ready for anything.

Mercer, Leyland and Lilywhite entered the lift. There was an awkward silence as the three were propelled toward the thirty fourth floor. To the showdown of showdowns.

"Why did she have to die?" Leyland broke the silence. "I mean these guys have been ruthless. But what possible fight or trouble could she have made for them once she had given up the stick and the emails? Why kill her?"

Lilywhite stared straight ahead and took in a deep breath

"It was an accident," She revealed.

"What?" Leyland was taken aback.

"A bloody accident?" Mercer repeated. "How do you accidently shoot someone three times exactly?" He questioned.

"She struggled. Panicked. Tried to get away. In the bundle she managed to take one of Petrov's guys down. Got him right in the nuts. Grabbed his gun but he got a hand to it as well. Before you know it they struggled. Four or five shots went off. You know how many she took. It wasn't intentional. But that's how it happened. Not intentional. Not that it matters."

"What's on the stick that makes it so valuable?" Questioned Leyland.

"Accounts. Communications."

"For what? For who?"

"The law firm she worked for. They were laundering money for Petrov. She found out. Somehow."

"Laundering how?" Leyland wanted more. They were interrupted by the ping of the lift reaching the floor. The doors opened.

"O.K. Let's get this done. He and Leyland concealed their weapons as they exited the lift and walked slowly along the corridor. It smelt of new carpet. Lilywhite was tagging behind. Scared.

"First left," she informed. She touched Mercers hand before they went any further.

"Guv. I'm sorry. If the shit hits the fan then just get out. I can take the heat."

"I think you've done enough sweetheart." Mercer answered simply. He nodded for her to knock the door and go in. She complied, knocking and opening the door.

"Ahh Roxanne!" exclaimed Petrov.

"You don't have to put on your red light," sang Mercer as he paced into the office behind Lilywhite with his gun raised at Petrov. Leyland followed in quickly and covered Vas with his aim. Petrov, for the first time in a very long time, was genuinely surprised.

"Well, I see you've bought guests Roxanne," he had his hands raised at shoulder level. Leyland advanced forward and shook down Vasilievitch, relieving him of his pistol from inside his suit jacket, sticking it in the back of his belt. Leyland tapped his shoulder.

"How's the wound?" he asked, hoping that his contact hurt him.

"You carrying dick head?" Mercer threw out to Petrov.

"No officer, no," he grinned, Mercer checked him over. He was clean.

"Drink?" Petrov offered to Mercer. He considered for a second or two.

"Why not. Been a long night," Mercer answered. Petrov opened a desk drawer and pulled out another shot glass, choosing not to touch the pistol concealed inside. All in good time.

"You O.K. love?" Mercer asked Felicity with a wink.

"So glad to see you both," She smiled. Mercer dialled into his phone.

"She's coming down. Intercept please." And ended the call. "Get yourself off and we'll have a good old catch up in a bit," She didn't need telling twice and despite her painful hobble she left the office, glancing back to smile at Leyland. A smile tinged with concern.

She was alive and free. Leyland felt a massive sense of justice and nodded warmly at her to keep going. Whatever happened now, they had kept their promise to her.

Mercer sat in Felicity's vacant chair and Petrov pushed the shot glass to him.

"Cheers," he thanked.

"Na Zdorovie," exclaimed Petrov. Leyland's ears pricked up at the language.

"So, what are the chances of you two coming quietly?" Mercer asked, fishing a pair of handcuffs from his belt. He already knew the answer.

"Not very good," Petrov confirmed. "You see we were planning on taking a little trip," he added and looked to Leyland.

"Would you like to drink with us old friend?"

"No thanks," Leyland replied quickly. "And we're not friends. Old or otherwise."

Petrov looked surprised.

"Come," persisted Petrov. "Come sit and share a drink with the guys who got you here. On the verge of stardom. Your biggest arrest ever," he teased.

"I think you've had enough. You're all confused obviously," Leyland assessed. "It's affected your mind Petrov."

"The man that changed your life forever offers you a drink and your poor manners mean you refuse? How very unBritish."

"Changed my life? I don't think so. Ruined lives, definitely."

Mercer's eyes narrowed. He could sense that there was something behind this chat.

"I'll take his," Mercer demanded sliding his glass back across to Petrov.

Vas had a smug grin on his face.

"So, where were you planning to go when this all went tits up? Which it has, just in case you weren't completely sure," Fished Mercer.

"Officer."

"Call me Phil."

"Well, Phil, in the office next door there are some suitcases. In one sits about a million Euros."

"That's a serious amount of holiday money," jested Mercer as Petrov slid another Vodka to him.

"Quite. Maybe if you and our friend here were to walk out with it we could all go about our business?"

Lilywhite shifted uncomfortably. She knew as well as anyone that Mercer couldn't be bought. And Leyland wanted payback for Connor and Rix. And not of the money kind.

Mercer turned to her.

"Check it out," he ordered and she slinked away to the office next door.

In it were three identical black suitcases on wheels. There was a big crimson patch on the carpet that caught her eye. Petrov wouldn't get his deposit back on the offices if he left that there. He could afford to lose it.

She undid the first case which contained clothing. Neatly folded and well ironed.

She lifted the second case onto the desk and unzipped it. Bingo. Wads of neatly banded notes. The case was full to the brim with them.

She took a couple out and sniffed them. In the gap she noticed a pistol had been concealed amongst the bundles. She froze for a second and then looked over her shoulder. Clear. She grabbed the gun and tucked into the back of her jeans and pulled her blouse down over it.

Taking the two bundles in her hand with her she made back to Petrov's office.

"It's true," she confirmed, throwing the wads onto the desk.

"You see Phil. everyone can walk away from this richer than when they came in. Nobody else needs to get hurt." he rested his chin on his fingers, made into a point.

Mercer necked his Vodka.

"Sorry Viktor. Some people just can't be bought." Mercer flashed a sarcastic grin. Lilywhite looked at her feet.

Vas held his smile at Leyland.

"What about you? Compensation for your leg perhaps?"

"How would you know about that?" Leyland questioned.

"You truly don't remember me? How disappointing."

"I don't know you, prick. Nor do I want to. I know enough about the sort of pussys you are when I saw the girl's body." He turned to Mercer.

"Come on Phil. Time to take them in." He was growing frustrated at the time wasting and bullshit talk.

Vas wouldn't let it drop.

"You were the only one still alive when I checked after the crash. You owe me. I could have popped you off just like Curtis." Vas's grin had morphed from annoying to evil.

Leyland's head, his whole world began to slow down and spin. His guts lurched.

The crash. The person. The foreign language. It was this fucker. A cold sweat had hit Leyland and he was struggling to hang on to his stomach. His hands shook.

"Oh fuck," mumbled Mercer. "Time to go lads," he threw the cuffs at Petrov and produced another set for Vas like a magician, keeping his Glock trained on Petrov at all times.

"Leyland. Get him cuffed. Get it together lad," Mercer ordered.

Leyland stood fast, stuck to the carpet. Frozen.

"NOW," bellowed Mercer. It did the trick and Leyland snapped out of his thought pattern. A look of pure hatred spread across his face. He reraised his Glock seventeen at Vas.

Vas dropped his grin and held his good hand up.

"It was business," he pleaded as if it made a difference to the situation.

"All of these things have only ever been about business. Never personal."

Leyland's hands were shaking badly. Rage was burning in him as he re ran the crash in his mind. McGuinness. Curtis Smith. Connor.

"Leyland!" Mercer shouted. It didn't get through.

"Detective Sergeant!" Mercer stepped over and grabbed him. In the split second confusion Petrov darted his hand to his desk drawer and grabbed the pistol within it. He pulled it up and aimed at Mercer.

"Drop it, Phil," he demanded cooly.

Lilywhite revealed her trump card, and pulled the pistol from her jeans and covered Petrov.

"Everybody shut the fuck up and put your weapons on the floor. Now!"

Mercer was aimed at Petrov. Petrov was aimed at Mercer. Leyland was aimed at Vas. Vas had nothing. Lilywhite was switching between the three. A major spanner in everybody's plans for the evening.

Mercer looked at his watch, raised his gun less hand.

"O.K. take it easy." He lowered himself slowly and placed his gun on the carpet.

Lilywhite turned to Petrov. "Now you," she demanded. He complied.

"And you," she ordered Leyland. He wasn't moving. He wasn't dropping his aim at all.

"Go on. Take the shot," Vas goaded. "Take revenge for your colleagues. You've lost enough. Do something about it."

"Leyland. Just put it down. Don't let the prick turn you into something you're not," Lilywhite exclaimed. "Just put it down and we can sort this mess out."

"Just remember how much money we've put your way Roxanne," Petrov warned with steely eyes.

Mercer griped Leyland's arm. "Come on lad. Drop it or we'll all end up dead. His time will come."

Leyland fixed his stare on Vas's smug expression, but let Mercer take his weapon, which was promptly thrown onto the floor.

"Everyone in the corner." Lilywhite signalled to the corner furthest from the door behind Petrov's desk. They all moved slowly.

"What's your plan love?" asked Mercer casually. "You know how many are around the building. They know the score with you. Where are you going to go eh?"

"There's more than one way in or out of here Phil," she revealed.

"And I reckon a million Euros will see me far away before anyone catches up."

Mercer nodded.

"Yeah I guess you've earned it with how busy you've been fucking everyone over for these couple of pricks."

She arched the gun to his head.

"You think you know what it's like once they have a grip on you? You think I wanted to do those things? He threatened my family. Threatened to turn me in. You name it, it was threatened. So yes, I've earned it."

"Spend it quickly, bitch," warned Vas.

"You've earned this Vas," commented Lilywhite, pointed her gun to his chest and fired.

The bang made Leyland step back to the wall and pull Mercer with him. Petrov didn't seemed disturbed.

Vas fell to the floor clutching his wound, bleeding out. Blood formed in his mouth and he slide to support his back against the wall as he descended, gasping for breath.

"That was for you Leyland. Enjoy watching the fucker suffer."

Nobody had really paid attention to the office door still being open. Until a familiar 'ping' of the lift rang out. Reinforcements from downstairs?

"Fuck," exclaimed Lilywhite. She took her attention off the men to look around and in an instant Petrov flicked his hand out sending the Vodka bottle hurtling towards her. She screamed in shock, instinctively jumped back and dropped her weapon as she put her hand out as protection.

The three men moved like lightning. Mercer jumped forward and went into a roll. Petrov ran into Leyland who tried to restrain him. Petrov's military training kicked in and enabled him to spin Leyland on the spot twisting his arm behind his back and slammed his head into the Walnut desk hard. Leyland was out for the count and slipped clumsily to the floor.

Petrov scanned for a weapon as Lilywhite regained her composure.

The pistol she had dropped was next to her on the floor. Shattered glass had sliced into her arm. She reached down for the weapon. Phil Mercers forward roll sent him tumbling into Lilywhite.

Petrov bent down to grab Leyland's Glock seventeen. In a second or two he could empty the magazine into Mercer and Lilywhite. His hand made contact with the grip. Lilywhite was set off balance again as

Mercer pushed her aside while reaching for her gun. Felt it. Raised it. Petrov had the drop on him.
Vas was still alive and cowering.
Bang. Pfft pfft pfft. A normal gunshot and three silenced rounds fizzed in the room.
Leyland came around. Hs vision blurred and his senses stunned. He scanned the view in front of him.
"What the fuck? You? You? No, how?" He looked in horror at the figure at the door. He shook his head in disbelief and then fell into unconsciousness again.

Twenty Three.

"Wake up lad."
"Wake up. No sleeping on the job," Mercer was tapping Leyland's cheek and he slowly came to again. He jolted into life, scared.
"The shooter. The shooter," he exclaimed.
"Don't panic lad. Just sit and get your bearings back." Mercer helped to support him as he got up and stumbled into Petrov's chair.
"Just sit for moment and get yourself together. We need to clean this situation up. Quickly."
Leyland scanned the room nodding. "O.k. O.k."
Lilywhite had been hit. She was sitting, propping herself up against a filing cabinet. Crying quietly. A massive patch of crimson had spread across her blouse.
Vas hadn't moved. He was deathly pale and staring into space. Close to the end.
Petrov was on the floor to his left, a hole in his head. The exit wound of the bullet removed a huge chunk from the back of his head. To say he was out of the game would have been the understatement of the century. Then Leyland's eyes hit those of the shooter at the door. He shook his head in disbelief.
"Hey buddy," came the familiar Louisiana accent. "How you doing over there?"
"Stan?!" Leyland's head was still swimming from the hit on Petrov's desk and he couldn't quite process the obvious. He felt sick.
"How? Why? You?" Confusion reigned in his brain.

Stan's eyes dropped to the floor. "I'm sorry my friend. When I cracked the emails they took me straight to the guys who killed Nathan."

"Petrov?" Leyland questioned.

"Yep. Petrov and his piece of shit number two over there."

Mercer was tending to Lilywhite. He knelt beside her.

"What were you thinking you stupid stupid girl?" His anger and disappointment had subsided. In the melee she had pushed him out of the path of Petrov's shot and taken the bullet herself. She smiled.

"I owed you that much at least. I'm so so sorry guv." Tears rolled from her eyes. She didn't have long. Mercer shook his head in disbelief at the scenario at that point. He had Stan's gun in his hand. An old school Browning nine millimetre with a silencer attached. Lilywhite's hand gripped his.

"Finish me off Phil," she asked. Mercer look horrified.

"Don't talk bloody daft. We can fix you up," he exclaimed. He stood up.

"Right. What a bloody mess. You two need to get out of here. Stan how did you get in past my team downstairs?"

"There's a second basement entrance. It's kind of a concealed one." Replied Stan.

"Then you both take that way out. I'll deal with the team. As far as anyone is concerned we weren't here, got it?" They nodded to Mercer.

"Right, go. Go now." Barked Mercer.

Stan made to help Leyland from the chair, an offer he refused. He looked at Stan and his expression was different. Leyland felt betrayed, but that wasn't the time to get into it.

"This way," Stan pointed and Leyland followed.

"We need to regroup at my place. We need a serious chat Stan, but thank you for turning up when you did." Mercer's parting shot came with a glare as he pulled his mobile out. He needed to stand down the team and sort out what he could up here.

"How did it feel?" Leyland asked Stan as they weaved through the corridors.

"To betray us? Use us? Just for your own ends?"

"It wasn't like that buddy. It really wasn't I didn't know I would find them. The information just hit me in between the eyes."

"But you have your peace finally, yeah?"

"Not exactly. I didn't feel like I thought it would. Through here," he indicated to a dark passage.

Mercer sat down next to Roxanne Lilywhite and put his arm around her as she faded fast.

"You've been with me since a rookie," he reminisced. "Was it really all so bad that you couldn't come to me?"

"They threatened mum and dad Phil. You know how mum has been with the cancer. I couldn't let those bastards anywhere near them." She rasped.

"They need help. They need financial support. Without me they have nobody to help them. Help sort it guv Please?" She looked into Mercer; her eyes were large and childlike. Frightened.

"We'll make sure it's sorted out love. Don't you worry."

"Need to sort out the loose ends Phil. Get my prints on that gun and it all ties in to me. Nobody need know any different."

Mercer stared at the gun. He smiled and pressed it into her hand. He cradled her. He could hear the ambulance sirens coming. But it was too late. He cradled her and wiped her tears as she slipped away. A tear dampened his own cheek. A tear of his own making.

"You silly girl. Didn't have to be this way," he whispered and gently kissed her head and laid her down.

He looked around the office, at the shitstorm of a mess. He would have to put it down to Lilywhite, as she wanted in the end. He would owe it to her to paint her in a decent light. Considering how she saved his life. He owed her, and her parents, that much. It would hopefully satisfy any likely ensuing enquiry. The Met and the press loved a hero. Especially a dead one.

And what of Stan Carmouche, he considered. Jesus. The press, top brass and anyone in-between would have a turkey shoot if his connection came out in any way. Christ, they'd crucify Mercer. And that would just be for breakfast.

They would have to keep a close eye on Carmouche and make sure he stuck to the cover story they would have to weave for him, just in case. He'd got his revenge. It was unlikely he would make waves for the guys. And Leyland would need guidance. Especially after the revelations. The next few days would be stormy at best.

Ghost Track: Melissa

Mercer needed to get out. Lilywhite looked so peaceful. He pulled Petrov's suit jacket from the back of his chair and carefully placed it over her face after kissing her forehead.

In amongst the blood and bullets the cover up had to begin.

Twenty Four.

The streets of the city were a bit less busy than usual. It was raining hard and as such had put off the less hard-core of the city dwellers. It was getting late as well, but for Detective Sergeant Leyland Francis sleep was a far flung memory. An unknown desire.

He sat in the American themed diner with his large latte. He was stirring in the sugar bomb he had put in. His attention darted to the door, a bell rang every time it opened and Leyland had jumped a hundred times as he awaited his guest. The tall figure of Stan Carmouche stood in the doorway. He took his pork pie hat off and raised it in Leyland's direction.

"Black coffee please ma'am," he ordered kindly and walked slowly to the table.

"I got your message young buddy."

Leyland smiled lightly. "How are you Stan? Please take a seat." Leyland gestured to the space in front of him. The two unlikeliest of friends sat opposite each other in a silence to a background of the rain tapping its summer night tune on the large window. Stan noticed the heavy bruising that had appeared on Leyland's forehead and around his eyes.

"That looks pretty painful."

"Looks worse than it feels I think."

The waitress padded over with Stan's coffee, which he acknowledged with his trademark smile. He waited until she was out of earshot.

"Hell of a mess up on that floor."

Leyland stared into his drink. They hadn't spoken since escaping the Wharf complex unseen. Like ghosts. Over the past forty eight hours the young detective hadn't slept much. Had run through a harvest of questions in his head.

"How did it feel Stan?" He began. Carmouche sipped his coffee and placed his hat on the table.

"To get Petrov? Finally? It didn't feel like it should have."

Leyland screwed his eyes up in confusion. It hurt his head to do so.

"In what way?"

"It was meant to be straightforward. In and out. Get revenge. I had played the shot out a million times in my head over the years. A clean headshot. No mistake. No resurrection. Game over. The commotion in there, seeing you. It took that feeling away instantly. It became, very quickly, about saving the good guys." He sipped again.

"If it wasn't for you and Phil I would have completely forgotten what good guys look like. The sort of people that good people can be. You opened my eyes to that again, after so so long."

Leyland sipped on his latte, taking in every word from Stan's lips.

His banging headache wouldn't subside and it was painkiller time again. He popped a couple out of a blister pack onto the table and slipped the pack back into the inside pocket of his immaculately tailored suit.

"Did you know we could lead you to them? Did you use us from the word go?" Leyland questioned.

"Absolutely not," Stan defended.

"My offer to help was genuine. I knew the girl, remember? It wasn't until I was going through all those emails that a picture began to build. Names. Places."

"So rather than come to us, you used it for your own purposes? I bet you weren't half surprised to see us up there?!"

"I used the information, yes. I didn't give it up. Hell I thought you guys would consider that they'd turned on themselves. I couldn't believe how close you had got when I walked into that office. But I shouldn't have been so surprised. You and officer Mercer are outstanding detectives. I had split seconds to react. I had to take that shot for Phil. To save him. There is a different feeling to a shot like that."

Leyland wanted to tear into him. Had prepared to do so for a while. But Stan was right. He had saved Mercer. And there had been enough anguish.

"How'd that mess get cleaned up?" Stan asked.

"The female officer that died. Roxanne. She has been credited with attempting to apprehend the two Russians, killing them and being killed in the process."

Stan nodded slowly as Leyland continued.

"She is being buried with full honours next Wednesday. Buried a hero."

"Despite being on their payroll?" Stan queried.

"Yep. Ironic isn't it. Mercer figured that she was under serious duress. Her family had been threatened. She needed the money for her mum's treatment. All got too much for her I guess. Maybe she didn't really have a choice. Doesn't make it taste any better when good men had been lost because of her."

"And I'm reassured and appreciative of the fact that you and Phil have kept me covered. Thank you buddy," Stan had been given an alibi by Mercer when they regrouped at his flat. Leyland had been hit hard about the revelations regarding the crash and he simply couldn't get his head into gear. Mercer had taken care of everything. Including Stan.

Leyland looked out of the window. It was dark, stormy and brooding outside. It matched his mood very well indeed.

"We talked about the crash before, Stan," Leyland reminded the big guy, Stan nodded confirmation while slurping his brew.

"Petrov and Vasilievitch were responsible. Told me as much in that office."

Stan's eyes widened.

"Where's my vengeance? My payback for what they did?"

Stan rubbed the bridge of his nose and then fixed Leyland with a stare of such intensity he felt the urge to run away.

"Listen to me. Carefully. You have to let it go. Let...it...go. You know. And that's more than you had before. At least you know. Don't start on the path that I did. You're young. You have a life to live. You can't focus on revenge you'll never get. It will destroy you and you're too switched on to let that happen. I know it. So leave it where it was. In that office." Stan's seriousness made his words penetrate Leyland's heart.

"You got yours?" He snapped.

"Did I? That shot was for Mercer, not for Nathan. Not for revenge. And I'm glad. I don't know if I could have taken it under any other circumstance other than saving a hell of a good man."

"Has that given you peace?" Leyland asked.

"To know they're gone and you and Phil are still here? Yes." Stan could see the frustration and anger in Leyland and he was fighting hard to get him to rest it.

"What you have to look at, concentrate on every day is what you did for that girl. And her sister. You saved Felicity's life. You solved her sister's murder. All the things you could have promised her, that would have meant everything, you made good on. Regardless of who takes the credit. Who lived. Who died. How it has to be covered up. You lay your head on your pillow every night and sleep the good man's sleep because you did what you set out to do. That, my very good buddy, is a gift."

Leyland's thinking went onto tangent. In the shitstorm of Petrov's office he had forgotten that they got Felicity out safely. Melissa's murder had been solved. Justice, of a brutal kind, had been served. What was left of the Marshall family could live with some degree of peace.

He still had Felicities number. He would call her in the morning. His Latte was begging to be drained and as he did so he could feel the weight lifting from his shoulders.

"What do you know about ghosts, Stan?" He asked out of the blue. It took the old man by surprise.

Ghost Track: Melissa

"Ghosts?" He repeated "They're all around us," he added looking puzzled.

"Meet for a drink tomorrow night?" Leyland asked. "I have a ghost story to tell you and maybe you could help me." He guzzled the last of his coffee and stood. Unaided. The crutches were officially history.

At the door and looking at the rain he flicked the collar up on his light raincoat and with a step he was out into the sodden night.

Lightning flashed over the city and thunder rumbled the pavement as Leyland made for the underground, ready for home. And bed.

Stan raised his hat to Leyland as he passed the big window. Leyland raised his hand to his friend and wondered how he would react to Leyland explaining his 'gift' Time would tell.

A much lesser effort in recent times got him to the tube and given the time and weather conditions it was virtually deserted on the platform and in the carriage.

As the train picked up speed and headed into the sooty tunnel the air chilled. Leyland felt it and remembered the sensation from before almost immediately.

His stomach lurched slightly but he tried to remain calm. Focused.

The lights flickered. Then again. Leyland focused after the third flicker and she was in front of him. She was as beautiful as he had believed her to be when he thought she was real. Alive.

She smiled at him and mouthed some words to him. There was no sound, but Leyland caught them in one, the movement of her lips as tears built up in his eyes.

Thank you. She said thank you. The carriage jolted and the lights flickered again. She was gone.

The carriage warmed quickly again.

Leyland wiped his eyes and he felt an enormous sense of peace wash over him. He couldn't put his finger on it, couldn't explain it. Didn't want to explain it. He had made good on exposing what happened to her. Honoured her memory. Despite being branded a lunatic. Despite the massive struggle he had with his own feelings.

Bed was calling and he hadn't slept properly in days. His mobile vibrated, and as he opened the message from Mercer.

'Investigation into the crash has officially been reopened'

Leyland couldn't help but feel the stable door was being slammed shut long after the horse had bolted. It felt like an anti climax. He wouldn't communicate that to mercer though. He knew that his good friend had battled hard in light of the revelations in Petrov's office to get the investigation reopened. The fact was that Leyland had his justice in a way. And he had to learn to be content with that, and anyway his bed was calling.

Tomorrow was a new day.

Coming soon...

Ghost Track: Judas Kiss

Book Two of the Ghost Track Series.

Facebook.com/ghosttrack14

Printed in Great Britain
by Amazon.co.uk, Ltd.,
Marston Gate.